THE LAST TANGO
OF
DOLORES DELGADO

Also by Marele Day

The Life and Crimes of Harry Lavender
The Case of the Chinese Boxes

THE LAST TANGO
OF
DOLORES DELGADO

Marele Day

Hodder & Stoughton

First published in Australia in 1992
by Allen & Unwin Pty Ltd

First published in Great Britain in 1995
by Hodder and Stoughton
A division of Hodder Headline PLC

10 9 8 7 6 5 4 3 2 1

British Library Cataloguing in Publication Data

ISBN 0 340 61349 1

Printed and bound in Great Britain by
Mackays of Chatham PLC, Chatham, Kent

Hodder and Stoughton Ltd
A division of Hodder Headline PLC
338 Euston Road
London NW1 3BH

acknowledgments

thanks to everyone who was there on location
for their various contributions—George, Don, Fiona,
Michael, Stuart, Patrick
and, especially this time, Elizabeth and that big bottle of gin

I'd never met a woman quite like Dolores Delgado; I'd certainly never had a client like her. She had smouldering eyes, high cheek bones and luscious lips that appeared to be permanently on the verge of a kiss. Strong dancer's legs, slim hips and small plump breasts. Even in the posters sensuality oozed out of her. There were probably more skilful dancers in the world but she was the most flamboyant, the one with the most pizzazz.

She danced with a knife in her garter, like the first tango dancers; she danced the story of tango—its beginnings in the bordellos of Buenos Aires, through tango teas in Paris to finally arrive in the ballrooms of high society. In a way it was her own story.

Off the dance floor what Dolores did with flamboyance and pizzazz was go shopping. She could spend $500 between here and the corner even though there weren't any shops. But she didn't shop merely to spend money. Dolores turned shopping into an art form.

That's where I came in. She hired me to go with her to nose out places that sold the most fabulous dresses, clothes that were exclusive, the unusual, the glamorous. To find fabrics that might have been specially woven for royalty, for rock stars; designers who would create masterpieces just for her. Dolores could discuss for hours the details of a frill, the right shade of red, the plunge of a neckline. Shopping with Dolores opened up a whole new world for me.

Dolores had done everything and been everywhere. She was larger than life. She thought nothing of dancing all night in Rio then flying to Paris for breakfast in a private jet. She hinted at a mysterious past—a family scandal, a man who had died protecting her honour, of how she could never go back home.

Dolores Delgado's life was cut short. I would like to have known her longer because everything about her intrigued me— her glamour, her seductiveness, the hint of tragedy in her past. What intrigued me the most about Dolores Delgado was whether there was anyone there at all under all that bullshit.

I guess you could say that Dolores came along at the right moment. The way things had been going in my life at the time I met her I was ready to do almost anything. I'm a private investigator. People think my life is exciting. I used to think so too.

The only work private investigators were getting was buying information from Social Security and the Motor Registry and selling it to banks and finance companies. They used it to collect on debts. I drew the line at that.

So I was sitting around with nothing much to do. Things were so bad that I'd seriously considered getting a regular job. But there wasn't a lot to choose from. They were tough times, and they were tough all round.

My personal life wasn't faring much better—Steve was in Germany and apart from a postcard telling me he'd arrived safely there was still no word from him. We hadn't parted on the best of terms. He was visiting hospitals there to familiarise himself with the latest developments in pacemaker research. His daughter Annicke lived in Germany. With her mother. I lay awake at night wondering whether pacemakers were the only things he was being familiar with.

I also lay awake thinking about my kids. It was the school holidays and for the first time Amy and David weren't coming down to spend them with me. They were going white-water rafting on the Nymboida. All I had to offer was Sydney. The

3

holidays were only two weeks long but without the kids they dragged on forever.

To top everything off, my mother had started dressing up as an ostrich again.

At least getting back into 'show business', as she called it, made her cut down on the cigarettes. She used to do her ostrich act at the Tivoli. For some reason she had decided to dust off her feathers and try it again. She really did look like an ostrich. Her head tucked away under splendid black and cream feathers, while one arm, clad in a long flesh-coloured glove, rose out of the feathers as the ostrich's neck. Her legs were the giveaway— they were far too shapely to be ostrich legs.

She entered a talent quest at the Bondi Pavilion and they loved her. In theory I was all for it, I wanted to be still kicking up my heels when I got to her age. I was glad she wasn't vegetating away in front of the TV. But you know, watching her shake her tail feathers or seeing her surreptitious little wave in my direction, I couldn't help feeling she'd be better off home in bed sipping a nice hot cup of Milo. I'd feel better if she was anyway.

She'd done so well in the talent quest that she'd been offered a two-week engagement at the Tropicana.

That's where I met Dolores.

The club was in Newtown, up a set of stairs that looked like nothing special. But once inside it was a different world. Club Tropicana—where every night is New Year's Eve, where all the boys and all the girls came from Ipanema. Tall and tanned and young and lovely. If you could bottle it you'd make a fortune.

There were palm trees and multicoloured birds suspended from the ceiling, dusky pink lighting that flattered every face, young or old. The club attracted inner-city trendies looking for a late night venue, people from the suburbs who got dressed up and made a night out at the Tropicana a special occasion, South Americans, friends and relatives of the management who came to speak Spanish and indulge in the old ways. And out-of-work private investigators whose mothers dressed up as ostriches.

People drank pina coladas from hollowed out pineapples, and

sangria by the jugful, even though sangria comes from Spain not South America. But you needed to have a degree of multi-culturalism to recognise that. The customers didn't care, it was all atmosphere to them.

After Mina had done her ostrich act, Amadio would introduce the main attraction: 'And now, bringing to life the passion and fire of tango, direct from Buenos Aires, Dolores and Ramón'. The characteristic sound of the bandoneón announced the tango. Dolores and Ramón entered from opposite sides of the stage. She in a red dress that dripped sequins. She'd had it made especially for her. I'd taken her everywhere to get just the right sequins. The back was low, even lower than the waistline. The skirt consisted of red and silver panels that allowed the audience to see the full length of Dolores' legs as she danced. And the flash of the knife in her garter. Her dancing shoes, with straps around the ankles, were also covered with red sequins. Ramón wore tight black pants, black patent leather shoes, a white shirt with armbands, and a red satin vest. His sleek black hair was combed straight back to show to full advantage his handsome features and the look in his eye that let every woman in the place know he was available for private lessons. Very private lessons.

The dance began. Ramón moved towards Dolores like a matador approaching a bull. Dolores was just as challenging but you'd never be able to pour a bull into that dress.

Mina's two weeks at the club finished but I stayed on. I'd watched Dolores and Ramón's performance many times but it never lost its appeal. Watching these two, every fibre of one body alert to the body of the other, eyes flashing fire and lust, it was easy to imagine why some people had wanted the dance banned.

Dolores missed one step, then another. Ramón's smile seemed to set in his face. Dolores' left arm slid down and dangled loosely. Her head rolled, she brought it upright again, though it seemed to take forever. The music played on. There was a collective murmur in the audience and people started looking at each other. She was making an effort to follow the steps, as if her life depended on it. She was in pain, panting now for breath. Saliva was coming from her mouth. Dolores' head rolled back as if her neck had been snapped, jaw slack, eyes open. Ramón brought his arm up to support her head. He held onto her as if she was a life-size doll, still keeping up some pretence of a dance, manoeuvring her to the wings. He held her tight, pushing her legs with his. He kept up the pretence till he was right off stage and the music was over.

I did a quick scan of the club on my way backstage. Amadio had assured everyone that everything was all right and had organised a conga line. Some people were asking questions about Dolores but most simply joined in the conga line, either too young to remember that it was the dance equivalent of flared trousers, or not wanting to admit that they could remember.

In the dressing room Dolores was slumped in a chair with Cilla lightly slapping her cheeks and feeling for a pulse in the neck. Ramón was sitting on another chair, panting and swallowing air. In between breaths he was talking Spanish to Cilla. It sounded like an argument but judging by the hand movements it looked like he was explaining what had happened out there. When he saw me come in he switched to English. 'I don't know, I don't know how this happened. I didn't do anything to her,' he said as if he had to justify himself. 'There was nothing different, she didn't say she was feeling sick. Nothing.' His whole face seemed to be a lather of sweat, as if he'd run a hard race or had a narrow escape from something. He wiped his hand across his eyes. There were tears as well as sweat.

'We'd better lie her down on the mat,' I said. 'Cilla, call 000 and ask for the ambulance.' I knelt down close beside Dolores and felt for a pulse. There was nothing. I could hear Cilla say 'Club Tropicana', 'Newtown', 'unconscious', 'no blood'. She told them they could park behind the club and someone would be waiting for them at the back entrance. It was as easy to get a stretcher out that way as it was out the front. And there wouldn't be any crowds.

There was no blood. But saliva was trickling out of Dolores' mouth. 'Did she eat anything unusual, or drink anything?' I asked.

Ramón took his hand away from his face and turned his palm upwards in a gesture of hopelessness. 'Nothing different, same as usual before the show—a black coffee and the bitters.'

I brought my cheek down close to her nose and mouth to feel if there was any breath. There was none. There was still the warmth of life though, and the sheen of perspiration on her forehead. I pressed the place near the sternum and began a rhythmic compression of her heart, replicating the heart beat, trying to crank the motor up again. I'd seen Dolores up close before but this time it was different. It was as if everything was magnified. The pores of her skin, the hollow of her neck, her slender arms, slightly raised veins on the hands, long fingers ending in long red nails.

I turned away. Dolores had her body almost permanently on show, she was proud of it, but it didn't seem quite right to be looking at it now, looking at it without her knowing. I guess she wouldn't mind me looking at the parts that were on public display every night on the dance floor but I'd seen something else—near her ears and around the hairline were the telltale little scars of plastic surgery.

By the time we heard the ambulance siren Ramón had stopped panting and swallowing air. He looked up briefly when the siren stopped and Cilla went to meet the ambulance officers. He leant over and put his hand out to stroke Dolores' hair but couldn't bring himself to do it. I kept on trying to pump the heart into action. But Dolores was showing no more signs of life now than she had ten minutes ago when I started.

When Cilla showed the ambulance people in with their equipment I moved away. There were spots of blood on my hand. I couldn't understand, there'd been no blood. What were those shiny red spots? As I turned my hand the light caught them. It wasn't blood, they were sequins from Dolores' dress. Involuntarily I closed my hand around them. I kept holding onto them even after I realised the action was futile.

The ambulance officers were a young guy who looked like he spent most of his days at the beach and a woman with freckly skin who looked like she'd seen this kind of thing a million times—in doorways at the Cross, in the streets of Darlinghurst. Cilla had already told them what had happened but the young guy asked Ramón anyway. They turned her arms over looking for needle marks. 'You're wasting your time,' I said in a hard voice. I'd never seen Dolores use drugs but that didn't mean she didn't. Nevertheless I felt affronted, as if somehow by doing their jobs they were violating Dolores.

I turned my attention to Dolores' dressing table. There was more make-up than I'd ever seen in my entire life, some of the things I couldn't even begin to guess what you might do with them. Among more familiar items was nail polish—bright red like she had on tonight, blue with silver flecks in it, black. There were pencils every colour of the rainbow to use on your eyes and mouth and anything else you needed to highlight. And there were creams and lotions to take it all off again. Near the mirror was a framed photograph, a black and white that had been coloured. It was signed Nelida y Eduardo, 1953. Dolores had told me they were the best tango dancers in the world. I said she must have been only a child then. She said, maybe I got the photo much later. In general Dolores steered clear of any discussion of birthdays. 'I wasn't born, I created myself,' she said, chucking me under the chin. I had to admire her, there were very few people who would even think of chucking me under the chin.

The young guy was now using the oxyvibor. It was routine procedure—check the air passages are clear, airway management they call it so it doesn't sound too human. The freckly woman started compressing the heart, a little too severely I thought. The shiny red sequins were still embedded in the palm of my hand. I wondered whether any of Dolores' red sequins would find their way onto her hand as well. Cilla and Ramón were talking quietly outside.

The dressing room looked untidy but no worse than it normally did. There was an empty pizza box that Dolores had been using as a waste paper bin, piled high with tissues, bits of used cotton wool and cotton buds, as well as a few cigarette butts. They were filter tips but that was about all I could tell. Dolores didn't smoke. Someone could have been in here and rifled through the drawers and you wouldn't notice any difference. Some of the drawers were partially open with various items of clothing peeking out. One of the drawers contained bottles of Angostura bitters, most of them empty. It wasn't as if she was collecting them, it was just that she never got round to throwing them out.

Dolores had this thing about bitters. Said it sharpened her performance. She'd take a nip straight from the bottle, pull a face, wince then finally say, 'Ah, much better.' A person who could drink bitters straight, you'd think there'd be nothing that could kill them.

Ramón came back into the room just as the ambulance woman was preparing to jab a needle into Dolores' arm. 'What are you doing?' he demanded.

'She's not responding,' she said, as if that explained everything. 'I'm giving her an injection to stimulate the heart.'

They'd tried, as I had, to get air into the lungs, to manually stimulate the heart. We'd gone through all the motions and nothing had worked. Now they were injecting the body with asystole drugs, the ace heart starter of them all. If that didn't work . . .

The ambulance officers waited but Dolores didn't respond. They exchanged looks then the woman asked us to call Dolores' doctor. Neither Cilla, Ramón nor I even knew whether Dolores had a doctor. Cilla said, 'What do you need a doctor for, you're the ambulance, no?'

Then the woman told us why they needed the doctor. To sign the death certificate.

Ramón put his hand up to his face, covering his eyes. Cilla and I looked at each other. There was nothing left to say.

'We're not authorised,' I could hear the woman's voice, softer now, kinder, 'you need a doctor to fill in the form. We'll take her to hospital, you can come if you like.'

I wanted to laugh. I had a mad hope that taking her to hospital would make her well again. That she'd wake up and everything would be all right.

Dolores was dead. I heard what they said, I'd seen it with my own eyes. But it would take a while before the full impact of the message got through.

Possible cause of death: myocardial infarction?

I knew what myocardial infarction meant—death of the heart muscle. That wasn't the problem. The problem was the question mark.

As usually happens in a case like this the hospital had called in the boys in blue. Actually, what turned up was not only a boy but also a girl. Her eyes were almost the same light blue as her shirt and her hair was pulled back in a ponytail. She looked like she was about seventeen. I wondered if I was getting old. Cops seemed to get younger and younger with every encounter I had with them. All except for Carol, that is. It wasn't that Carol ever looked any older, it was just that she'd lost that fresh-faced look. About twenty years ago. The boy in blue had an olive complexion and eyes that were so dark you couldn't see the difference between the iris and the pupil. He did all the talking.

'You relatives?'

'A friend,' I said.

'How long have you known her?'

'A few weeks.'

'And you, sir?'

'The same,' replied Ramón. He was lying.

The cop asked him to describe what had happened on the dance floor. He did that fairly accurately but when the cop asked him questions about himself he started lying again. His answers were short, non-committal. He didn't want to talk to them.

'Has the family been notified?'

I assumed any relatives would be in Buenos Aires though I didn't know how to go about finding them. Dolores had lived everywhere but Buenos Aires was the place that cropped up more in conversation. We talked a bit about families but not that much. She knew Mina, my mother, of course from the club. When I told her about Guy, my father, and how he'd become a dero she'd said, 'Nothing wrong with the gutter, there you learn the wisdom of life. My mother was from an important family in Argentina, my father from the streets. He played the bandoneón. When tango became respectable my mother's family would summon the group to come and play while the ladies and gentlemen danced. My mother and father fell wildly in love. At sixteen she became pregnant. He wanted to marry her but her father wouldn't hear of it. They sent her away to the country and her lover was found dead in a back alley. The family honour was saved but my father is lost to me, same as you.'

'Think notifying the family is going to be your job, constable.'

'What's her full name and address?'

'Dolores Delgado. She's staying at the Royale in the Cross. I don't know what her permanent address is. Was.' Ramón of course didn't know either.

The constable was having a hard time filling in the P79A form, Report of Death to Coroner. All that he'd filled in so far was the name of the deceased. I told him my name and address, adding that yes, it was my permanent address even though it was a pub. They needed only one name and address. Which let Ramón off the hook.

'Can I give you a lift somewhere?' Out in the real world Ramón's pants looked too tight, his collar too wide and his shoes too shiny. Off the dance floor, without Dolores, he looked sad and lost.

'Which way you going?'

'Back to the club,' I said.

'I live at Five Dock.' It was a bit out of the way but not too much. Besides, I had a few questions I wanted answers to.

Before we had even left the hospital car park he had lit a cigarette. By the time we hit Parramatta Road he still hadn't ashed it. I don't know why it hadn't detached itself from the body of the cigarette. It was holding on, defying all the laws of gravity and my patience. It was probably just the grief making him so distracted he didn't notice, I told myself. I pulled open the ashtray on the Daimler's dashboard. 'Do you want to use this?' I suggested.

'What? Oh, sorry.' He wound down the window and ashed the cigarette. None of it blew back into the car. He left the window open now and ashed absentmindedly from time to time.

'Why did you lie to the police back there?'

'Lie?'

'Yes. About how long you'd known Dolores.'

'What does it matter how long I know Dolores? Doesn't make her come back to life.' He wiped his hands across his face. 'Turn left here.'

I turned left into a wide avenue. 'And what about all that stuff about just arriving in the country?'

'It sounds better, you know like Amadio says—"Direct from Buenos Aires". Just here,' he said about halfway along the street.

I pulled up. 'Cops think people who lie have something to hide.'

'Why are you talking about this? Do you know what happened tonight? Dolores . . . died.' The word came out as a cry.

I eased up.

'What happens now?' he asked, after a while.

'They'll do an autopsy, try to determine the cause of death.'

'But they know already, no? Heart attack.'

'Yes. But what caused the heart attack? Dolores was healthy, she was young.' I thought of the little scars around the hairline. Not that young, I said to myself. But too young to die of a heart attack. 'You spend a lot of time with her? Outside the club, I mean.'

'Enough.'

'How much is enough?'

'We practise the routine, go dancing in other clubs sometimes.'
If there was anything more to it than that he wasn't giving
anything away.

'What are you going to do now, Ramón?'

'Do some work at the club,' he sighed, his heart not really in
it, 'as a waiter; look for another partner. I think Dolores would
want the dance to keep going.' He looked me up and down.
Not leering, more of an appraisal. 'Yes,' he said after some
consideration. 'You've got the legs, you've got the body. Change
the hair a little, the make-up, the right clothes. You could do
it.'

'Get some sleep,' I said softly, 'it's been a long night.'

I phoned Cilla and said I'd be coming back to the club for
Dolores' keys. The cops needed to see Dolores' passport to get
the necessary details to trace her family. Then I phoned Carol
and asked her to meet me there.

When I arrived at the club I told Cilla how it had been at
the hospital. She poured a couple of Pernods and handed me
one of them. I sat on a bar stool. My shoes, my going-out-to-
night-club shoes, looked a lot better than they felt.

'Did you know Dolores very well?'

'You think it's possible to know Dolores well?' she asked me
back.

'What do you know of her background? She didn't come here
straight from Buenos Aires, did she?'

'"Direct", like Amadio says? No. She'd been here before, to
the club. She and Ramón danced together before. She comes
and goes, to Tokyo, Paris, America . . .'

'Where had she come from this time?'

'Coffs Harbour.'

'Coffs Harbour?' It hardly seemed like the entertainment
capital of the world. An international star like Dolores was
supposed to be, wouldn't she work the capital cities? I couldn't
image that Coffs Harbour was anything more than a fly speck
on the map to her. If you had any imagination at all and you

couldn't spell, Coffs Harbour sounded like a safe haven for people with tuberculosis. That must have been the attraction—Dolores had a lot of imagination and she couldn't spell.

'What was she doing there?'

'She's a dancer, I assume she was dancing,' she said offhandedly. 'She goes to other places, I don't ask; it's none of my business. And Claudia, maybe it's none of your business too.' Cilla took a sip of Pernod and pressed her lips together. She wasn't dismissing me, she was just letting me know which subjects were open for discussion and which weren't.

It was the ones that weren't that I was more interested in. 'She must have talked about it though—where she went, people she met.'

'Sure. I listen to Dolores' big talk. About celebrities she meets, places she goes. But with Dolores the talk is like bubbles. You try to grab hold of one it disappears.'

'At the hospital Ramón said he'd known Dolores for only a short time. He got any reason to lie to the police?'

Cilla curled a strand of her dark blonde hair behind her ear. 'You got questions about Ramón, you ask Ramón.'

'I did. He said it didn't matter.'

'So maybe it doesn't. What is this, the Spanish Inquisition?' She was beginning to get annoyed. Cilla and I got on well. I spent a lot of time at the club but she hadn't really seen me in work mode. She hadn't really had to. Till now.

'I'm a private investigator. I ask questions for a living. The police may come and do the same; consider this a dry run.' I didn't know whether the police would be around or not. They'd need some reason to mount a homicide investigation. That's why I'd phoned Carol. I wanted to talk to her because she was my friend. I also wanted to talk to her because she was a Detective Inspector with the Homicide Division.

I finished off the Pernod. 'I'll get Dolores' keys,' I said. 'If my friend arrives, I'll be in the dressing room.'

I had a quick look through the things on the dressing table and the drawers but didn't find anything that shouldn't have been there. I could see now that the butts in the ashtray were

Kents. That's what Ramón had been smoking in the car. Didn't mean anything though, he was often in her dressing room.

The key card for the hotel room was in the pocket of her jacket. It was a black jacket, beautifully tailored, made from leather so soft it could have come from a new-born calf. It had been made specially for her, so she said, in Italy.

I tried the jacket on. I could almost feel Dolores' warmth still in it. It felt good, like a second skin. I checked it out in the mirror. Ramón's parting comments came back to me. Change the hair, change the make-up . . .

The door opened. It was Cilla. She was looking at me looking at my reflection in the mirror. She looked startled, almost as if she'd seen a ghost. She had her mouth opened to say something but nothing came out. I turned around.

'Your friend is here,' she finally said.

Carol was sitting at a table, gazing at the macaws suspended from the ceiling. She wasn't entirely impressed.

'How was the Mozart?' I greeted her.

'Fine.'

'Noni enjoy it?'

'Yes.'

The small talk was minimal. Carol knew I hadn't asked her here to discuss her night out at the Opera House.

'Something happened here tonight,' I began.

Carol waited for me to continue.

'I had this . . .' I didn't know whether to say client or friend. Carol ran her finger round the rim of her martini glass, letting me take my time.

I took a breath. 'Dolores Delgado was a dancer in this club. She had a heart attack here tonight and died.' It seemed easier this way, to announce it like this, matter of fact.

Silence drifted between us.

Carol waited. 'And?'

'And something about it doesn't seem quite right.'

'Sure that's not just an occupational hazard?'

'I don't know. Maybe. I haven't been having much occupation

to hazard lately. I wasn't working at all when I met Dolores.' I told Carol how I was 'minding' her, how the minding mostly consisted of taking her shopping.

'You were hired to go shopping?' she said, as if I'd just told her I had leprosy. 'You left your husband and kids to end up taking some tango dancer shopping?'

'So what's wrong with shopping?'

'It's an indulgence,' she said dismissively.

'An indulgence, Carol? It's the expression of a primeval urge. They hunt, we gather.'

Carol rolled her eyes up to the macaws but she wasn't going to find any allies there.

'You collect antiques and Persian rugs,' I reminded her.

'But that's not shopping.'

'No? Where do you get them from? Go out and shoot them?'

Normally Carol would have had a comeback but she must have been tired. God knows we were all tired.

'Is there any reason why you should be suspicious?' she said, bringing us back to business.

All I was supposed to do with Dolores was go shopping. But I ended up acting more and more like a bodyguard. When she wanted me to I'd bring her to the club, take her home again. I'd come to the dressing room before the show and tell her what the crowd was like. 'Anyone interesting for me to dance with tonight?' I'd describe potential partners in the audience, and where they were sitting. She didn't really need my protection. Nothing ever happened that she couldn't handle herself. Maybe it made her feel more of a celebrity having a bodyguard around.

'I don't know, nothing definite.' I searched around for something, anything to give substance to the feeling. 'She was . . . when she died. There was a lot of saliva.'

'You mean frothing at the mouth? As if she'd been bitten by a mad dog? Someone came at her with a ricin-tipped umbrella, the way that Vatican banker died? Poison pygmy darts?'

I smiled. 'No, not like that, kind of dribbling. It wasn't the sort of thing Dolores would do.'

'Heart attack isn't the sort of thing people go out of their way to do either. Maybe that's all it was, a heart attack. People don't always react to it in the same say.'

But they never mention excessive salivation as one of the symptoms. 'Look, maybe she drank something or ate something. Maybe someone slipped something into her coffee, her pizza even.'

'Was there opportunity?'

'Yes, it's easy to get backstage.'

'Someone from the club you think?'

I thought about it. 'Perhaps.'

'Ramón?'

I was surprised she knew his name. 'I saw the posters outside,' she said. 'Looks like he could bring on a few heart attacks.'

He did have opportunity. And he'd lied to the police. But I wanted to find out why before I handed him over to Carol.

'He seemed genuinely distressed about what happened.'

'They sometimes do,' Carol said. 'Thinking about it's one thing. Doing it and seeing the results is another.' She held the martini olive between her lightly varnished nails and shaved a morsel off with her small white teeth. I imagine this is how piranha do it. Backwards and forwards, backwards and forwards they go till all that's left are bits of sashimi floating down the Amazon. 'You know what I think?' She shaved off another piece. 'I think you liked this woman, Dolores. She died, you're asking yourself why. I've listened to what you've been telling me, I'm sorry about what happened. But frankly I don't see any official reason why I should be here. Testing for poisons takes time and money. God, you eat a pizza you take your life into your hands. I can't get a full investigation going unless you can give me something I can put on paper. You know what police paperwork is like. It's not something you enter into lightly.' She put her hand over mine. From a non-tactile person like Carol this was a rare and grand gesture. 'Claudia, you're not the first person to feel like this. Someone you know dies you want to do everything you can. You lost a friend.'

'I lost a client.'

'She wasn't just a client though, was she?'

Carol was a good listener. She had to be. She asked a lot of questions and she heard a lot of answers. She heard what people said and she heard what they didn't say. Spend enough time with Carol, sooner or later you confess.

Dolores wasn't just a client. 'She was different. I've never been around anyone like that. Even though I didn't believe half of what she said, she was exciting, dramatic, there was something about her, she was larger than life.'

'You want larger than life, read a book.'

Dolores was better than a book. With Dolores I didn't even have to turn the pages. I smiled. 'I didn't know you read, Carol.'

'Not any more than I have to. Some nights I don't sleep. I think tonight is going to be one of them.' She looked at her watch. 'There's not enough time left in it for a start. I've got to be sitting in front of my desk in a few hours.'

'It's big enough for you to lie down on and be "in a meeting".'

'Don't you worry about that.'

The sex workers were hanging out in William Street, shifting from one foot to the other, trying to keep their bare legs from freezing off. Cars cruised by checking them out. A couple of brawls broke out, there were kids up back alleys doing things. It was business as usual at the Cross.

I knew the way to Dolores' room and no-one asked if they could help me when I walked into the foyer of the Hotel Royale. The staff here were used to seeing me coming and going. If you wanted to be pedantic about it you could say that the Royale was in Potts Point rather than Kings Cross. It sounded more genteel, didn't carry with it the notoriety of Kings Cross. We had the same thing in Balmain. Certain residents would never admit to living in Balmain, they always gave their address as Birchgrove. More genteel. The irony was that Balmain was getting more and more like Birchgrove. Most of the pubs in Balmain have been tastefully renovated. I told Jack the day he started thinking about renovating would be the day I moved out.

The Hotel Royale had a terrific facade—bright red bricks with clean white mortar separating them. It was curved so that every room had a view and there were two sweeping staircases that came together in the middle with a balustrade of classic white columns. All it needed to complete the picture was for Fred and Ginger to come dancing down the stairs.

20

It felt strange standing outside Dolores' room, putting the key card in. I'd stood at this door a lot during the last couple of weeks. She usually unlocked the door but I went in first. 'After you,' she would say grandly. Now I was going in alone.

Dolores' suite was pink. She reckoned they'd done it specially for her. I would have thought that reds and golds would have been more to her taste. 'On stage yes,' she said. 'When I sleep I like to sleep in pink rooms. You know Barbara Cartland? She told me pink gives you romantic dreams. She always dresses in pink. She is rich, she is old. For an Englishwoman she is very glamorous.' Dolores then pulled me close and whispered in my ear. 'She gave me a pair of her eyelashes.'

I thought about the eyelashes because they were the first thing I noticed when I entered Dolores' hotel room. They sat like centipedes on the pink dressing table. I don't know why I picked them out amongst the myriad of detail there but I did. They looked so forlorn, so forsaken. Sitting there faithfully waiting, for someone who was never coming back. Well, at least they had each other I reminded myself.

If I hadn't already been familiar with the mess, I would have said the place had been burgled. I don't know how a person could get a place so untidy, especially when a maid came and tidied the room once a day. Drawers were open, the bed was unmade, and of course the dressing table was in the same mess as the one at the club. I looked through it all but I couldn't find Dolores' passport.

I opened the wardrobe. This wasn't a mess at all. In fact it was practically empty. Except for the suitcases. They hadn't been there before. The dresses were gone but there was a brand new set of red suitcases. They were heavy. I took one out and laid it on the bed. Dolores would never have done that—put a red suitcase on a pink bedspread.

It was unlocked and snapped open fairly easily. It was full of dresses, most of which had previously hung in the wardrobe. I had a good idea of what this meant but I didn't want to believe it. I opened the second suitcase. It was full of clothes too. I had to believe it—Dolores was planning a move. Maybe she was just changing rooms, or hotels, I told myself. And just because she hadn't told me didn't mean she didn't intend to. Did it?

I'd been looking for her passport but this put a slightly different complexion on things.

I found the passport—in the inside pocket of a beauty case on the top shelf of the wardrobe. But that wasn't all I found. There was something else behind the lining, about the same size as the passport only a bit thicker. I got one of Dolores' hairpins from the dressing table and started to unpick the lining. What was hidden in there was another passport—in the name of Valerie Estevez. Different name but same photo as the one in the Delgado passport. At least the Spanish theme was consistent. In a travel wallet at the bottom of the beauty case was a Thai Airways ticket to Bangkok. One way. Date of departure was the day after tomorrow.

She was going to tell me. She was going to have a little party after the show and tell us all. A surprise party. She didn't like farewells so she was just going to say 'Oh, and by the way . . .' It was a mistake, she wasn't leaving at all, she'd changed the date of departure but still had the old ticket. There was a reasonable explanation for it.

I reached for the pink phone beside the bed and rang through to Thai Airways. I said I was Dolores Delgado confirming my flight. There was a brief silence while the person on the other end brought the details up on the computer. He confirmed the flight arrangements.

I knew the reasonable explanation—Dolores was checking out of here and she wasn't telling anyone.

My heart sank. I knew most of what Dolores said about herself wasn't true. Despite the fact that her stories were bullshit, the sheer gusto with which she told them made them entertaining, appealing little diversions.

But now I'd uncovered a deeper layer of deception.

Was I the only one being deceived? I rang the Tropicana. Anna answered the phone. She studied microbiology during the day and cleaned the Tropicana three nights a week. Cilla had left already. I rang her home number. The phone rang for a long time before it was answered. Cilla had just got in. I asked her how long Dolores' present engagement was for. She said another couple of months. 'Do you know if she was planning any trips before that?' Cilla said sometimes on her days off she went somewhere. 'To Bangkok with two full suitcases and a one-way ticket?'

There was a silence. 'Cilla?'

She asked me what I meant. I told her I had the ticket in front of me and that I'd just confirmed it with Thai Airways.

'It's for when?' she asked.

'Day after tomorrow.'

There was an even longer silence. Then she swore. I couldn't understand all of it but it had something to do with Madonna and pigs. Finally Cilla remarked that at least Dolores had chosen a Sunday to piss off, the club was closed Sundays and Mondays. That gave them a couple of days to find a replacement act. Not much time but better than nothing. Neither of us mentioned the fact that Dolores was now dead and the club would have to come up with something else anyway.

Why didn't you tell me, Dolores?

I examined the clothes in Dolores' suitcases more carefully. There weren't just dance dresses, there were also more tailored numbers—crisp linen business suits that didn't really seem Dolores' style. I opened the wardrobe to have a better look around. On top of the wardrobe I noticed a book. I reached up for it. It was called *Doing Business with the Japanese*. That wasn't Dolores' usual style either. I opened it and something fell out. Another passport. This one for Lola Montana. One hidden in her beauty case and one on top of the wardrobe. Looked like Valerie was going with her but she was leaving Lola behind.

In the bottom of the wardrobe was a black plastic garbage bag. There was a sticker on it as if it was a bag of laundry. The name written in block letters on the sticker was Yasmina. Another of Dolores' names? I untwisted the bag. In it were some clothes I'd seen before and a pair of boots I hadn't seen. But they weren't new. They had mud on them. It hadn't rained in Sydney for months.

I couldn't make sense of it. I was tired, overloaded. I'd had enough surprises for one night. I'd come back later, when I'd had some sleep. When I wouldn't be taking it all so personally.

Right now what I had to do was get Dolores' passport to the cops. Before they came looking.

I took the passports with me and left everything else more or less as I'd found it.

I was just about to get in the lift when I heard a phone ring. I ran back. It was Dolores' phone. I got the card out, stuck it in the slot and raced into the room. Just as my hand reached the phone it stopped ringing. I picked it up anyway and listened. All I got was the dial tone.

The young constable wasn't there when I fronted to Newtown Police Station in Australia Street. The desk sergeant said he'd be back sometime that morning. I asked where he was. He said, 'Who wants to know?' I told him. He said the constable was at the morgue. I guessed he was checking Dolores in. I had all the passports with me but I thought better of handing them all over. They could try their luck with Dolores Delgado. If that didn't produce a result I could always tell them about the others later.

'I need to photocopy this,' I said, meaning the Delgado passport.

'Why?' asked the desk sergeant. He didn't sound too suspicious, just curious. It was too early in the morning to start being suspicious.

'For my records, that's all.' I showed him my private investigator's licence. That seemed to satisfy him. I photocopied every page that had something on it. Then I asked him for an envelope big enough to contain the passport. He gave me a bright yellow one with NSW POLICE stamped on the top left-hand corner. I slipped the passport into the envelope and wrote Const. Loukakis on it. The desk sergeant assured me it would get to him. I got out of there as quickly as I could. Despite my line of business I don't feel any more comfortable in police stations than the average person.

It was raining when I stepped out onto the street. First bit of rain in months and all it was was a misty drizzle. Just enough dampness to be aware of it as I hurried down the street to where the Daimler was parked. As I leant down to unlock the door I caught a glimpse of myself in the side mirror. My glamorous nightclub dress from last night was looking a bit the worse for wear and just to top everything off, the rain had made my hair go frizzy.

Unfortunately when I got back to the pub Jack was taking a delivery of kegs. I had hoped to sneak upstairs without being seen.

'Night out on the tiles?' he asked in a voice he thought was knowing.

'Do I look like a roofer?'

'You're gonna give my place a bad reputation,' said Jack suggestively as he and the delivery guy rolled another keg down into the cellars.

'What, the lawyers aren't bad enough?'

Normally it was just a bit of light banter but this time it felt like wading through mud. I wasn't feeling particularly sociable right now, I just didn't have the heart for it.

'Ready for a liquid breakfast with Wayne and me?' he said.

I ignored him and started up the stairs.

Jack knew that something was up. 'Hang on, mate,' I heard him say to the delivery guy. 'Claudia, you all right? You want a cup of tea?'

'I'm all right,' I said without much conviction. 'It's just . . . something happened tonight. I'll tell you about it later.' I found my key and put it in the lock. 'G'night, Jack. Thanks,' I said for no particular reason.

He waited while I opened the door and went inside.

'I'm fine,' I assured him. 'Really. Tell your mate the joke about the greyhounds, that'll make his day.'

'The two greyhounds in the pub?'

'Yes,' I said desperately.

Jack went downstairs, not entirely convinced.

Maybe I should have accepted his offer of a cup of tea, that was probably as close as I was going to get to any sympathy. The answering machine wasn't blinking. No-one had rung. I played it back just in case but all I got was old messages. I lay on the bed. There were people I could talk to, Carol, for instance, but the only one I wanted at the moment was Steve. Who called me Magnum but never told me to keep my chin up, to be a big girl. Who would put his arms around me and hold me till I fell asleep.

But he wasn't here and I didn't even have a number where I could reach him.

I tried a karate breathing technique—slowing the breath and focusing the attention inwards. I tried counting sheep but they wouldn't jump over the fence.

I had only one trick left. When the nights get really tough and nothing else works I go for the Scotch. It wasn't night anymore, it was seven o'clock in the morning. Nothing strange about drinking Scotch at seven o'clock, my father did it all the time. Maybe still does, if he's still alive.

I dragged the bottle out and took a look at it. It was a little dusty—it had been a while—but it was more full than empty. I went to take a swig but thought better of it. My father again. Him drinking himself to a misery hadn't shied me off alcohol, it was the drinking straight from the bottle that I shied away from. One more step and you're in the gutter, Mina had said. Guy had taken that step too.

I went into the kitchen and selected a whisky glass. I don't have much in the way of personal belongings but I do have glasses of every shape and kind. There are bonuses to living above a pub. I put ice cubes into it. Then I carefully poured in the Scotch, watching it slip and slide over the ice. I was to repeat this process several times before I collapsed on the bed, though after the third shot I no longer bothered with the ice.

The Scotch smelled lousy, like the pub after everyone has gone home, and all that's left are the swills. That's the thing about taking a drink at seven o'clock in the morning. And there was another problem—the grey drizzle had been replaced by a sun that made everything blindingly bright. And it was going to stay like that for hours. I didn't want another day crowding in on me just yet.

I pulled the curtain across and switched on the bedside lamp to give a gentler light. I slipped Astor Piazzolla into the cassette deck. My computer friend Otto said I should update to a CD player. I said when my income updates I'll think about it.

Astor Piazzolla sounded like tango to me but Dolores had told me that when they first broadcast his music on radio in Buenos Aires the traditional tango musicians had threatened to knife him.

What did she get out of all those stories? Why did she feel the need of all that embroidery? It was obvious she knew how to dance. And she was good. Wasn't that enough for you, Dolores? What were you hiding behind those stories? Who are you really, Dolores–Valerie–Lola?

I took Astor out and put in Dolores and Ramón's dance music. That way it didn't feel so much like drinking alone.

'She wants to meet you.'

I hadn't come to Mina's opening performance, she'd wanted time to settle in first. With a two-week engagement there was hardly time to settle in before she'd have to settle out again. I rang up and asked her how the first night had gone. She was so excited she could hardly talk. The audience had clapped and cheered and wanted encores. She was even thinking of polishing up her fan dance to expand her repertoire. I groaned inwardly. The ostrich dance was one thing; having your mother appear naked in public was another. Even if she did keep on her flesh-coloured leotard. I asked her what the club was like. 'There's another dance act, you should see it, a South American couple, they do the tango. It's just marvellous, Claudia, such style! Reminds me of the Trocadero. Dolores—that's the girl—is a big star overseas, she's even given a royal command performance for Prince Charles.'

I might not have used the same adjectives but the club certainly had something going for it. It was definitely an improvement on staying at home. My mother was right about the crowds loving her, she was right about Dolores and Ramón.

After the show, when she had assumed human form again, my mother came over to my table. 'She wants to meet you,' she said proudly, 'Dolores wants to meet you. Backstage.' Mina was impressed. Backstage held even more of a fascination for her than frontstage. The dancers getting ready, all the girls talking, helping each other with their costumes; I grew up on my mother's stories of backstage.

'Ah, the famous Claudia.' I thought three cheek-kisses was the maximum but Dolores almost smothered me in them. Her skin was warm, glistening, a faint subtle perfume surrounded her. About the only thing that was subtle. 'Have a seat. Ramón, get her a drink.'

'Hi,' said Ramón, as if that had been our introduction, 'what do you like?'

Well, you're not bad for a start, I thought. Great to look at but then just about anyone looked good in here.

'I've been drinking Bloody Marys. I'll continue in the same vein.' Ramón pursed his lips together. I thought he was going to kiss me too but instead he said 'OK' and left.

'Sit, sit, sit,' insisted Dolores, once we were alone. I sat on a scrappy-looking metal chair.

'Your mother has told me everything about you,' she burbled.

I could imagine.

'Private detective! That is so exciting, so glamorous, like James Bond.'

'It has its moments.' The moments were OK; it was the hours that were long and boring. 'Your life's pretty exciting too, from what I hear.'

'You heard about me? In Paris, New York, Tokyo, everyone knows me. I didn't know I was famous in Sydney too.'

'Actually my mother told me.'

'Oh,' she said. But that little thimbleful of water wasn't going to dampen her spirits. 'She is so cute, Mina. And such a fantastic ostrich! We have birds like this in South America.'

But I hadn't been summoned here to discuss bird life.

'I have a job for you. Are you available?'

Was I available! I'd been nothing but available for the last month or so, not even any boring insurance surveillance had come up.

'Depends what it is,' I said coolly.

'Very easy and very nice. I want you to go shopping with me.'

I sat staring into the bottom of the third Scotch for a long time. Shopping had never particularly grabbed my interest. I could never understand how women could spend so much time on it. But then I never understood how the blokes in the pub could stand there for hours talking football. It was a different matter once I learned the rules and came to recognise a virtuoso player in action. And she was a virtuoso. Dolores Delgado was the Mal Meninga of shopping.

I turned the cassette over and played the other side. Three Scotches and I could see all sorts of things in the bottom of that glass. The music played on, a soundtrack to a flickering film. It was the track called 'Danzarin' that brought back one particular image of last night. That was the music for the audience participation number. I had been dancing with Ramón so I didn't see it happen but I heard Dolores' reaction. 'Jerk,' I heard her say. Ramón and I danced over to her.

'What happened?'

'Some jerk pinch my bottom,' she said, rubbing it. It wasn't the first time something like that had happened.

Ramón let go of me. 'That's it, Dolores. We don't dance with the crowd no more, OK? It makes trouble for you. And it's no fun for me either. I never know when you are going to finish. Always one more then another and another.'

Dolores pulled Ramón forcefully to her, the same way he did to her at the start of the performance. Dolores' eyes were full of fire but her voice was hard as ice. 'Enough. This is a perfor-mance, we are performers. You want to fight we fight after. Now we dance.'

My eyes flicked round the room looking for a potential bottom pincher. But all I could see were people partying and having a good time. Whoever had done it had probably forgotten all about it by now.

This wasn't the first time I'd seen the two dance partners have a disagreement. Disagreement is putting it mildly. Ramón never liked this part of the routine but Dolores said she always danced with her public and nothing was going to stop her. The arguments were usually about the routine but not always. One night there'd been an argument about something else. I recognised a couple of words of it—*mujer*, woman, and *dinero*, money. They stopped as soon as I entered the room. When they argued about dancing they didn't do that.

For some reason I thought the bottom of a fourth glass of Scotch would reveal even more. It didn't. After the fifth I didn't even bother looking.

I t was close to midday when I woke and despite the fact that the room was still darkened I felt as if I'd been lying out on the Nullarbor for forty days and forty nights. During some of those days and nights several coachloads of tourists had driven over me. What ever had given me the idea that drinking a bottle of Scotch was going to help any?

I opened the curtains and let in the day. It wasn't that bad except that everything was far too white. I opened the doors and looked at the geraniums on the balcony. They were very red. I would have liked to be lying in a pool of very clean water in the middle of a tropical paradise.

Instead I made my way to the bathroom where I underwent physical torture. I scrubbed several layers of skin off with the loofah then stood under the shower and subjected myself to steaming hot needles of water. By the time I'd finished with the cold water treatment I was fairly bristling.

That was on the outside. On the inside clouds swirled round. I felt dismay, disappointment, regret, curiosity, all at once. There was mystery surrounding Dolores' life and not all of it was made up, some of it was real. She was involved in something, she or Lola or Valerie. A drug courier? Smuggling? What does a girl with three passports do? I felt cheated. Robbed. I'd hardly begun to get to know her and suddenly she wasn't there anymore.

People who live mysterious lives sometimes die of natural causes but I felt sure this wasn't the case with Dolores. You don't hire a private investigator just to have someone to go shopping with. More than that, it was the way she died. A dramatic collapse, yes. But dribbling, in public during a performance? Dolores would never have done that if it had simply been a heart attack. If she was still alive I'd be asking her exactly why she hired me. I smiled ruefully—she probably wouldn't have given me a straight answer anyway.

I combed out my wet hair. If she were still alive . . . She couldn't answer any questions dead but if she were alive . . . Maybe she could be alive. Her death wasn't public knowledge yet, on the dance floor it just looked as if she collapsed. There'd be no funeral till the relatives were contacted, there was nothing in the papers. The cops knew but I didn't think the killer would be phoning the cops to find out. If whoever killed her thought they hadn't succeeded or weren't sure, maybe they'd try again. Only Cilla and Ramón were there to know that the ambulance had failed to revive her.

Maybe I could revive her. Wear her clothes, do the things she did, step into her life. By finding out about her life maybe I could find out about her death. It was going to be risky leading that life, it was a life that had ended in murder. But I'd taken risks before.

I phoned the hospital and the cops. They remembered who I was. No-one had enquired about Dolores and even if they had they wouldn't have been told. If someone had died it was policy not to answer queries concerning them over the phone. Good. Those leaks seemed to be plugged up.

'Dolores collapsed of nervous exhaustion and is having a few days off.' I explained the story to Cilla. Not surprisingly she wasn't at first willing to go along with a lie of such mammoth proportions. It didn't appear to be a moral dilemma, she just didn't want any trouble at the club. 'It won't be good for business if cops start coming to the club and they will start coming if I hand over the evidence I found in her hotel room.' I explained about the false passports. 'Oh,' she said. She asked a few more questions. I told her I would appreciate her cooperation, that I thought Dolores' heart attack wasn't due to natural causes and that I was investigating her death. I told her I could keep the investigation nice and quiet or she could have a big noisy one. She opted for the former.

The club was closed for the next two days anyway, it was just a question of extending Dolores' days off, I reasoned.

'What about Ramón, have you told him?' she asked.

'Not yet. Do you have his number?' I didn't think Ramón would be any trouble. I had the impression he'd prefer a nice quiet investigation as well.

'I'm seeing him today. I'll tell him if you like.'

I liked. The story would probably sound better coming from Cilla.

Meanwhile I would put the plan into action. Nervous exhaustion or not, what Dolores did on her days off was go shopping.

Rule number 1. First dress for the occasion. 'Dress the best you can to go shopping, image is everything. If you dress in dull clothes the shop assistant will try to sell you dull clothes.'

I put on a hip-hugging black miniskirt and black lace camisole. I took out my black boots then had a better idea. The mock alligator ankle boots. Dolores had insisted on buying them for me. They weren't really my style but they would look just fine in Oxford Street. I was as careful with my appearance as a candidate for a job interview, or an actor going for an audition. I plastered on so much make-up it didn't look like my face anymore. I put on Dolores' jacket and had a look in the mirror. I looked great.

Except for one huge oversight—my flaming red hair.

I took it all off and put on the clothes I wear to go up to the shops in Darling Street.

'Morning, Jack,' I said on my way out.

'You're looking a mite chirpier than you did earlier. By the way, it's afternoon.'

I looked at my watch. 'Only just.'

There were several chemist shops in Balmain but Soul Pattinson was the biggest. I went in there.

Rule number 2. 'Look at everything. Compare and contrast.'

Having never been previously interested in the subject I didn't realise what an array of colours there were in hair dyes. Even something as basic as black came in about seven different shades. As well as that, different brands called the same shade a different name. This could take all day.

Rule number 3. 'Once all items have been examined, make a choice. Never go home emptyhanded.' I finally settled on 'Raven'.

Back in my room I read the instructions, put on the plastic gloves that were part of the kit and applied the black paste to my hair. During the twenty to forty minutes I had to wait for it to work I range Cilla again and asked if I could pick up some of Dolores' things. She said she'd be there tomorrow afternoon, why didn't I come over then?

Then I reached into the pockets of Dolores' jacket and pulled out the cards. As well as the key card there were credit cards. If I was going shopping as Dolores, for the sort of purchases I had in mind, I was going to have to learn to forge her signature.

There was Amex, Visa and another. It had Dolores' name on it but it also had a company name–Royal Dolphin Enterprises. Except briefly last night while I was looking for her key card, I'd never seen her credit cards. She kept a tight hold on these little beauties, as if she'd turn into a pumpkin without them. Now I could look at them as long as I pleased.

I went to the phone book. Royal Dolphin Enterprises had a 008 phone number. I tried it. 'Royal Dolphin Enterprises, Melissa speaking.' I asked to speak to Dolores Delgado. Melissa asked me to repeat it. I did. She informed me they had no Dolores Delgado working there. I asked them what their address was. She gave me a Gold Coast address. I asked if they had an office in Sydney. Then she started asking who wanted to know. I hung up.

I tested a strand of hair. It didn't look raven to me, more russet; but it was definitely darker than it was when I started. Another twenty minutes should do the trick.

Amex and Visa are pretty ordinary, everyone has them. But the other one had her name on it though they'd never heard of her. How did she come to have it? Was this another piece of false identity?

I sat down at my low lacquer table with the card and a magnifying glass. I was faintly amused, the magnifying glass made me feel like Sherlock Holmes. But this was the first time I'd ever used it. I kept it because it belonged to my grandmother. She used it for reading, forever optimistic that her eyesight would get better and she wouldn't need something as permanent as glasses.

I got out a big sheet of drawing paper I keep for when the kids visit. They weren't going to be needing it these holidays, I reminded myself. I took a pen and started forging Dolores' signature. Maybe it was just as well they weren't here, I wasn't setting a very good example. I practised writing it larger than it was on the card. For the flow. I put on Dolores' leather jacket, played some tango music and practised it some more. To get the feel. Then I practised it without looking. I got up, walked around, sat down and did it again.

The alarm went off. Twenty minutes had elapsed. It was time to test another strand of hair.

Perfect. Raven as it could be.

I rinsed it out then used the special sachet of shampoo. When my hair was nearly dry I arranged it the way Dolores arranged hers. It took some time to get it to look as if basically nothing had been done to it.

Then I put the clothes back on and touched up the make-up. I picked up the Royal Dolphin credit card and put it in the jacket pocket. Ready to go.

I studied myself in the mirror. I looked terrific, Dolores would have been proud of me. Now all I had to do was get out of Balmain without anyone I knew seeing me. I hoped I wasn't going to get run over. It might be all right for Dolores but I didn't want to be seen dead wearing mock alligator ankle boots.

Her sunglasses were in the other pocket of the jacket. She wore them practically everywhere, except when she was actually dancing. They looked like the sort of sunglasses Madonna wore. Walking along the street one day we'd gone past a record store with a poster of Madonna in the window. Dolores stopped, and had stopped me by laying her hand on my arm. She gave the poster an approving appraisal. 'Not such a good dancer, not the best voice in the world, but style! Madonna makes herself. She has created her person.' Then Dolores had drawn me close to her and spoken seductively into my ear: 'But a naughty girl. You know what I mean?' I could feel Dolores' hot little breath on my cheek, it was not entirely unpleasurable. 'I met her once. New York. You know what I like best about Madonna? The armpits. Beautiful armpits. Smooth like avocado, then the little muscle on the arm. She does lots of aerobics and eats rice cakes. I prefer pizza.' She looked at the poster again, hand on her hip and the other one on her chin. 'The eyebrows are no good,' she said dismissively. 'Overdone.' Dolores herself had fine slim eyebrows. Each small fine hair individually etched on.

I walked up to the cab rank in Darling Street without too many heads turning. I usually catch the bus if I'm going into the city. It's not far and if you do it out of peak hours you get there in about the same time as it takes to drive, with no parking problems at the other end. I don't mind public transport. It gives me time to think and there's always the oddball on board who makes it interesting. I know, because they usually sit next to me.

There were three cabs in the rank, the drivers reading newspapers or eating snacks. I got in the first cab and told him I wanted to go to Darlinghurst.

He put his newspaper down. ' 'Nother developer gone to the wall,' he commented as we drove up and stopped at the only set of traffic lights in Balmain.

'Yes,' I said.

'You wonder when this recession's ever going to end. Weather's good but, isn't it?'

I said yes, trying not to give him any more lead-ins. He was a nice enough bloke but I didn't feel particularly chatty. I always thought it would be a good idea for cabs to have No Talking signs, the way they have No Smoking signs.

Today was bright and sunny. The only way you could tell it

was winter was by looking at the calendar. Darling Harbour sparkled. A westerly wind was blowing all the pollution out to sea. It'd all come back eventually but on days like this planet Earth looked a mighty fine place to be. It felt so good I almost stopped thinking about the unnaturalness of the weather. The meteorologists were telling us it was because of *El Niño*, a weather phenomenon from South America, but we all knew in our heart of hearts it was ozone damage; we'd done it to ourselves. Yet another endangered species—*homo sapiens*, only not so *sapiens* as we thought we were. Winters in Sydney used to be cold and wet. Now it rained all summer and in winter it was fine. It wasn't normal. Something was happening to the world. The spring bulbs in the pots on my balcony were already out. I'd even seen a blowfly. In June. In Sydney. And the cockroaches, those staunch little creatures who would inherit the future, had begun reappearing.

'Think it will rain?' asked the cab driver. There was not a cloud in the sky.

Just be polite, Claudia, the guy's only trying to make conversation, you don't have long to go now. 'Eventually. In summer.'

He kept talking, about the weather. All the way through the city centre and up Liverpool Street. He was still talking about the weather and I was still grunting yes, no, when we went through the lights at Whitlam Square. We were nearly there. I could get out now.

No, I couldn't. If I was Dolores I wouldn't be coming from my place I'd be coming from hers. I got him to drive me to the street behind the Hotel Royale. I came round the front and stood there conspicuously looking for a cab. Cabs cruised Kings Cross all the time. I didn't have to wait long.

Oxford Street was booming with life—skinny black tights, multi-studded ears, pasty faces and hair that needed washing. Drivers of cars followed me with their eyes, some of them leaned out and made comments, one car even cruised along slowly beside me. I didn't go much on uninvited looks and comments myself but I was pleased. It was working—Dolores was provoking her usual reaction.

I walked into the dress shop, through a central doorway with display windows either side. The shop was carpeted and quiet compared to the street, as if they wanted to hear you spending the money. The carpet was soft dove grey. The whole of Sydney seemed to be carpeted in grey. It was the carpet colour of the eighties but still around in the nineties. The recession. Carpet was the last thing you spent your money on. I hoped I wasn't going to feel guilty about spending money because that's exactly what I was here for.

The walls were grey–blue, there was a bit of chrome but it wasn't overdone. On the racks were the street clothes. A lot of them were black. I'd been here before with Dolores and I knew where the real treasure lay. Upstairs.

On the landing where the stairway to heaven turned, like a promise of things to come, was a mannequin in a strapless dress with fitted top and the equivalent of the entire GNP of a third world country invested in the skirt. The top was rich red brocade and the full-length gloves were the same. The skirt was layers and layers of red and black net. It was Dolores personified. But this was only the entrée. I went further up the stairs, to the accompaniment of wispy summer clouds on a blue background.

I came to the last step and entered dress heaven. The wispy clouds followed me in, as did the dove grey carpet. There were muted spotlights embedded in the ceiling. The change rooms were either side of a full-length arched mirror with a classic Greek edging in white plaster. The whole interior was designed to make you feel like a million dollars. When I saw the price tags I understood why.

The dresses were grouped together in shades of the one colour. Every shade of the spectrum except bright yellow but there was enough gold to make up for that. All the big names were here. Lots of strapless numbers with hectares of skirts. Brocade, velvet, silk, taffeta. It was luscious. Magentas, indigo, midnight blue. It was better than a complete set of Derwent coloured pencils.

There was no-one else here, just me and Dolores' credit card.

We both roamed the range, glutting ourselves on excess. It seemed to go on for hours till I became aware of someone softly speaking to me. I turned from my multicoloured daze to see a shop assistant who looked as if she'd be more at home selling Laura Ashley. I hadn't seen her in here before. That was good—it meant she hadn't seen me in here before either. She too was soft and pastel, with no strain in her face. Must come from working in places where the only sound is the sound of the machine sliding across the bankcard.

'We're having a . . . sale,' she whispered as if it was a dirty word. 'Don't worry about the prices, just pick the dress you really really want.' She breathed. 'Once you have found the dress you have fallen in love with tell me and we'll do you a deal.' She must have been in her stride now—deal didn't seem anywhere near as distasteful to her as sale. 'We can throw a pair of gloves in, or you can pay less for cash.'

'Ask her questions, make comments, tease her, don't let her think you're an easy sale, stretch it out, play with it.' I could feel Dolores hovering at my shoulder. But I already knew which dress I was going to choose. I dispensed with the foreplay.

'The one on the mannequin.'

'Oh,' she said, 'I'm not sure that one is for sale. One moment please.' She floated down the stairs to confer with some invisible decision maker. Sorry, Dolores, I couldn't help myself. But at least choosing the one on the mannequin had teased the transaction out a little.

When she returned I could already see by her smile that the answer was yes. There was a slight problem though, it was a one off, there weren't any other sizes. 'We can alter it,' she said, 'if it doesn't fit.' She looked me up and down. 'It looks about your size actually. You might be in luck.' She smiled her Laura Ashley smile, careful not to wrinkle her eyes. Her optimism was contagious and I was prepared to buy the dress without even trying it on, especially as I was spending someone else's money. But I thought I'd better go through the motions. No-one buys a dress that expensive straight off the mannequin. This one was so expensive it didn't even have a price tag.

She unzipped the dress and peeled it off the mannequin. And the gloves. She carried it carefully, delivering it to me as if it were a wedding gown. A far cry from what I wore at my own wedding. I think I had flowers in my hair but that was about it; they came from Hyde Park where we went after the Registry Office and got drunk.

The dress looked fabulous. Especially when I breathed in. In the mirror I hardly recognised myself. 'I'll take it,' I said.

Laura Ashley smiled again. 'Is it cash or charge?' she whispered.

Now was show-and-tell time. All that was standing between me and the dress was Dolores' signature. I'd come this far I had to go all the way. Into the valley of death rode the $500 limit.

'Charge,' I said.

'It's $2700,' she whispered in an even lower voice. 'If you're really really in love with this dress we can throw in the gloves as well.'

'I'm in love, I'm in love,' I reassured her.

I unzipped the dress and took it off. I didn't know how she was going to wrap it, it didn't looked like an ordinary sized plastic bag would accommodate it. But shopgirls have their tricks of the trade. When I came back out of the change room there was a large extra-strength plastic bag on the counter. Miraculously the skirt had folded down to a reasonable size and as long as the handles didn't break it wouldn't spring out to its full glory.

I gave her Dolores' card. 'One moment, please,' she whispered. $2700 was a large amount. She discreetly made the phone call to check the credit rating. Everything seemed to be in order. She put the card through the machine. Then handed me the pen. I signed without hesitation. She gave the signature a cursory comparison and handed me the carry bag. Mission accomplished.

Me, my card and my dress floated back down those stairs.

Oxford Street was just as grimy, just as pasty, but I didn't care. I'd brought Dolores back to life, doing what she liked doing best—shopping. Spending the company's money. Best of all I had a stunning new dress. But there was more to it than that.

I'd done it. I'd carried out the deception and got away with it.
And I didn't feel the least bit guilty. On the contrary, I felt
fantastic, exhilarated. I had carte blanche, I could do anything.

Cars could follow me down the street, drivers could lean out
and make comments, I didn't care. I floated down Oxford Street
to Crown. The WALK sign was a lovely shade of green. Even
the lights are in my favour, I thought, as I floated along.

I was almost halfway across before I was suddenly jolted back
to earth. 'Look out!' someone screamed. I spun round. Jesus
Christ! There was a grey Celica almost on top of me! I dived
out of the way just in time.

The road smelled cold and stony. A grey-haired man with
grey stubble on his face helped me up. My father would have
grey hair by now. If he was still alive.

'You all right, love?' He smelled of stale wine. I didn't know
who was shakier, him or me.

'Yes, thanks,' I panted.

'You just sit here till you catch your breath.' He sat me in
the gutter. 'Here's your shopping,' he said, handing it to me. I
sat there staring at it. The bag was split and the black and red
net cascaded out. The net was ripped. Was God punishing me
for forging Dolores' signature?

'Bloody fool,' the man said to the little crowd that had
gathered. 'Went straight through the red light.'

I looked up. 'Did you get his number?'

'Sorry, love, it all happened so quick. It was a grey car, that's
all I saw.'

I stood up and brushed myself off. My stockings had holes in
the knees. This was how a lot of people dressed in Darlinghurst
but mine weren't intentional. 'Did anyone get the number, see
who was driving?' I asked desperately.

No-one had. I hadn't really expected to be that lucky. I was
grateful just to be alive.

Carol's red Subaru was parked outside the pub with Carol sitting in it reading something that looked like a report.

I bent down and tapped on the window. She looked up, a little quizzical. 'Yes?'

'Carol, it's me.'

'Claudia? What are you doing behind all that make-up, and your hair, it's gone black.' She put away her reading material, got out of the car and took a good look at me. 'It's the dancer,' she said dumbfounded, 'you're dressing up as that dancer. Well, isn't that a coincidence. I've come here to give you some news about her. I've been to the morgue.'

'Oh?'

'Yes. Very interesting. I could have phoned and told you but then I wouldn't be able to see the look on your face. Well, have you lost your manners, aren't you going to invite me in for a drink?'

Must have been big news for Carol to be here in person. 'Come in.'

We went into the pub. 'I thought you weren't interested in Dolores.'

'You're right, I wasn't. I was there on another matter. Let's have a drink, shall we?' She was bursting to tell me her news but she wasn't going to give it to me straight away; she wanted to dangle it in front of me for a while. Well, she could dangle it for a while if she liked, it didn't bother me. I was interested, but I could wait. I had other things to think about, such as grey Celicas going through red lights to run me over. Run Dolores over.

I got Jack's attention. 'VB and a dry martini,' I said. He leaned over. 'I recognise the voice but not the hair. What happened to that redhead that used to live upstairs?'

'She's gone on holidays.'

'Undercover, is it?' he said in a low voice.

'Something like that.'

Jack shook his head and went away to get the drinks.

Carol had a connoisseurial taste of her martini before registering her approval. It had taken Jack a couple of goes and a few complaints from Carol but now he knew just how to make the martini to the degree of dryness Carol liked. And he never forgot the olive. It didn't really make a blind bit of difference to Jack whether she approved or not. It wasn't as if she was keeping the place afloat.

'Been shopping, have we?' asked Carol, eyeing the split bag with the dress in it.

'I have. I don't know about you.'

'She's gone, Claudia, you don't have to keep doing it.'

'Maybe I don't want to stop; maybe I've developed a taste for it.'

'Well, all I can say is that I hope this bimbo phase is only temporary.'

'I'm a bimbo because I go shopping? Listen Carol, you've been sucked in, that's the official view, the party line. You know why it's considered trivial? Because it's something women do, same as housework. Come to think of it, it's not only women who shop, men do it too. They go out picking up little treasures to bring home. The British Museum is full of men's shopping. Only they don't pay for it.'

'Yes, all right, you don't have to beat me over the head with it,' she grumbled. 'Don't you want to know what my news is?' she said, ready now to deliver it.

'I'm dying of curiosity.'

'Dolores has caused a minor sensation at the morgue, everyone's talking about her.'

'I'm listening.'

'Well first of all you might be interested in knowing how your friend died,' she said, taking a sip of her martini. 'Cause of death was myocardial infarction.'

'I could have told you that.'

'Let me finish. My forensic colleagues aren't completely satisfied, they're sending specimens to the labs at Lidcombe.'

'The labs at Lidcombe?'

'Diagnostic Analytical Laboratories. They analyse poisons. Amongst other things.'

It didn't come as a complete surprise.

'That's not what everyone is talking about. Actually, it's funny you dressing up as Dolores because that's what she, or rather he, did too.'

'He?'

'Dolores Delgado was a transsexual.'

I was speechless. Even dead, Dolores had one more surprise. I couldn't believe it. The deception had been complete. I was dismayed, disillusioned. I'd been completely taken in. All those little lies; they were so obvious. But she was a lot smarter than that. The real truth, the depths of her being, remained hidden. The camouflage had been complete. 'She had no ovaries, there'd been . . . alterations, surgery,' I heard Carol say. Till now, till the body that had been so carefully put together was being pulled apart.

Carol was smiling happily. The look on my face must have been worth the trip.

Only in retrospect did I start adding it up and then it didn't always tally. The little scars, the small plump breasts, the lavish care with her appearance, make-up, the 'girlie' things. The shopping.

The reason it didn't add up was that I was trying to fit Dolores into a stereotype, a drag queen whose high camp mannerisms become a parody of women—the clothes, the make-up, the false eyelashes, the flamboyance. I was thinking transvestite rather than transsexual. Dolores' gender was more than skin-deep; it wasn't a caricature, it was her. The only slip-up was to have been born into the wrong body. But Dolores fixed that. As she had told me more than once, she made herself. It didn't matter that she had no ovaries, it didn't matter that, as Carol reported, the body had been altered—Dolores was Dolores.

I hoped the morgue workers hadn't made too many jokes when they cut open her body. I knew why they made the jokes, same reason surgeons in operating theatres do it—to keep themselves one step removed from it. It's not normal to stare this closely at death every day. And it reminds you. One day you're going to be lying on that slab too.

I didn't really want to think about that. The body being cut open, dissected, handled, bits taken out, as if she was no longer a person, just a collection of parts.

I looked at the things that belonged to Dolores: the sunglasses, the leather jacket, even the new Carmen Miranda dress I'd bought. These were parts of Dolores too, part of the persona she projected, part of the image she created. But she didn't need the clothes or the body anymore. I could almost see her hovering around at the morgue while they were cutting up the body she'd had specially made for her, waiting to see the look on their faces when they discovered the additions and subtractions. 'Come right in, suckers,' I could hear her saying, 'and be sure of a big surprise.' They might make jokes about her but it would be Dolores who'd have the last laugh.

While the big news had eclipsed almost everything else, Carol was also professional enough to remember the humdrum details of the autopsy and unprofessional enough to tell me.

There were injection marks on the thighs and buttocks, possible site of entry of poison, if indeed it turned out to be poison. They could have been caused by hormone injections. That'd be where Dolores would do it, not somewhere visible such as the arms. Carol started pointing out the alternatives. 'It could have been an accident, an overdose of hormones.'

'Is that possible?'

'You can certainly OD on steroids,' she suggested, 'it does

affect the heart muscle. Don't you remember that footballer at Cootamundra a couple of years ago?'

The injection marks mightn't mean a thing. Poison could have been administered in another way, in food or drink. There was always the bitters. She said it put hairs on her chest, ironic considering the hormones she must have taken to keep them off. It tasted awful but it kept her alert, sharpened her performance, she said. It tasted awful already; if a drop or two of poison had been added to it she wouldn't have even known the difference.

Need it have been something that had been administered that night? Maybe it was something slow-acting. My thoughts were going round in circles without getting anywhere. It was all conjecture till the analysis showed some results—the kind of poison in the system, how long it took to work.

'How long does it take for the results to come back from Lidcombe?' I asked Carol.

' 'Bout three weeks under normal circumstances,' she estimated.

'God,' I moaned, 'we could all be dead by then.'

'Under normal circumstances,' I said. Seeing that she's everybody's darling down at the morgue and they want to know everything there is to know about her it'll probably go through in a few days.' Carol snorted, as if remembering a funny joke. 'Come to think of it, she's every darling's body.'

Carol was quite pleased with herself. Sometimes she can be really funny. This wasn't one of those times.

I had a dilemma. I needed to know the results of those tests as soon as possible. I also needed those laboratories at Lidcombe to test the Angostura bottles for poisons. Carol and her 'official channels' could easily satisfy those needs. But I wasn't sure I wanted this to be an official case. If the cops started sniffing around the club, Dolores' room, whoever had had a go at me in the grey Celica would get scared off. They'd come after the bait once. I wanted them to try again. This time I'd be ready. I'd get them on the hook and, when the moment was right, reel them in.

Carol had finished her martini. She was looking at me shrewdly. 'You're up to something, aren't you?'

'What do you mean?' I hoped the enquiry sounded innocent.

'It's not grief that's making you dress up as Dolores, you're up to something. Now what would a private investigator be doing— investigating perhaps?'

I said nothing.

'Tell you something, if you have grounds for suspicion I don't really want to know at the moment. The question of treating this as a homicide has come up in my department. Was it natural causes, an accident or homicide? Suicide? A case can languish in the red tape while the powers that be decide who should deal with it. So if you do have a little investigation going you just go right ahead. When you find something concrete, outside of your emotional involvement in the matter, then I think we should know about it. If you do find anything, that is.'

'So you want me to do your work but you don't want the responsibility.'

I'd hit a nerve. 'I wouldn't say that.' She recovered her composure. 'Besides, if you really wanted us in on the case you would have made it perfectly clear before this.'

I didn't want this to be an official homicide case and neither did she. 'Well,' I said, 'it seems that things are to our mutual satisfaction.'

'Indeed.' She stood up.

'One more thing, Carol, before you go.'

'What is it? I hope it isn't going to spoil the happy ending,' she said, as if some bad news was about to come her way.

'Can you let me know as soon as the labs have a result? If I did happen to be carrying out an investigation it would help enormously.'

'Always willing to help a friend,' she said magnanimously.

I packed a few things into a bag and set off for the Cross. I told Jack I'd be popping in every so often but if there really was an emergency he could contact me at the Hotel Royale.

He was still shaking his head when I walked out the door and got into the Daimler.

I arrived at the hotel just before six. The drive across town had been uneventful, despite the peak hour traffic. I spent a lot of the trip looking in the rear vision mirror but no-one followed me. I didn't see any grey Celicas following or not following. You'd think in peak hour traffic there'd be at least one.

Vicki, the receptionist, was just about to finish her shift. She looked up in surprise. 'D . . .' she started to say.

'No, it's Claudia, I've dyed my hair.'

Vicki had a round face that she tried to give some contour to by wearing lots of blusher. Her honey blonde hair was swept up from her face then cascaded onto her shoulders. She used a lot of mousse. I'd never really noticed about the mousse before but I was developing an eye for these things.

'Of course,' she said, back to her cheerful, efficient self, 'you're Dolores' friend.' Her tone changed. 'Is she all right? Someone's been phoning all day and she hasn't been answering. No-one's seen her either.'

'Well that's why I'm here. I came the other night but you weren't on duty. Dolores collapsed from nervous exhaustion and she's gone to a health farm down the south coast for a few days. She left me her keys and everything, said you wouldn't mind if I stayed in her room while she's away to keep an eye on things.'

'Ah . . .' She thought about it for about fifteen seconds. 'Yes. I can't see anything wrong with that.' It didn't take her long to make a decision. She was young, innovative and made sure the place ran smoothly without bothering the management with every little detail. 'Can I ask you a personal question?'

'Sure.'

'Is there any reason you dyed your hair black? From a distance it makes you look just like Dolores.'

There was no turning back now. 'Great! Dolores will be so pleased.' I got more confidential. 'Actually, while she's away she wants me to buy her some new dresses. We're about the same size so I could easily try them on for her, but I can't get a true sense of how the colour's going to be with red hair.'

The lying wasn't nearly as guilt-free as the shopping had been. Somewhere in the back of my brain was a little voice telling me what a tangled web I was weaving. Vicki seemed to go for it but I didn't want her to dwell on it too long, she might think up some hard questions.

'You said someone was ringing?'

'Yes. Do you want to take the call if anyone rings back?'

'That'd be the best thing. Just put them through and I'll explain what happened.'

Everything seemed to be all right. For the moment. I took the lift to the sixth floor.

Dolores' room was exactly the way I'd left it. The maid might have been in but she hadn't done anything. No-one had slept here so there was no bed to make. No-one had used the bathroom. Barbara Cartland's eyelashes were still sitting there on the dressing table. Despite the pinkness and the mess of things the room felt sad and empty.

I turned the radio on for a bit of noise and opened the doors that led onto the minute balcony. Over in the west the sun was setting. Down below cars passed slowly by. It was impossible to go fast in the Cross. I knew I'd be taking risks by adopting this course of action, by coming to stay in this room, by living Dolores' life. But I thought all the risks were physical. I hadn't counted on the emotional risks I was exposing myself to. It wasn't as if I'd lost someone close to me like the kids, or Steve. Carol even. Despite her little and sometimes extravagant lies I was fond of Dolores. But it wasn't as simple as that. I felt duped, disappointed, betrayed even. I needed to distance myself from her life to get a perspective on it. But instead here I was, right in the thick of it.

The sun was down now, I came inside. I'd be far better off doing something rather than letting these thoughts circle round and round. For a start I could unpack her bags. I took the dresses out one by one and hung them in the wardrobe.

At the bottom of the first suitcase was a photo. Of a child sitting on a bench, big brown eyes, legs sticking out of short pants, a rather tearful look on his face. Dolores' child? On the back of it in faded ink it said: Danny's first haircut. Aged 3. A photo of Dolores as a little boy?

Just as I was about to embark on the second suitcase the phone rang. I said hello in Dolores' voice a couple of times then picked up the phone.

'Hello?'

'Where have you been? It was a man's voice, with an urgent sound to it. 'I've been phoning the last two days, you haven't been in. Is everything all right?'

'Of course, why not?' I tried to make it sound buoyant, the way Dolores would, while all the while trying to glean what I could from his voice. Can you tell over the phone what kind of car a person drives and whether they tried to run you over in it?

'Your voice sounds different, a bit strained.'

I had to think fast. 'I have a face mask on, I don't want to move my lips too much.'

'I'll be there in twenty minutes, will the mask be off by then?'

'Sure.' I could hardly wait.

He was more relaxed now, seductive. 'Good, because in twenty minutes I want those lips to be moving. See you then.'

Boy was he in for a surprise! I was living Dolores' life but I wasn't going to go as far as moving my lips for her boyfriends. Well, probably not.

Twenty minutes. It was like going on a blind date. A mixture of excitement and uncertainty. It was more than the normal doubts about blind dates, this one could be with Dolores' murderer. I fussed around, checked my make-up, threw some of the mess into the cupboard but not too much. I wanted it to look like Dolores still lived here.

Fifteen minutes later I was watching from the balcony, to check out any cars that drove up, to see if I could catch a glimpse of the gentleman caller on his way in.

Twenty minutes later there was a knock on the door. I took a breath. 'Who is it?'

'It's me.' Oh great. It sounded like the man on the phone but I couldn't be sure.

'Just a minute,' I sang. Very quietly I unlocked the door. Then I stood behind it so that when he came in I could check him out. 'Come in.'

He came in. Dark hair greying at the temples, late forties, expensive casual gear, not very discreet. He'd made money rather than inherited it. A boyish face beginning to show signs of age. Jogged in the mornings but not enough to get rid of the thickening at the waist.

He did have something in his hand but it wasn't a weapon unless you call a bunch of red roses a weapon. Some people would.

'Where are you?' he sang as if his lover was playing a game with him.

I closed the door behind him.

He turned; and stopped dead in his tracks. 'But you're not . . . Are you her sister? She never mentioned a sister.'

'I'm Claudia, Dolores' friend.'

He relaxed a little, the name obviously rang a bell. 'Yeah, I think she's mentioned you. Your mother's the ostrich, right?'

'Right.' I was feeling slightly peeved. Was my biggest claim to fame the fact that my mother was an ostrich?

'So what's going on?' he said, looking around, 'Have you girls arranged a little surprise for me?' he asked.

Not the sort of little surprise you've got in mind, I thought. Be pleasant to the man, Claudia. You wanted to do it this way, you've got to take what comes along.

'Actually Dolores is away for a few days, I'm just here keeping my eye on things. Didn't they tell you at the desk?'

He smiled majestically, 'I don't go to the desk, I know my way around. Where did she go?' he asked.

'She's convalescing. Nervous exhaustion.'

'Really? She seemed fine last time I saw her.'

'When was that?'

'Three, four days ago. I've been away on a business trip. Just come back.'

'It happened quite suddenly, two nights ago. Just collapsed on the dance floor.'

'Is she in hospital? Can I go and see her?'

'She was there one night but then she went to a health farm on the south coast. She didn't tell me the name of it, said she wanted to be completely isolated.' I hoped he was going for it. Dolores would really have to be sick to want to be on her own. 'She'll probably ring here to let me know how things are going. Probably ring you too.'

'Well, it'd have to be on the mobile phone. She can't really ring me at home, you know how it is,' he implied, as if I did know.

OK, so you're married and you're having an affair. Surprise, surprise.

'If she rings, let her know I called in.'

'And what name can I give?'

'How many boyfriends does she have?' he joked confidently.

Don't get so cocky, I thought, there could be more than just you. All of them thinking they're the only one.

'Is there anywhere I can get in touch with you if I need to?'

'*I'll* be in touch with *you*,' he said. 'In the meantime, why don't you have these?' He held the roses out to me.

I went to take them then thought better of it. 'Just leave them on the table,' I said.

'You allergic to them?'

'Not normally.'

'See you soon.'

He left.

I unwrapped the roses, careful not to touch them. Gingerly I looked through them, separating each rose with a pen. There were no nasty little surprises in there. The guy seemed harmless enough but it was better to be sure.

I phoned reception. It was Patrick, the night-time receptionist. 'Hi, this is room 621. The guy that was just here, did he leave a name?'

'What guy?'

'He's only just left, you must have seen him.'

'No,' said Patrick, 'no-one's come through reception.'

'But you must have seen him come in, 'bout fifteen minutes ago. Maybe he went straight to the lifts.'

'No, no-one's been through reception in the last half hour.'

'Is there any other way of getting in? The fire escape?'

'You can get out that way, into the parking area, but you can't get in from the outside, the door's locked, you'd need a key.'

'Thanks.' I hung up.

So maybe the guy was still here, lurking around somewhere. I went out into the corridor. There was no-one about. I went back into the room and checked the balcony. You could probably reach it from the balcony next door but you'd need mountaineering equipment to do it. I came inside again.

I turned the light out and lay on the bed listening. I wished Steve was here. If the guy was still around I could handle him; it was the lying in the dark on my own that was getting to me.

I reached for the remote control and switched the TV on. There was a late night movie. There was probably nothing to worry about. The guy *seemed* OK. And if by chance he was Dolores' killer he knew now that I wasn't her. There'd be no point in killing me. Would there?

In the bright light of day Steve wasn't looking as good as he had in the darkness of last night. It had been a month now and still no word apart from the brief postcard on arrival. Thinking of you, it said. He could think of me as much as he liked but I wasn't receiving his thoughts, Germany was a bit beyond my range. All that seventies bullshit about being cosmically connected didn't wash with me anymore. I wanted to see a bit of effort being put into it; I wanted hard copy. If that's the way it was, if it was all starting to be an effort, maybe we had passed our use-by date. Not a particularly inspiring thought to have while waiting in the traffic for the lights to change. Those lights at the intersection of Darling Street and Victoria Road must be the slowest in the world.

They did change, eventually. I drove across the Iron Cove Bridge heading for Five Dock where Ramón lived. There were a lot of Italians living there but it didn't have the restaurants or colour that Leichhardt had. Five Dock was more residential, some areas of it had what every home buyer in Sydney wanted—water views. The views were of the Parramatta River rather than the harbour but at least it was water. And you didn't have to put up with the inner-city trendies who had invaded the cafés of Leichhardt. Inner-city trendies were very thin on the ground in Five Dock.

I turned left off Victoria Road and drove into Five Dock. Some of the houses were new blond brick two-storey numbers with arches and patios but Ramón lived in a street full of older style liver brick houses and front gardens. Most of the gardens looked like they were their owner's pride and joy—roses, neatly clipped lawns, paving stone paths.

It was the middle of the day and the street was quiet. There were no flowers in Ramón's front garden, only a dense patch of kikuyu. Standing round the edge of the grass was a whole gang of gnomes. They were all shapes and sizes with different expressions on their faces. They didn't blink an eye as I walked up the garden path but I knew they were going to talk about me later.

I pressed the white buzzer. It set off a dog barking on the other side of the door, a loud throaty bark, from the sort of dog you hope gets fed regularly. It continued to bark till I heard footsteps and a human voice say, 'Down, Christopher.' The barking became sporadic. 'Down.' Then it stopped.

A shortish blond guy opened the door. He had very pale eyes, a nose with a bump in it and a small chin. He was wearing a towel round his waist. A few blond hairs curled on his chest and there was a subtle roll of skin above the towel.

'Yes?' he said somewhat warily. He had that bleary look of the caffeine addict who needed a cup of coffee in the morning to kickstart the heart. And the morning only had a few more minutes left in it.

'Is Ramón in?'

He eyed me suspiciously. 'Who wants to know?'

'Claudia Valentine. He knows me, from the club.'

Just then another towel-clad figure emerged from the room. It was Ramón, scratching the stubble on his chin. Christopher the dog leapt up and was quickly ordered down. Ramón smiled an embarrassed smile and looked out from under those long black lashes. The whites of his eyes were very white for someone who'd just got out of bed. 'Come in,' he said, opening the security door.

The blond guy didn't seem too pleased but he stood aside to let me in. I knew who was wearing the pants in this household. The house smelled of dog. And stale smoke.

Christopher bounded down the hall, pushing past all the humans. At the end of the hall was a dining room with a high ceiling. The dining table had a black glass top and chrome legs. Bad colour black, shows everything up, including the specks of white on the table. Perhaps it was icing sugar. Then I noticed the money. You don't use a rolled up $50 note to ice a cake.

Ramón shook a cigarette out of a soft pack of Kent. He lit it with a black lighter lying on the table and started to smoke. He didn't offer one to anyone else. 'Your hair,' he commented, as if he'd just noticed it. 'It's good,' after further appraisal, 'all you need now is the dresses.'

'Don't worry, I'm working on it.'

The blond guy stood by keeping his eye on me. He wasn't leaving till he knew what I was here for. Ramón was flirting with me and the blond didn't like it. I knew as soon as he'd opened the door that I'd interrupted something. But, hey, it was practically midday, how long can a person stay in bed? All day, I recollected. At the beginning, when everything was rosy, Steve and I would spend whole weekends in bed, only getting up to fetch another bottle of champagne from the fridge.

The first drag of the day must have made Ramón feel human. 'Coffee?' he said, flashing his winning smile.

'Why not?' I replied. 'Long and black, thanks.'

'Greg, make us some coffee,' Ramón said beguilingly.

'Oh that's fine, isn't it!' said Greg sarcastically. 'I have to make coffee for your visitor. It's not the first time,' he said to me. 'He treats me like the maid. He seems to forget whose house it is,' the last comment directed back to Ramón.

I could feel a domestic shaping up here and being the third party to a domestic is never a good idea. Either side inevitably tries to win you over as an ally so that you can be called on as a witness to the supposed atrocities of the other side. And if you do, they join ranks and the only person on the other side is you.

Ramón made a noise with his tongue against the roof of his mouth, rolled his eyes and walked into the kitchen. The blond guy glared into space for a minute then flounced into the kitchen himself. 'I'd better do it. He's probably still trying to light the stove. Doesn't realise it's electric.'

Voices were raised and before long the door was slammed. This caused Christopher, who had settled in under the dining table, to leap up at the door. I didn't know which room was the lesser of the two evils. In here with Christopher trying to claw his way into the kitchen, or in the kitchen with the boys trying to claw each other.

Eventually the door opened, the dog bounded into the kitchen and Greg stormed out, right out of the house in fact.

Somehow though during all of this, coffee got made. Ramón came out with it. He looked down the hall after the blond.

'C'est la vie,' he philosophically. He put the coffees on the table, sat down and pointed me to a chair. His body was bronzed and his chest almost hairless. Just the way I liked it. Trim, taut and terrific. His nipples were large, flat and seductive, the colour of fine dark Dutch chocolate. I tried not to look at them, even though they were looking at me.

What a sly young dog he was. All that come-on to the women in the audience, all that self-promotion as some kind of Casanova and here he was living in the suburbs with a wife, a dog and domestic arguments. Even if the wife was a boy.

He seemed to take his domestic arguments with a lot more calm than he took his fights with Dolores. She egged him on, riled him. Maybe it was too early in the day for him to be fully revved up. It had been a big night judging by the debris on the table. Maybe it was because Dolores was more of a match for him. Maybe with Dolores it was the common background. It's a lot easier to argue in your native language.

Did she rile him enough for him to kill her? Not in cold blood. I could see him using a knife but not poison. You don't administer poison in the heat of the moment. He didn't strike me as the killer type but what did I know? Killers aren't types. They are your husband or your wife or your lover. Your dance partner.

I could have started with small talk but Ramón knew I wasn't here merely to pass the time of day. I'd never been inside his house before. We got on fine at the club but before this morning I knew virtually nothing of his private life. The blond in bed had come as a bit of a surprise. In my job I knock on a lot of doors. I get surprised all the time.

'Cilla told you we were going to say Dolores was away for a few days?'

'Yes,' he said. 'Good idea. People won't feel sad about her that way.'

'And the cops won't come round.'

'Yes, and the cops won't come round.'

'You wouldn't like that, would you?'

He shrugged. 'It's nothing to me, it's bad for the club to have the police visit. Everyone starts talking.'

'Let's leave the club aside for the moment. Let's talk about your relationship with the cops.'

'Relationship? I don't have relationships with cops.'

'And you don't want them to know you. Why?'

'Is this about what I said at the hospital? I told you, it was just a story.'

'Did you know Dolores was a transsexual?'

The question surprised him. His answer surprised me.

'How do you know?'

It wasn't the fact that she was a transsexual, it was the fact that I'd found out.

He'd known all along. He was pretending, trying to make it sound like a surprise but he'd known all along.

'The autopsy. You know something? I like you but you're full of shit.'

He was taken aback. I felt sorry for him as soon as I'd said it. Because I wasn't saying it to him. I was saying it to Dolores. Because I wanted Dolores to be here answering the questions. Right now I knew precisely how I felt about her—mightily pissed off that she'd left before I could even ask her the questions.

'OK, so I knew,' he admitted.

'How long?' You told him, Dolores, why didn't you tell me?

'It was the time before when she came to the club. One day I saw her with a needle, putting it in here,' Ramón grabbed a piece of his thigh. 'I think maybe it's drugs, I'm annoyed that she's doing it at the club. She explained then that she was a transsexual, that she was injecting hormones. After that I don't see no more needles. Dolores is very careful.'

'And no-one else knows?'

'I don't tell other people, it's none of their business. I have other friends who are transsexuals, they don't care if people know. But Dolores didn't want people to know, that was her secret.'

'And what's your secret, Ramón?'

'No secrets,' he smiled, 'I have nothing to hide.'

I picked up some remnants of the white powder and rubbed it between my thumb and forefinger. 'So you wouldn't mind a little police search of the house.'

'How come a nice girl like you asks all these questions?'

'Because a nice boy like you keeps lying all the time. You know what I think? I think that you and Dolores were using the club to move a bit of substance. What were all your fights about, you weren't getting your fair share? What weren't you getting your fair share of, the drugs or the money? Remember a week or so ago a fight you had with Dolores? As soon as I came in you both stopped. When you were fighting about something to do with the performance you didn't take any notice of me, you just kept on fighting. But this time was different. I didn't catch much of it but I have learned the odd word of Spanish hanging around at the club. I seem to recall hearing the Spanish for "woman" and "money". Am I right?'

'No, you're wrong,' he protested. 'There's no dealing drugs at the club. What do you think, we're all Colombian drug barons?' He glared at me. 'That woman with the money, I don't really know what that was about.

'It was early in the evening, no-one else was there. I went to the dressing room, there was a woman, a pretty woman, sitting with Dolores. When I open the door I see a pile of money on the dressing table. About this thick. Dolores is very angry, she says how dare I walk straight in like that? It's what I normally do, but this is the first time she says anything. After, I ask her what's going on. She says none of your business.'

'And this,' I said, waving my hand over the table, 'this is your business?'

'I don't need to do that shit. OK, last night we have a few friends come by, we use a little cocaine, but I'm not dealing it.' Then more quietly he said, 'Anything I need I get from Greg.'

'He's dealing?'

'No. He packs shelves at Woolworths, he's the supervisor.'

'And the pay is good enough to give you guys anything you want?'

'He doesn't need to work, he inherited money.'

'Five Dock isn't exactly Point Piper,' I remarked.

'You know why he bought this house? Because he wants a normal life—a normal life in the suburbs.'

'That what you want too?'

'I want excitement I've got the club. And here, I don't pay rent.'

'So you're being kept, like a mistress.'

He pursed his lips. 'I don't think of it this way.'

'Is that why you told the cops you'd only just arrived in the country? So they wouldn't ask you about your domestic situation?'

'Not exactly,' he said warily.

'Well, why then?'

He looked at me, shaking his head in disbelief. 'You're incredible, incredible. In my country, when they interrogate a prisoner they won't let him sleep. Night after night they wake him, leave him alone for an hour then wake him again. It never happened to me but now I know how it feels. OK, OK,' he said, putting up his hands, 'I confess, I confess. You know why I don't want to talk to the police? Because I am an illegal immigrant. I am not "direct from Buenos Aires", I have been here two years. If the police find out I get deported.'

'Does Cilla know?'

'Yes, yes, she knows.' He was heartily fed up with my questions. 'Are you satisfied, do you want a litre of blood as well?'

The doorbell rang. Christopher raced up the hallway, his bark echoing off the walls. Ramón followed. A few words were exchanged at the door then Ramón came back to the dining room. With Greg. Why did he have to ring the doorbell if he lived here? Then I remembered. He'd walked out in such a huff he'd forgotten his key. He'd been away about half an hour. Where does a man go to in Five Dock wearing only a towel?

He looked at me darkly. It was time to leave. Ramón saw me to the door. 'Let me know if you think of anything and if anyone asks about Dolores, you know the official story.'

'Sure. I still need a dance partner. How about it?' He nudged me, back to his flirtatious self. 'If you dance as good as you ask questions you'll be sensational.'

I stopped off in Leichhardt and had a tuna and artichoke focaccia. I liked the filling but it beats me what anyone sees in the rest. It tastes like stale sponge cake without the sugar. Funny thing is that this thick white bread is eaten by people who wouldn't dream of buying a loaf of Tip Top sliced white. The coffee was good though, and the atmosphere. Brown wood panels, fishing nets and markers draped from the ceiling, and an odd assortment of knick-knacks. Old style Italian–Australian kitsch. I liked it, it had a kind of innocence about it. At least it wasn't one of the new wave Italian cafés with tiled floor, white walls and chrome that made you feel as if you were sitting inside a fridge.

Leichhardt was on the way to Newtown and the Tropicana, where Cilla said she'd be this afternoon.

Even though it was three o'clock in the afternoon, when the roads are relatively quiet, King Street was chockers. Trucks heaved their gears and hissed their brakes, cars banked up behind them at the traffic lights at the big intersection near the station. To top it all off, just about every side and backstreet of Newtown was now one-way or no through road. Motorists looking for a quick bypass of King Street are condemned to an eternal wandering in a labyrinth of which there is only one way out—leave the car and walk. Which is what I did once I was safely parked in the parking lot behind the building the Tropicana was in. There were a few other cars in the lot, none of them grey

Celicas, but the one that really caught my eye was the 1966 Thunderbird, a 360. It was a beauty, sky blue, white upholstery, immaculate condition.

I walked up the stairs, the red carpet not quite so plush during the day as it was at night. It got darker the further up the stairs I went. I could hear rumba as I pushed open the door. Even from this distance it sounded terrible. The plastic palm trees and leaves hanging around the place weren't looking their best without the benefit of coloured lighting either. The place smelled of cold cigarette ash. At night you didn't seem to notice it. Nor did you notice scuff marks on the walls. Amazing what a little atmosphere will do.

I heard Cilla say something to the band. From the tone of her voice, and the tone of their playing, it didn't sound like they were going to get a job in this club. The band started packing up. They looked like they were straight out of the seventies. Flared trousers and Cuban heels. The lead singer even had frills on his cuffs. He was a weedy looking gentleman with hollow cheeks and a drooping moustache. The rest of them had black curly hair and softly sculptured features—just the way I like it. Pity they couldn't play.

Cilla was sitting on a lone chair in the middle of the room. It was the apex of a triangle, the base of which consisted of the two speakers. She had her legs crossed and between her fingers was an unlit cigarette. She uncrossed her legs and stood up when she saw me.

'Hi. Come to the bar.' She went behind the bar and poured two short black coffees, in small brown cups with small white saucers. She slid one across to me and popped two cubes of sugar in her own.

'Cubanitos,' she complained, bringing her well-shaped eyebrows together, 'they think they are born with the music in their blood. They see Desi Arnaz on television they think you just have to stand up on a stage and hey presto, God makes you a musician. They have no idea. Hey, Claudia, what did you do to your hair? You come for the job of replacement act?'

I liked the way she pronounced my name, making it sound like a cloud rather than a claw.

'A change is as good as a holiday.'

'You want a holiday, go to Rio. Girls in Rio kill for red hair.'

'Wouldn't be much of a holiday if I was dead. Not having much luck then with the replacement act?' I commiserated.

'So many musicians, so little talent,' she remarked. Her face brightened. 'Seriously, why don't you do it? You got the legs.' She grinned. 'And now you got the hair. Ramón can teach you. You're a natural.'

I was good with my legs, that'd come from years of karate training. I'd done a few rounds on the dance floor with Ramón, and my mother was a dancer, it wasn't that far-fetched. I was warming to the idea, like someone at a karaoke bar who just needs that extra bit of encouragement to get up on stage. If one more person suggested it to me, I just might do it.

'I've just been to see Ramón, actually. He said a woman came here, 'bout a week ago, to see Dolores. You remember that?' While I talked Cilla tapped the still unlit cigarette against her lip.

'Yeah, I remember her. I remember because she don't look like a woman normally goes to clubs.'

'What did she look like?'

'Pretty, well-dressed, good clothes. Like she don't go to clubs much but she wants to make a good impression. Not a young girl, though. This woman is 40, maybe 45. Australian accent. She asked to see Dolores.'

'She said Dolores? Not Dolores Delgado? Not the tango dancer?'

Cilla thought for a moment, playing with the cigarette. 'Yes, just Dolores. I told her Dolores is pretty busy before the show. She said, "Tell her it's Margaret Shaver, I think she will see me." '

'Margaret Shaver?'

'Yes. Dolores looked very surprised but very interested.'

'Got a phone book?'

'Which one you want?'

'White pages. L–Z.'

She dragged it out from under the counter and gave it to me.

There was only one Shaver in the Sydney phone book. Shaver, S. Short St, Balmain. I rang the number and asked for Margaret. There was no Margaret there. 'I'm looking for Margaret Shaver, do you have any relatives called Margaret?'

'No, I don't,' said the voice at the other end, 'and if this is direct marketing I'm not interested.'

'You sure about the name?' I quizzed Cilla after the person hung up on me.

'She said Margaret Shaver. You want me to ask for the birth certificate?'

'It'd be helpful. Maybe next time. Can I have a look at the bookings for the night Dolores died?'

Cilla swallowed her coffee in one gulp. I'd already finished mine but Cilla liked to drink hers cold. 'Sure. It's by the phone.'

I didn't really expect a murderer would ring up and book but there was no harm in checking the bookings. Maybe I'd see a name that would trigger something off. I didn't see Margaret Shaver or any other name that I'd heard before.

It did trigger something off though. Dolores had complained that someone pinched her that night. The autopsy showed injection marks on the thighs and buttocks. Dolores had been rubbing her bottom. Could an injection feel like a pinch? Maybe. Particularly if the area had been hardened by other injections. You'd feel nothing more than a little pinprick. Or a pinch. In rubbing her bottom, was she unintentionally rubbing the poison in?

The list of names didn't help but a photo might. The Tropicana had lots of birthday parties, wedding anniversaries and other big nights out that people wanted a memento of. Jimmy took care of the mementos. Actually his name was Jemal but Jimmy was easier for the customers to remember and he wanted to make it as easy for them as possible. He was the club photographer. He'd take snaps of the groups, snaps of people dancing with Ramón and Dolores, and have them back in an hour. They didn't have to buy if they didn't want to but once they saw the print they usually did. Jimmy did everything for them, they didn't have to ring and order, they didn't even have to wait. All they had to do was put their hand in their pocket.

'You got Jimmy's number?'

'The photographer?'

'Yes. I want to buy a print of every photo he took that night.'

'Jimmy'll be pleased. That's a lot of money.'

'Dolores can pay for it. I'm sure she'd be only too willing to help me find out who murdered her.'

I explained about the credit card and how I was using it to go shopping. She thought it was a great idea, only trouble was she didn't think I could keep up Dolores' pace on my own. 'Maybe you need a little help,' she said. 'There's a cashmere sweater at Strathfield Plaza that whispers to me every time I go there.'

'You busy the day after tomorrow?'

'The morning I'm free,' said Cilla.

'Fine. Let's go shopping.' She was right. I was doing my best but I couldn't keep up Dolores' pace on my own. Besides, it was more fun shopping with someone else. I was curious to know just who was paying for all this; Royal Dolphin Enterprises might prove interesting. I looked at my watch. I didn't have time to do a company search today. The ASC, Australian Securities Commission, would be closing by the time I got there and I hadn't finished my business here yet.

'Has anyone enquired about Dolores?'

'Ah yes, I nearly forgot. You ask so many questions,' she remarked. 'A man came in with the Cubanitos I thought he was one of them but he has blond hair and not dressed like they are, from the seventies. Maybe he's the manager. He went out back. I followed. I found him in the dressing room. What do you want? He said he wants to leave a present for Dolores. It's a flower in a box, an orchid, with ribbon and everything. OK, leave it with me. He said no, I'll come back tonight and see her. She's sick, she's having a few days off. Where can I send the present? he asked. I don't know. You must know, he said. He asked again, same question all the time, where is she?

I think he's trouble. Then the singer came to say they're ready to start. I asked him in Spanish if he knows this blond guy. He said no. So I said to the blond guy, time you left. He could see I'm getting suspicious. He puts his hands up and says OK, I'm leaving.' Cilla played with the cigarette, getting more mileage out of it than any smoker ever would. 'You know, I don't think he came here to give Dolores a present. He wants something.'

'What did he look like?'

'Blond, not tall, not short, no moustache. In the beginning he looked OK but when he kept asking where she is and I must know, his eyes started to get strange, as if another person is living in his body and is at the window looking out.'

Cilla had to be letting her imagination run away with her. I pressed her for more specific details but she just kept saying strange. He'd arrived with the band, I arrived just as they were finishing. 'How long did the band play for?' I asked Cilla.

'I let them play maybe ten minutes,' she estimated. 'It didn't need that long,' she added, 'I can tell after half a minute they are not good.' So the guy had left maybe ten minutes before I arrived. I could have passed him in the street.

A blond, not tall, not short, no moustache. Terrific. Could have been anyone. Could even have been Greg, Ramón's boy-friend. Surely Cilla would recognise him. Or was he a well-kept secret?

'Do you know Greg?'

'Ramón's friend? He tell you about Greg?'

'I was at Five Dock today. Ramón told me a lot of things.' Eventually.

'Yeah?' said Cilla, trying to gauge how much I knew.

'Yeah. We had a very long talk. Most of it I've forgotten already. I've forgotten how long he's been in Australia and that he's working illegally. I've forgotten the name of the club he works at. That's none of my business. My business is finding out who killed Dolores.'

She understood what I wasn't saying. 'You want another coffee?'

'Maybe later. I'd like to have a look at the dressing room.'

'One minute,' she said. The boys in the band were all packed up now and ready to leave. She went over, thanked them for coming and again told them she'd be in touch. She didn't offer them a drink. She was brisk and efficient. They were off the premises as soon as possible.

We went to the dressing room together. My heart sank. I guess it had to happen, you couldn't keep it forever preserved in aspic. 'When did the room get cleaned?' I asked.

'Today, before the band came,' said Cilla. 'I had to do it. It has to be ready for when we get a new act. Don't worry, I kept her things for you.'

'What did you keep?'

'Come, I show you.'

We went out the back. The fabulous dresses were lying on top of a cardboard box. They were still on the coathangers. I picked them up in one pile and put them over the back of a chair. Inside the box was her make-up. I scrummaged through it. There were no telltale scraps of paper with phone numbers on them, no business cards, no envelopes of matches from places that Dolores might have visited. I don't know why I expected the matches, Dolores didn't smoke, but sometimes people souvenir these things.

What wasn't in the cardboard box was the collection of Angostura bitters bottles. I asked Cilla about them.

'In the garbage,' Cilla said. 'And also in the garbage is old Kleenex and cotton wool. I don't know how she can have that mess around her. You know what else I found? A syringe. I put that in the garbage too.' Cilla looked disgusted. 'I don't like to think this goes on in my club.'

'It was probably hormones,' I explained.

'You mean like the footballers take?'

She didn't know.

The irony of Dolores taking something to make her look like a footballer amused me. 'Female hormones. Dolores used to be a boy, she was a transsexual.'

Cilla stared at me in disbelief. 'It can't be true. No. No,' she went on denying it. 'She had breasts, she had nothing in her

pants, just flat,' she made a movement with her hand to empha-
sise the point. 'Her face is smooth. No. No. I don't believe this.'
The more she denied it the more the realisation dawned.

'She had operations, she had hormone injections to give her
the right body.' Cilla kept shaking her head, then she started
laughing. 'All those men going for her, all those men who dance
with her, the customers, if only they knew they were dancing
with a man!'

'They were dancing with a woman,' I said. 'Dolores was a
woman, she was just born into the wrong body.'

How did that feel to be in the wrong body, Dolores, before
the operations, when you were growing up, how did that feel?
I would have liked you to tell me because I can't even imagine
that.

The closest I've come to feeling uncomfortable about my body
was when I was in fourth grade and tall enough to be in high
school. I was awkward, I bumped into things, the other kids
looked at me as if I were a freak and the teachers expected a
big girl like me to be more sensible. By the time I was sixteen
I felt a lot better. I'd stopped growing and everyone else was
catching up.

'The stuff you threw out, is it still here?' I asked Cilla. I was
not looking forward to my next task, especially as it involved
a used syringe.

'Yeah, in the garage bins out the back,' said Cilla.

She unlocked the back door. It had a glass panel in it and I
could see outside over rooftops. The door opened onto a small
landing and a set of old wooden stairs. Down below in the yard
I could see my car, and the four or five others. Between the
Thunderbird and my Daimler there was a black Barina with
black-tinted windows. It looked so incongruous between the cars
either side of it, like a Chihuahua trying to be an Alsatian.

'Who owns the cars?' I asked.

'The BMW is from the electronics business, the others I don't
know. Except for the Thunderbird—that's mine,' she said with
a cool flourish.

'Very flash,' I said. 'New?' Last time I'd been here Cilla was driving a clapped out little Honda. I didn't think business had been that good.

'Yes, my uncle died, my father's brother. He left me the car. Never been out of the garage for fifteen years. Now everything is going to be different. I'm going to show that car a good time.'

Behind the cars were enclosures that looked like greyhound boxes, not that I could recall Newtown being a big spot for greyhound breeding. I asked Cilla what this building was before. She had no idea and wasn't particularly interested. She unlatched one of the enclosures. Inside were four large garbage bins. 'The cats,' she said answering my unasked question, 'very big cats, big as tigers some of them. The garbage is always all over the place. Here,' she took the lid off one bin, 'here is the garbage from Dolores' room.'

I went to my car and opened the glovebox. I must be the only person who actually carries gloves in the glovebox. I took out some garbage bags and laid a couple of them out on the floor. Then I put the gloves on and tipped the garbage out. Cilla didn't offer to help, but then neither would I. I picked up every bitters bottle I could find and sifted through the rest looking for anything that might be of interest. Apart from the syringe there was nothing. I put it aside with the bottles.

I'd gone through garbage only once before in my life and then I didn't have the protection of gloves. It was a garbage bin on George Street in the city. I'd just finished eating an apple and as I lofted the apple core into the bin the car keys followed. And do you think they would have rested nicely on the surface so that all I had to do was pick them up? Not on your life. After poking my fingers in substances that defied description, I found the keys.

Of course digging around in the garbage was only half the nightmare, the other half was the fact it was in the middle of the city. You could be lying dead on the footpath and people would just step over you and continue on their way. But me going through a garbage bin? That was a different matter. Everyone who went by turned around again when they were at a safe distance to have a good look. Some even stopped. There was quite a little group forming.

My face was very red, from embarrassment or frustration or a combination of both. 'I suppose you're wondering why I've called you all here,' I said in a very loud voice. 'I have an announcement to make, I'm not looking for food, OK? I've dropped my car keys in here and I'm looking for them. Anyone like to give me a hand?' That seemed to scatter the gathering but my troubles weren't completely over. There were the deros to consider as well. They had territories mapped out that no-one else knew about. Maybe I was muscling in on someone's bin. My father's even. I wondered if he had a round of bins he regularly went through. That was the worst part of all. That I was doing what my father did routinely every day. I didn't like doing it and I didn't like to think of my father doing it either, with the people in the street staring, thinking what they thought. Maybe he didn't care about that. But I still did.

And now I was going through someone else's garbage looking for syringes and empty bottles.

I carefully wrapped up the syringe and the bottles, then put all the other rubbish back where it came from. Cilla and I went back upstairs. I picked up the dresses and make-up and came out again.

I dumped my load in the boot and squeezed past the Barina. I always get the urge to peer into cars with black-tinted windows but there was nothing much to see in this one; it looked like it was straight out of the showroom.

People walked past the yard, hurrying home from their day's work. I had the whole night ahead of me but I wasn't particularly looking forward to it. I was going to visit my mother. What I was going to tell her warranted more than a phone call. I was going to have to tell her about Dolores. Not only that she was dead but that I was treating it as murder. Worse than that, I was going to have to ask her questions.

If Carol had to interview her mother in relation to a homicide she would probably assign the task to someone else. I would too if I had someone who could do it for me. No matter how good at my job I was, no matter how smart and street-wise I was, for Mina I was eternally in fourth grade.

I drove out of the yard and up the side street. It took ages for the traffic to trickle into King Street. It wasn't till we were in Cleveland Street that I spotted the black Barina.

T he Barina was with me all the way along Cleveland Street and still there when I followed the traffic into Anzac Parade. At the lights at Anzac Parade and Alison Road I caught a glimpse of the number plate. I slotted it into one of thᴗse brain cells I keep free for information like this. We drove past the racecourse on one side and Centennial Park on the other. It's a nice wide road with a gentle curve. In the middle of the night you could tear along here pretending you were at Le Mans, or Monte Carlo. Now, at 6 p.m., while you weren't exactly crawling you were hard-pressed to go over the speed limit.

By the time we hit Belmore Road the traffic had got congested again. But the Barina was still with me, right up close, breathing down my neck almost. I had a vague feeling of unease, as if the little animal that lies curled up in my stomach had stretched out and yawned, without quite waking up. That little animal called fear. The tail was up too close to be a professional; these main arteries were well-lit enough to stay five or six cars behind and still not lose sight of the target. That was more worrying. With a professional it's just a job. Anyone else doing it they've got a personal reason. They're involved, they take risks, make mistakes. That makes them dangerous.

It had to be the same Barina parked next to me at the club but where had the driver been? I hadn't spotted anyone hanging around there. There was no-one in the car, I'd looked in. Was

74

the driver somewhere close by, waiting round the corner, then running back to the car when they saw me drive out? Or were they in the yard with me all the time? In one of the other enclosures, watching and waiting. Listening.

Had the grey Celica turned into a black Barina, same driver watching and waiting for the opportunity to have another go at me? Or was there a whole gang of them, one picking up where the other left off?

The lights were red. I preferred to be moving. I preferred the evening was over and done with altogether. I wasn't looking forward to what was ahead of me—telling my mother about Dolores—and I certainly didn't like what was behind me. I had been going to use the drive to work out how best to approach Mina. Now I had a more immediate concern. I reminded myself that this was exactly that I wanted. But now that I had it I was less than overjoyed. I could drop the whole thing. Stop the investigation, the impersonation, go back home and change my hair back to its normal colour. But it was too late for that. I couldn't just turn around and say look, it's a case of mistaken identity, I'm not Dolores Delgado, I'm Claudia Valentine. They knew I was involved, I'd gone too far now to take the mask off.

On the other hand I hadn't gone far enough. I didn't know enough yet. If I turned around and confronted them there were two possibilities—they could kill me or they could run. Either way I'd never find out who they were and why they wanted Dolores dead. I'd known in the beginning this way was risky. I had to run with that risk. They were on the hook now. I just had to make sure I wasn't the one to get caught.

The lights turned green and I continued down the other side of Alison Road. Though most of the traffic went for Belmore Road, the Barina followed my path. As long as I kept going so would the Barina. I was in control I reminded myself, I had hold of the line, the Barina would follow wherever I went. I didn't, however, want it following me right to my mother's front door.

I parked outside an old cemetery a few streets away from Mina's. The cemetery was small but its spooky atmosphere was enhanced by the orange lights from Belmore Park across the road. The light made the pencil pines in the park look ghostly as well. It was different from how I remembered it. There was a lot of park renovation going on in Sydney. Most of them looked quite good but I couldn't see what had been wrong with them in the first place. So what if it got muddy under the swings when it rained? That was the way kids liked it. Oh well, it kept landscape architects in work. God knows, we all needed work at the moment.

I watched the Barina park further up the street. I slipped off my boots and put on a pair of joggers. I took my time getting out of the car and going through the ritual of locking it. The driver wouldn't get out of the car till I moved away from mine.

I made my move. These legs aren't just for show. I sprinted across the park and started jogging down the street. They would be able to see a shadowy figure crossing the park but they'd have to be moving fast to follow me down the street. On foot I was in my element.

The Daimler is easy enough to spot but once I'm out of it I'm invisible. I usually hire a car if I'm tailing someone but that wasn't on the cards when I set out today. Funny thing, even though the Daimler was getting on she liked the thrill of the chase. And her conspicuousness wasn't always a disadvantage, today she was earning her keep—while I didn't want them coming to my mother's house, I didn't want to lose them altogether.

On the other side of the park I looked back. The driver was out of the car now and approaching. It looked like a man, medium height and build. He was wearing one of those windcheaters with a hood that had become fashionable, but this one wasn't. It was doing its job though, it obscured his face and the colour of his hair.

I kept going. I knew the neighbourhood and the short cuts well. I didn't always like coming back to it but I did know my way around it. I scaled the fence into Panadopoulos' back yard and broke a capsicum plant as I landed. I crouched down and didn't move. Through the palings in the fence I could see a figure stop and look up the lane. It could have been the same guy but there were no street lights here and it was too dark to tell. He would have to have been fast on his feet to have caught up this quickly. Maybe it was just a passer-by. There must have been some people on the streets who weren't following me. He paused then walked on.

I squatted in the capsicum patch for a while longer. There was no sign of life. No-one else paused at the top of the lane, no-one walked past. When I'd waited long enough I started scaling the fences and going from backyard to backyard. I'd played in most of these as a child. I didn't know all the people anymore, they came and went but the backyards stayed basically the same, except for one family that concreted theirs then got it all dug up again because of the drainage problem.

The Greeks immediately next door to Mina had packed up and gone back to Skiathos. She had Korean neighbours now and I'd never met them. But tonight was the night. The man was just coming out of his garage as I landed in his backyard. 'Evening,' I said. 'I'm Mina's daughter. Just passing through.' And continued on my way. It seemed better in the long run than trying to explain myself.

He stood at the garage staring at me. By the time I was knocking on Mina's backdoor, he'd come over to the fence. The top half of his head was visible over the palings. It stayed there even after I called out to Mina. If you had a neighbour who dressed up as an ostrich, you'd be curious to see what her chicks were like. Especially if they'd just run through your backyard.

I called out because I didn't think she could hear me above the loud music. It wasn't like Mina to play her music that loud. I knocked and called out again. Still she didn't come.

That little creature in my stomach woke right up this time. The music might be up loud to hide the sound of something else. Maybe the guy had tracked me here anyway. Jesus, I thought, how could I have been so stupid as to have called out to her?

Very quietly I turned the door knob. The door was unlocked

and opened easily under my hand. I heard my mother's voice coming from the lounge room. It didn't sound like her at all.

Something was up. I grabbed the umbrella from behind the door and crept up to the lounge room. I stayed close to the wall then sprang into the doorway holding the umbrella in both hands, like the police do on TV with guns.

Then I stopped in my tracks. My mouth fell open in surprise and I stood there gaping. I couldn't believe my eyes. A man was kissing my mother. A man that I knew!

'Brian! What are you doing here?'

Brian Collier was a journalist. He and my father had worked at the same newspaper, he was a friend of the family. If you could call it family. I'd met up with him again years later and we'd stayed in touch. He was a good contact and we'd become friends. I always had a sneaking suspicion he was carrying a flame for Mina but I hadn't realised he was actually stoking the fire.

'Evening, Claudia.' If embarrassment could have been person-ified it was Brian Collier at that moment. He looked as if he'd been caught with his pants down. But all he had off was his tie. My mother was another matter altogether. She was wearing one of her old Tivoli outfits. The ones she wouldn't let me dress up in when I was a kid, the ones that stayed in her wardrobe year after year. It was mostly net with a few strategically placed sequins. They would have been strategic thirty years ago, they weren't so strategic now.

I'd stumbled into some kind of party. They were dancing, if you could call what Brian was doing dancing. I was, to use one of my mother's own words, flabbergasted.

'Claudia!' said my mother, tippling towards me. 'Your hair's gone black. Never mind, have some champagne.'

'But Mum, you don't drink!'

'She doesn't drink and I don't dance so I guess that makes us even,' said Brian. I had never seen him so sheepish. The way I looked at it that was a big point in his favour. My mother had said that Brian had stood by her when my father finally drank himself into oblivion. She didn't say anything about him being a gentleman caller.

'Mum, what's going on?' I asked in a voice halfway between a bewildered child and a stern parent.

'Oh, for heaven's sake, Claudia, loosen up,' she said with gay abandon.

Loosen up? My mother never says loosen up.

'She's tipsy, Brian, you've got my mother tipsy,' I accused him. It very well nearly looked like he was going to take advantage of her as well.

My mother lurched towards me in high heels that looked like they could do a lot of damage. 'It's all right, dear,' she consoled. She tried to pat my arm but ended up patting the air. 'We're just having a little dance and a little drink, just a little celebration.'

'Celebration is it? You're not getting married, are you? They tell me the daughter's always the last to know,' I said sarcastically.

I marched off into the kitchen and put the kettle on for coffee. No-one followed me in there and I was pleased for that. It was the only thing I was pleased about. I leaned against the kitchen cupboards and stared at the opposite wall. She still had the seed painting I'd done in second grade. It was a childlike house with a path leading up to it. A couple of lentils had fallen out of the path about twenty years ago and never been replaced. Every time I came here I noticed those missing lentils and every time I thought of fixing it up but never did. Like a painting that's askew—leave it there long enough and it grows on you; the idiosyncrasy becomes endearing.

In all my childhood my mother had never entertained a gentleman caller though there had been plenty of admirers of those Betty Grable legs. When I got to be a teenager and started having boyfriends myself I asked her why not. 'I'm perfectly happy with the way things are,' she'd say. And that was all there was to it. When people started telling her she ought to go and see the movie *Shirley Valentine*, and not only because of the surname, she said, 'You don't have to go to Greece for that

79

sort of thing, you can find it right in your own backyard.' I'd always assumed it was a kind of little joke about the neighbourhood but now I was beginning to think otherwise.

More importantly I was thinking what a fool I'd been. Barging into the lounge room like Rambo, armed with an umbrella. I always wanted Mina to go out and enjoy herself, I know the reason she didn't drink was because my father had done so much of it. But now she was enjoying herself I felt . . . What did I feel?

'You going to turn that thing off?' It was Collier. The kettle was boiling. Furiously.

I turned it off.

'You're not going to believe it, but this was the first time.' He was still sheepish, apologetic, as if I was Mina's mother, not the other way around. His tie off, the strands of hair that he slicked back with water coming unstuck. I thought I had problems. It was a toss-up who was more embarrassed—him or me.

I was beginning to see the lighter side of the situation. 'I don't think I'll have a coffee at all. I might join you in a glass of champagne and don't make any comments on how crowded it would be, Brian.'

'Looks like boiling the kettle served its purpose,' said Brian. 'Welcome back to suburbia.'

Fortunately Victor Sylvester's Dance Time had stopped and even more fortunately Mina hadn't noticed. Still, there was plenty of noise. Mina told me the whole story of the day's events, how Brian had invited her to the races, haven't been for years, how they'd won a pile, bought some champagne to go out to dinner but had ended up having 'just the one' at home. Mina wiggled into the bedroom, she had something to show me. 'The winnings didn't extend to Moët?' I asked Brian when she'd gone. 'She wanted the Minchinbury,' Brian said out of the side of his mouth.

'Isn't it lovely?' she beamed. She was holding a gold and emerald necklace up to her neck. I looked at Brian quizzically. 'You?' Not me, he shook his head.

It wasn't really my style but Mina liked chunky gold. 'Suits you,' I said. 'Part of the winnings?'

'Dolores gave it to me. I'm going to wear it tonight.'

I felt terrible. Here I was, come to tell mother that Dolores had died and she was all set to go out wearing Dolores' necklace. I hadn't been looking forward to telling her in the first place, it was even worse now. She handed the necklace to me for a closer look. 'She gave it to you?' I repeated weakly.

Mina sat down on the couch and patted the space beside her, inviting me to join her. 'She's got a rich sugar daddy,' she said confidentially, 'a big business tycoon. Gordon somebody. He gave it to her but she didn't like it much. She asked me if I wanted it. I asked her if she was sure, she said "Of course!" You know the way she talks, Claudia. She said she was just getting rid of a few things before she went away.'

Dolores had told Mina she was going away? I knew the way she talked all right but it seemed Dolores had been doing a lot more talking to my mother than to anyone else. She hadn't told Cilla, she hadn't told me. But my mother knew. If I hadn't already seen the ticket I would have thought this was just another of Dolores' stories.

'Dolores told you she was going away?'

'Yes,' Mina continued blithely, 'to Spain.'

To Spain? But the ticket said Bangkok.

'Not Bangkok?'

'What would she want to go to Bangkok for? She said she was going to Spain, I'm positive she said Spain.'

'When was she planning on leaving?'

'I don't know. Soon, she said.'

'And was she going alone or was this Gordon going with her?'

'I don't know, why don't you ask her?' she said impatiently. 'Good Lord, anyone would think I was a suspect the way you're firing questions at me.'

I put the necklace down on the couch. 'Mum, I can't ask Dolores those questions,' I said in a quiet steady voice. It was the kind of voice my mother had used when she had explained about my father and why he wasn't living with us anymore.

She must have recognised the tone. She sobered up considerably. 'Something's happened, hasn't it?'

'Yes,' I said simply. 'Dolores had a heart attack at the club. They tried to resuscitate her but . . . they couldn't do anything for her.'

A look of consternation passed across her face. 'She died?' Somehow the words always need to be said. 'But . . . but . . . she's so young for a heart attack.' She sat there staring at the necklace, the shock waves working their way through her. 'She must have had a bad heart, it was almost as if she knew it might happen,' Mina said in a small voice, 'giving away her jewellery and things. It was almost as if she knew.'

'It wasn't a normal heart attack. I think someone murdered Dolores.'

'Oh dear God,' she cried. 'Not murdered, surely not.'

I didn't normally discuss cases with my mother, especially murder cases, but then she wasn't normally involved in them. She had a nice life. Murder was something she read about in the newspapers. It didn't happen to people she knew.

It had shaken her. She stood up and started walking towards the kitchen. 'I'm going to make a cup of tea. Brian, look after Claudia, will you?' she said superfluously.

Brian and I exchanged looks.

'She told me about Dolores, about the club and everything. I've got a lot to thank Dolores for. I've been asking your mother out for years, on and off. It's only since she worked at that club that she's said yes.'

'It's that kind of place.'

'You said she'd been murdered. Is there anything I can do?'

I knew exactly the kind of help Brian had to offer. He had mates. He was one of those battered journos you see around the place. He'd been a court reporter, he was now senior features writer, he knew Sydney's crime world as well as anyone who wasn't actually involved in it. And he'd weathered more storms than he'd had hot dinners. Funny thing is, I sometimes invited him to dinner with Steve and me, feeling sorry for the lonely bachelor. And here the sly old dog was going out to dinner with my mother.

'Don't know.' Brian's knowledge was local and Dolores wasn't a local. Yet she had a credit card from here. 'Actually, Brian, there may be something. Royal Dolphin Enterprises. Know anything about them?'

'Rings a bell. Can't remember if they're coming or going. You know when I started off in this game crime was break-and-enter, mugging, a killing now and then. Now it's all changed. It's gone corporate. The real crims are the businessmen. They order up big, have a good feed, then they leave the country without paying the bill.'

'I didn't get very far when I rang them up to ask about Dolores. The receptionist had never heard of her. And she wanted to know who was asking.'

'Listen, I've got a mate works at the Australian Securities Commission. You know it, corner of Pitt and Market?'

'I haven't been there but it's my next port of call.'

'Don't bother going in, you'll only be able to get the bare essentials. My mate can access ISIS, it's an intelligence database. Has all sorts of interesting information about companies. And their directors. You can key in the name of an individual and it tells you all the companies he's associated with. You won't get that over the counter. I'll find out what they've got and fax it through to you. What's your fax number?'

'Give us a break, I'm only just getting used to the idea of a mobile phone. Jack's got a fax, though, my publican. I don't think he'd mind. And Brian, thanks. I'm glad you've got lots of mates. I can't get by without them.'

Collier smiles. 'Some of my best friends are mates.'

'I've got one or two of my own,' I said, 'in fact I've got one or two on my tail. Even as we speak.'

'Good mates, are they?'

'I hardly know them but they tried to run me down. I think they know Dolores. They might even know why she died.'

'You catch the rego number? I can get it looked up.'

'Thanks, I can deal with that one. There is something else

though. You know anyone at the labs at Lidcombe, Diagnostic Analytical Laboratories?'

'Been a while since I've had anything to do with that mob. Why?'

'Thought I'd see how things were going. The morgue sent samples there.'

'Don't like your chances, you don't work in the system. Why don't you ask your cop friend?'

'Well, she doesn't really want to know about it yet. If I pressed her she'd do it. But by the time it went through all the official channels we could all be dead.' Dead felt like a hammer coming down on me. It was only a turn of phrase; why did it sound so ominous? It was time for me to go.

I went out into the kitchen to say goodbye to Mina. She was staring at the seed painting on the wall, she'd been crying. 'We ought to buy some lentils and fix that up, you know, Claudia.'

'Yes, we should. I'll give you a ring. Go and talk to Brian, I think he's missing you.'

I went out the same way I'd come in but I didn't go hurdling over all the back fences. I went down the back and peered through the palings. There was no-one about. I pulled myself up over the fence and jumped down into the lane. Back along the block of houses then across the park. Not even a dog barking. And it was only eight o'clock at night.

The Daimler was still there and so was the Barina. I checked the boot. Everything was still in place. I started the engine and pulled out onto the road. So did the Barina.

The Barina came all the way back to the Cross with me. He watched me drive into the Hotel Royale car park but he didn't come in after me.

I took Dolores' things out of the boot and went to reception. Patrick said there'd been no messages or phone calls for me or Dolores. 'If anyone makes any enquiries, any enquiries at all, will you let me know?'

'Sure,' said Patrick in his easy breezy style.

I went upstairs.

It felt odd hanging these dresses up in the wardrobe, considering that Dolores had taken dresses off the hangers and packed them in her suitcases ready to go away. It almost felt as if she was on her way back and I was preparing for her return. But she wasn't coming back. She wouldn't be opening the wardrobe, running her eye over the collection then carefully selecting the best dress for the occasion.

It was a bit pointless really but I didn't know what else to do with the clothes. This was still Dolores' room, these were her things. They belonged here. Eventually I'd have to do something, sell them or give them away. But not yet.

What I could do was tidy the mess. It was Dolores' room but I was the one living in it. I wasn't excessively tidy myself but I did like the horizontal surfaces to be at least visible. It was hard to think straight in a room this messy.

I sorted out her jewellery and put it into the appropriate

boxes. Dolores did have a system, she just didn't use it. There was a box for expensive pieces, but the really interesting jewellery, the outlandish fantasy pieces, were in the other box—well, it should have been. Most things were just lying on the dressing table. She'd shopped around in Paddington, Ahah Dodo in Glebe, places in the city. She also had jewellery designed for her. There were earrings that looked like wedding cakes, a pair of gold dancing shoes, a miniature replica of herself and Ramón dancing, one for each ear.

The ones in the other box, the expensive box, were showy but not very original. Chunky gold, like the necklace she'd given Mina. Mina had mentioned a name. Gordon, big business tycoon. Was he the guy who'd brought the roses? He didn't really look like a tycoon but then lately they were coming in all shapes and sizes. Maybe he looked bigger in a suit. There must be some reason why men wear them.

It was almost done. I wrapped the Angostura bottles securely in plastic, the syringe in tissue then plastic, and stashed the lot in my overnight bag.

Dolores' apartment looked supertidy for Dolores and not too bad for me. I'd thrown nothing out, just rearranged things. I made myself a gin and tonic from the bar fridge and leafed through the book on doing business with the Japanese. On a desert island with nothing else to read I'm sure I'd find it fascinating. But I wasn't on a desert island. I put it aside and turned on the TV. I wasn't really concentrating on it though. Not that you have to. I'd been back here over an hour and no-one had called. I rang Patrick at reception. No-one had made any enquiries.

My tail had disappeared.

It was almost ten o'clock and I was hungry. I didn't have to hang round here all night. I had a mobile phone, I was mobile.

I phoned my friend Lucy and asked if she wanted to join me at one of the brasseries in Bayswater Road. She said she'd love to but she was a bit strapped for cash at the moment. Times were tough, you know. I don't know why she was having a hard time. As far as I knew doctors were still being paid. I said it was no problem, I'd inherited a goldmine. She said she'd be there in twenty minutes.

I was planning on paying for dinner with Dolores' card. I was getting increasingly curious about Royal Dolphin and wondering just how much spending I had left before someone put a stop to it.

Lucy worked in the allergy clinic at Prince Alfred Hospital. Doctor by day, wild child at night. Lucy was small and slim. So is a stick of dynamite. Over dinner I asked her if she ever had any dealings with the labs at Lidcombe.

'Not really,' she said, 'why?'

'I need some stuff analysed. For traces of poison.'

The piece of grilled capsicum she was about to pop into her mouth remained on the fork. 'Poison. You trying to put me off my food?' she said, now attacking the capsicum with zeal, regardless. 'There are private labs, what about them?'

It seemed so much more efficient to go to Lidcombe where they were already analysing samples of . . . samples of Dolores. I was beginning to go off my food as well.

But not off the dinner conversation. When the antipasto was finished I went back to it. 'You know much about poisons?'

'A little,' Lucy said, lighting a cigarette. 'I know more about allergens but I've done some toxicology.'

'What sort of poison makes you salivate while having a heart attack?'

She thought for a moment, took a drag on the cigarette, watched an attractive waiter walk by then elegantly blew out the smoke. 'Muscle weakness?'

Dolores' movements had been floppy, like a limp doll. 'Possibly.'

'It's not my area, and I'd hate to have to stand up in court and swear to it but there's an indole alkaloid called bufotenine that has that effect. It's found in the skin glands of toads, in the seeds and leaves of some plants, oleander for example, and in *amanita* mushrooms. They're those lovely red ones with the white spots that gnomes and fairies live under.'

'You'd have to eat these things, then?'

'That's one way of doing it. Sounds very appetising—sautéed toads' legs in mushroom sauce with a salad of oleander leaves. Only trouble is it would taste like shit.'

'What's the other way?'

'If you knew what you were doing you could extract the bufotenine. It's soluble in alcohol so you could spike a drink with it. Or if you didn't like the taste you could inject it. Shall we go?'

As usual Lucy wasn't content with just dinner, we had to go out and rage. We ended up at a club in Darlinghurst. It wasn't that easy dancing with a mobile phone in my pocket but I managed. There wasn't anywhere else to put it. It had been a waste of time giving the number to Patrick anyway. There'd been no calls the whole night. At 2.30 I decided it was time to pack it in. I had an early start in the morning.

'C'mon, Lucy,' I said, 'no-one new's going to come.'

'No,' said Lucy, looking around, 'and the ones that are here aren't going to improve.'

I woke up bright and early the next morning despite the late night. I hadn't had too much to drink, I was feeling fine.

As soon as it was nine o'clock I called my mate Bernie at Motor Registration. He said long time no hear. I said in my business silence is a virtue. He said when were we going to have lunch together. I said whenever his wife invited me over. That sobered him up. He changed the subject and asked why I was calling. When I told Bernie I wanted some rego details I could feel the distance getting even greater. I didn't know what the problem was, I'd been getting rego details from him for years. 'Can't you talk at the moment?' I asked. I didn't expect anybody else would even be in the office yet.

The problem was that Bernie had been reading the papers and watching the news. Plus there'd been an office directive on giving out information to private investigators.

'Look Bernie,' I said, 'it's got nothing to do with the banks. You think I'd be helping the banks out with their debt collecting? They're practically running the country, own most of it anyway. Actually, I'm worried about my health, there's a car that's been following me.' I gave him the rego number. 'You're a public servant, I'm a member of the public. So serve me.' I held the phone away while he made the inevitable comments about serving me in other ways and put it to my ear in time to hear him say he'd get back to me later on in the day. 'I might not be at home though, I'm staying at a friend's place. But you can leave a message on my machine.'

'Don't I always?' he said. We exchanged a few other niceties then Bernie said 'Cop-u-later.' I was too slow, I usually hung up before he got to it. It had got tireder than a yawn on a Monday morning.

I went to the wardrobe and got out the bag with the things I was taking to Lidcombe. I opened the door to walk out and stopped. Right outside the door was a clear plastic box with a ribbon round the corner of it and one of those decorator's rosettes. In the box was an orchid, the type you see on Thai Airways.

Tucked under the ribbon cutting the corner of the box was a plain white card with a serrated edge. It said: 'Lunch. Today at the Ramada Renaissance, 1.30.'

Was it the guy who'd come to the club, the guy who brought the roses? The one in the Barina, the Celica? Were they all the same people?'

They must have been feeling pretty sure of themselves. How did they know I didn't have to break a lunch date with Tom Cruise?

I put the orchid in the overnight bag and walked to Kings Cross station. Lidcombe was a long way out. If you got a through train you'd be there in about the same time it took to drive it. On a train, you weren't as likely to be followed, either. I kept an eye out though, from the front entrance of the Royale, through the streets of the Cross, down the escalator to the station, onto the platform. Not till the train started moving did I sit back in the seat and relax.

The train stayed underground in the black tunnels till we got almost to Redfern. There were a few brief glimpses of city near

Central then we headed out west on the Campbelltown line. At Redfern we passed the brick railway sheds that now housed Paddys Markets. I liked the railway sheds, they were dirty and industrial, the windows had never been cleaned in their lives and you probably got grit in your lungs if you stayed in there more than five minutes but at least it was pollution you could see.

Houses backed onto the railway track and even the smallest of small backyards sported a Hills hoist. And this was only Newtown. Round Petersham the green, pink or buff-painted terraces gave way to liver-coloured brick bungalows. By Summer Hill the houses were getting bigger and there was a lot more greenery between them.

The railway graffiti out here was different from the graffiti you see on the walls of buildings in the inner city. Not so much slogans as patterns in paint that looked like Arabic writing as the train sped by. Maybe it was. People at the stations wore tracksuits, blue jeans instead of black ones, T-shirts with lettering on the front, and smoked more than they did in the city stations. Because the city circle stations had signs requesting you not to smoke or because once you're in the city you don't have time to smoke?

We stopped at Strathfield, where everything stops, even the country trains and the expresses. After Strathfield we passed Rookwood Cemetery. My grandmother, Mina's mother, was buried there. I gave her a silent wave.

Finally, we arrived at Lidcombe. I got off the train and walked up the station stairs. The smell of doner kebab mixed with the metal of train tracks. It was a clear day with a bit of breeze but the edge of the skyline was murky with pollution. From up here I had a splendid view of shops and two pubs, only a block apart. Not surprisingly, one pub was called the Railway Hotel. But you could only tell that if you were up high enough to see the deco lettering on the wall above the awning. Otherwise you'd swear the pub was called 'Tooheys on Tap'. It was like Randwick had been in my childhood only here there were fewer shops.

As I walked down the steps to the cab rank a big yellow CC's van pulled up. The driver pulled out a stack of boxes full of corn chips and, in a perfect balancing act, walked across the road with them.

I got in the first cab on the rank. No sign of a sheepskin seat cover but what was there far surpassed the humble sheepskin. Front and back seats were covered in acrylic leopardskin, black smudges on a white background. I'd seen Jackie Collins reclining on this kind of background in a magazine. Probably not in this cab though. I didn't feel inclined to do the same. The driver looked like Omar Sharif. I told him where I wanted to go and we pulled out of the rank. Omar wasn't much of a talker which was just as well—it was probably difficult to make yourself heard above the loudness of the seat covers.

Lidcombe Hospital was only about seven dollars away from the station. Buses were few and far between and the ones that did run along Joseph Street where the hospital was were private. Public transport barely managed to keep up with the suburban sprawl and in some places had given up trying altogether.

We turned left into the hospital grounds. The buildings were low and spread out. Occasionally there was a clump of native flora planted in the short grass. The grounds seemed to go on for miles. One thing there is plenty of out west is horizontal space. The driver knew exactly where the Analytical Laboratories were. We drove down an internal road flanked by a row of date palms. 'There it is,' he said, pointing out a two-storey building with vertical aluminium shutters. A sign board said DIVISION OF ANALYTICAL LABORATORIES, DIVISION OF OCCUPATIONAL AND ENVIRONMENTAL HEALTH, STATE POLLUTION CONTROL COMMISSIONER.

There was a foyer and a small reception area in front of double doors that had Analytical Laboratories across the middle in black letters. The receptionist was a woman in her fifties with a nice neat perm. The kind of person who in actual fact runs the place. She was attending to a man and a woman, cops, each holding onto large brown paper bags full of marijuana. Whole plants, recently picked. Surely they didn't have to get it analysed to tell what it was. The receptionist signed them in and they went through into the laboratories.

I went up to the desk, said my name, showed her my ID and stated my business. I hoped it all sounded as if I knew the drill. I wrote my name in the visitors' book, time of arrival, reason for visit and signed it, then proceeded towards the door. 'Just a minute,' she said. 'Are you from the morgue?'

'I've got some samples for testing,' I opened my bag and showed her, 'to do with a specimen that the morgue sent here.'

'Take a seat,' she said, pointing to two chairs either side of a small table with a stack of magazines on it, 'I'll get someone to come out and see you.' She put through a call. 'Matthew? Sylvia. Can you come out for a minute? There's a lady with some samples.' She listened to something he was saying then turned her back to me. But I could still hear what she said. 'Don't think so. Haven't seen her before.' There was some more conversation then she put down the phone. 'Matthew Davidson will deal with you, he'll be out in ten minutes.'

'Thanks.' Nobody gets through those doors into the labs without Sylvia's permission and she was letting me know in the nicest way possible. She was doing a job and doing it well. 'Worked here long?'

''Bout five years,' she said. Probably came back to the work force after twenty years at home bringing up children. No wonder she found this job a breeze.

Another cop came in, a young guy bristling with health. He was dressed in jeans and a bright green short-sleeve shirt, and was carrying a plastic bag full of white powder. Yep, cops were definitely getting younger. And better looking.

Meanwhile I sat on the chair and waited. I should have guessed there'd be some waiting involved. This was part of the public service. I watched the first ten minutes go by on the clock above the double doors. Boredom forced me to the magazines on the table but I soon gave up on them. Micro-filtration devices and packed glass columns didn't exactly make riveting reading. I spent the rest of my waiting time looking at Analytical

Laboratories on the doors and seeing how many words I could make from the letters.

Twenty-three minutes later the doors opened to let out a man in a lab coat. He looked at the receptionist and she looked over in my direction. He came and introduced himself. 'Matthew Davidson,' he said.

'Claudia Valentine.' We shook hands. He had white skin, black hair and a trim black beard. I thought of the first time I met Steve; he'd also been wearing a lab coat and it had also been in a hospital. But there was one big difference. This time my loins didn't flutter in the least.

'Come through,' he said. We went through the double doors and along a corridor. It smelled like hospitals used to smell in my childhood. When I asked him what it was he said, 'What smell? I don't smell a thing.'

A young Indian girl in a lab coat was getting something out of a storage room. I could feel the cold air as we passed and saw small glass containers of blood, urine, liver, brain and other things that weren't so readily identifiable. Parts of Dolores were in there. Seeing the actual samples was nowhere near as disagreeable as the thought of them had been at dinner last night. I had a friendly kind of feeling towards them, as if they were all parts of people that I knew. I wondered if the lab workers felt that way or if all it was to them was specimens and numbers.

We passed labs that looked like classic chemistry labs—test tubes, burners, pipettes, and others full of sleek apparatus attached to computers. Then he showed me into an office. 'What can I do for you?'

I'd thought about the answer to this question on the train trip out. What he could do for me was examine the bottles and the syringe for traces of poison. As Lucy had told me, I could get this done at a private lab. But a private lab didn't have Dolores' specimens. This one did. If they had the bottles and the syringe as well they could crosscheck. There were times when having all your eggs in one basket was an advantage.

There was only one problem. It was easier for a camel to pass through the eye of a needle than for a private individual to have these facilities made available to them. But I had made it through the doors. Eventually, after waiting, after being screened by Sylvia. That was the first step.

The train trip had given me time to work on lines of approach that would get me over the hurdles. Something I'd said to Bernie that morning had given me the idea for the first line of approach.

The Analytical Labs were a public sector facility, staffed by public servants. I paid taxes, indirectly I paid their wages so in a way they were working for me. I was a member of the public, they were there to serve me and if I had substances I wanted the lab to analyse, in theory they should analyse them for me. A kind of privatisation from the bottom up. It was beautiful—logical, efficient, simple.

I threw that idea out the window before the train even got to Newtown.

Which then brought me onto my second line of approach—ask not what they can do for me but what I can do for them.

I took the parcels out of my bag and placed them on his desk. Either he was dull or I wasn't as smart as I thought. For most people a parcel is an object of intrigue, almost everyone wants to know what's in it, particularly when someone lays the parcel out in front of you as if it is a gift. He didn't even muster up a hint of curiosity.

So I undid the parcels containing the bottles. They looked like a wino's breakfast in miniature. He waited. I unwrapped the parcel with the syringe in it. 'Yes,' he said encouragingly, as if he was indulging a child. 'Where did you say you were from?' He must have thought I was a sales person showing him a new line in laboratory equipment, or a magician with a bag of tricks.

I flashed my private investigator's licence at him. 'I'm working on the Dolores Delgado case. These were found at the scene of the crime.'

'I'm sorry?' he said mystified, 'I don't follow.'

And you don't really want to, do you?

'Some specimens were sent here from the morgue a couple of days ago. Dolores Delgado.'

He still looked mystified.

'The transsexual.'

That seemed to jog his memory. 'Ah, yes. I'm sorry I didn't recognise the name, all that information is on file but I'm a chemist, I don't deal with the paperwork. What exactly can I do for you?'

'It's what I can do for you,' I smiled charmingly at him. 'The bottles, the syringe, they were found in Dolores Delgado's room. I'm sure they'd help with your specimen analysis.'

'Why weren't they sent over at the same time?' he enquired.

'They've only just come to light.' I hoped it didn't sound as weak to him as it sounded to me.

'This is not the way we normally proceed. We're a government body, we do work for the coroner, the police, not private individuals. There are private labs . . .'

'I'm working with the police. Detective Inspector Rawlins, Homicide, South Region.' Being up front about it, giving him all the information. Ring up, check. Hey, I'll even dial the number for you.

'Where are the accompanying forms?' Uh-oh. It wasn't going to work. I wished I hadn't used Carol's name now. This was the wrong place to do it. He and Carol were part of the same system. He *could* ring up and check. And he'd find out that the police knew nothing about my trip out here today. Living Dolores' life was getting to me, the edges were getting blurred. I'd forgotten when to stop telling the lies. All I wanted to do was to get out of here.

'The forms?'

'Suspect items such as these should be submitted with the post-mortem exhibits. If they're not, if they don't come to light till later as you say, there should be appropriate cross-referencing. I'm sorry you've wasted your time but I can't take them like that, I can't accept the responsibility.' I'd hit the glass ceiling. Only it wasn't glass, it was forms. Stacks of them, as far as the eye could see.

'I'm sorry I've wasted *your* time. I'll get the appropriate forms and come back later.' I gathered the bottles and the syringe up and put them back in the bag. I had no intention of coming back later. I'd ring Carol and confess. Then, after she was speaking to me again, I'd tell her why I'd come here in the first place. If she thought it was worth it I'd hand the bottles and syringe over to her and she could fill in the damned forms.

I wasn't looking forward to it but it was better to get it over and done with. When I got back to the train station I rang Carol. They informed me she was in Mudgee for a couple of days. Shit.

I hoped the rest of the day would prove more fruitful than it had been so far. Otherwise I might just as well not have bothered to get out of bed this morning.

'Situated at the heart of the business district, the Ramada Renaissance is ideally placed for both efficient business and a wide variety of pleasures,' said the brochures. I wondered what lunch with my date was going to be—efficient business or a variety of pleasures.

It wasn't exactly the Medici palace but the decor wasn't too bad. Italianate but not over the top. Mosaic floor, the lighting was unobtrusive and the staircase of the three-tiered lobby went on forever. Up those stairs were various restaurants and bars, including the brasserie designed to make you feel as if you were having lunch on your grandmother's verandah, particularly if your grandmother happened to live in the Philippines. Cane chairs with cushion covers in earth shades, a decorative rattan wall sculpture that looked like a huge sun hat and lots of light coming through the bay windows. It was 1.18 and the brasserie was full of diners, many of them Japanese. I thought about Dolores' book again. What was the Japanese connection in Dolores' life?

The message hadn't said specifically where, just the Ramada Renaissance. I was a little early on purpose. I like to get an idea of the layout of a place, its exits and entrances, to know where the bullets might be coming from, or the poison darts; to know where to run.

I went upstairs and had a good look in the public areas, the bars, restaurants and club lounge with its heavy fake leather chairs and books in bookcases. Then I went into the ladies. It was spacious—dark grey tiled floor edged with a warm dusky beige mottled with black. Matching paper towels to dry your hands on. Even though it was spacious I was beginning to feel claustrophobic. It was awfully quiet and still in here. A person could be lying dead on those tiles for hours before the body was discovered. There was enough room to fight in but nowhere to run. I caught sight of my face in the mirror. It was a worried looking face. I listened at the door then slowly opened it and walked downstairs where there was safety in numbers.

1.30. A Japanese family were getting ready to go out somewhere, somewhere they were going to be doing a lot of walking judging by their footwear and the fact that the two little girls were wearing sun hats. It was winter, a bit chilly for the beach but the weather was unseasonably warm.

I looked at the orchid in the box. It looked dead, interred, in a little coffin on a bed of purple satin. Like a body that's been painted and prissed up for the funeral viewing, the cheeks too rosy, the lips too red. Almost lewd. Was this part of the message, that I'd end up dead like this? Time and place of death—1.30 p.m, Ramada Renaissance. A macabre little joke? Take it easy, I told myself, nothing's going to happen to you in front of all these people. They've been watching you, now they want to talk.

1.30 passed and I was still alive.

1.45. When the Japanese family vacated the comfortable-looking lounge chairs I sat down in one of them. A youngish Japanese man in smart casual gear sat down in the chair next to me. I looked at him and he looked at me. He looked at his watch. He was waiting for someone. I looked at my watch and looked at him again.

'Beautiful flower,' he said, looking at the orchid. 'You are a collector?' It was hard to tell if it was merely conversational or whether this was the lead in.

'Not really,' I said, 'but I have a friend who collects. Dolores,' I said.

'You are waiting for your friend?'

'I'm waiting for a friend who sent me this orchid,' I said more pointedly. If it's you, buster, make your move. You're already late, and there aren't a lot of bushes in here to beat around, except for the artificial trees. I remembered what it said in the book about business negotiations, how the Western gung ho attitude doesn't work at all. In a deal with the Japanese circumlocution is everything.

'I am waiting for a friend too,' he said amicably.

'Perhaps your friend is me.'

He smiled uncertainly. 'Excuse me?' he said. Before I had time to go any further a couple of young Japanese came up to him. 'Ah,' he said, and proceeded to greet them in Japanese. He pulled out a map of Sydney and they talked some more. They decided on something and he put the map away. 'Excuse me,' he said to me, 'do you know which ferry to Manly?' It wasn't him.

'I think it's wharf 3, you can check at Circular Quay.'

'Thank you, nice to make your acquaintance. I go with my friends now, OK?'

It wasn't him. I'd been there almost 40 minutes now and no-one had shown. I was getting a very bad feeling about all this. I waited five more minutes for the benefit of the doubt then went to the desk and asked if there were any messages for Dolores Delgado or Claudia Valentine. There was nothing for either of us. I thought about getting them to call me a cab but it would be quicker for me to run down to the rank at Circular Quay.

So I ran. My Japanese friend must have found the right wharf for Manly because I couldn't see him around. 'The Royale, Kings Cross,' I said to the cabbie. I didn't bother telling him to drive as fast as he could. I guess we could have gone through red lights and driven on the pavement but what was the point? Whoever had wanted me out of Dolores' room had probably found what they were looking for by now.

Things weren't exactly as I'd left them but it wasn't as if a bomb had hit it either. I'd had bombs hit before, in my room at the pub. That break-in had felt like a personal affront, as if I had been violated. They hadn't cared two hoots about covering their tracks. The job had been done by powerful people who didn't have to cover up after themselves, they could flaunt their power. The mess itself was a message: We've been here and there's nothing you can do about it.

This time it was different. There was none of that flagrancy. But it was just as bad, almost as if my negligence had allowed it to happen. Someone had been in here. I sat down on the floor, my back against the door, my hands resting on my knees, trying to take in the big picture. Christ, why hadn't I just stayed home today? I felt guilty but that wasn't going to help things now, the damage had been done. If indeed there'd been damage.

The thing that struck me most about it was how neat everything was. Neater than I'd left it. Neater than the cleaner leaves it—her job is to clean the room, not tidy up the personal belongings. It wasn't simply a cursory tidy up to make it look as if no-one had been there, it was systematic, as if the person who did it had spent time in the army. Or jail. Someone for whom neatness was a habit. Or an obsession. Who inspected the cutlery in restaurants; who couldn't let someone walk around with the label poking out the top of their jumper. But no-one would go to all that trouble just to tidy up. Besides, it wasn't technically a break-in, the door hadn't been tampered with, and by the look of it nothing had been smashed.

What had they been looking for? Had they found it? That was an added difficulty. At least with your own stuff you know what's valuable—not how much money a thing is worth but its importance. What was here that was important to whoever had come in? Would I notice if it were missing?

The things of most monetary value were the contents of the jewellery boxes. I looked through them. All the expensive items were still there and the junky stuff as well. Touching as little as possible I went through the wardrobe, checked under the bed, opened cupboards, the fridge. Nothing missing as far as I could tell. I went out onto the little balcony. An abseiler could gain access to the balcony, maybe fiddle open the French doors as long as they didn't mind the whole of Bayswater Road watching.

But a lot of things went on at the Cross, a break-in on a sixth floor would probably pass unnoticed. I looked at the ant-like people in the street down below. No-one looked back up at me, they all went about their business as if I was invisible. I came inside again.

The only place left was the bathroom.

Before I even opened the door I got a strange feeling about what might be behind it. The door wasn't closed when I'd left this morning but it was now. Another manifestation of the intruder's obsessive tidiness?

No, because this room wasn't at all tidy. For a start there was a vacuum cleaner left in the middle of the floor. Even more untidy was the body in the bath. Funny way to have a bath, fully clothed and with no water in the tub. I recognised her as one of the cleaners. She was unconscious but I could feel a pulse. There were no visible signs of struggle though her hair had fallen out of her clip. I carefully felt her head, no lumps except one just above the left ear. Maybe she'd slipped and fallen while cleaning the bath. In that case wouldn't the Ajax and the cleaning cloth be somewhere close at hand?

On the right side of her neck was a small spot of blood, the kind an injection leaves.

I called the desk and asked Vicki if she could come up as quickly as possible, then I called the ambulance. I told them the address and the problem. It all had a terrible familiarity. But at least the cleaner was still alive. She had a pulse and I could feel her outward breath on my cheek.

I went to the door when I heard Vicki knock. Despite the blusher that made her look like a rag doll with painted cheeks, she visibly paled when she saw the body. 'It's Yasmina,' she said, staring. The staring didn't last long, Vicki worked at the Cross, she'd seen this kind of thing before. She went to the phone.

'I've called the ambulance,' I said. She put the phone down.

Together we lifted Yasmina out of the bath and laid her on the bed. I told Vicki what I thought had happened and asked her if she'd noticed anything untoward. The Royale was as security conscious as any hotel in the Cross looking for the tourist dollar and Vicki was paid to notice. She said there'd been nothing out of the ordinary. Strangers couldn't just walk in off the street and go up to the rooms. I asked her then who had delivered the orchid I'd found outside my door that morning. She didn't know anything about it. The policy with delivery of flowers was that they were left at reception and a porter or someone else would take them up to the suites. But no-one had left any flowers for me at reception, I'd found it outside the door.

There was no sign of a break-in, no-one had left anything at the desk, there were no breaches of security, nothing out of the ordinary. I had eliminated all the possibilities I could think of, it had to be someone who didn't have to break in, who didn't have to pass security. It had to be an employee. Or a guest.

Vicki didn't go for the employee idea at all. They'd all been here at least six months, she knew them, no-one would pull a stunt like this. I wasn't quite so sure, most people had a price and most people could be conned. But why now? If they'd been here a minimum of six months there would have been ample opportunities in the past to rifle the room. Why now?

It was far more likely to be a guest, someone just passing through. Passing through on purpose.

The phone rang. The ambulance people were on their way up.

Vicki opened the door to let them in.

I couldn't believe it—one of them was the guy who'd attended to Dolores! He looked at me as if he knew me from somewhere but couldn't quite place me. I hated being caught up in life's little ironies. It kind of took the edge off the seriousness of each individual situation.

I pointed out the spot of blood on Yasmina's neck. He and his companion, this time a burly, sandy-complexioned man close to retirement, examined it closely. Then they stuck an oxygen mask over her mouth and nose. The older guy asked us what had happened. I showed him into the bathroom, explaining the position of the body and the circumstances. There was a low muffled moan. When we came back into the bedroom Yasmina was opening her eyes.

She was still groggy by the time they put her in the ambulance and wanting to know what had happened to her. So was I. How did she feel?, I asked her. Like after an operation, she said. By the time we were outside St Vincents Hospital I had the full story. Or as full as Yasmina knew.

She had just started vacuuming the room when someone grabbed her from behind. He'd put his arm around her throat and said into her ear, 'Don't struggle, I don't want to hurt you.' The voice was very soft, an Australian accent, she thought. His breath felt clammy on her ear. Did she catch a glimpse of him, have any idea what he looked like? No, he had her by the throat, she couldn't turn her head. She was too frightened to move or even open her mouth to scream. His arm then, the one around her throat, did she notice anything about it? Yes. He was wearing something knitted, a brown and black pattern, she could feel the coarse wool against her throat. Then there was a sharp stab in her neck, like a bee sting, and she couldn't remember anything else.

I asked her if she'd noticed anything beforehand, heard anything while she was cleaning the rooms, for example. Not really. With the vacuum cleaner it's hard to hear. Did she see anyone in the corridor? No. Everyone was out, except the man in room 617. He asked her to come back later. Did she see him? No, she knocked and said she was there to clean the room but he didn't open the door, he just said come back later. She closed her eyes as if her brain was hurting, her hands resting on the slight mound of her abdomen.

Yasmina didn't want us to call any relatives. Her husband worked nights and slept during the day. He got very angry if his sleep was disturbed. Was there anyone else we could call? No, no other relatives in Australia. She would be all right, she didn't want any trouble.

The bulge beneath her protective hands was barely discernible. 'You're pregnant?' I asked softly.

She took a sharp intake of breath, then let it out slowly. 'Yes.'

'And your husband doesn't know,' I guessed.

'He doesn't want a baby yet. Not till we buy a house. But I want this baby.'

Gary and I didn't have a house when Amy was born. In fact we never got round to buying one. Didn't stop us having her; and David a couple of years later. Oh, how rosy everything had been then, I reflected dryly. 'You didn't get pregnant on your own. Tell him, he'll come round.'

'I will tell him. When I am ready.'

I got the point and held my silence. It was none of my business. Whoever had knocked her out only meant it to be temporary. The hospital would have a quick look at her but then they'd send her home. There was always a shortage of beds, especially at St Vincents, especially in casualty. Around King Cross and Darlinghurst, the areas St Vincents serviced, there were lots of casualties, many of them due to the sharp end of a needle.

'Will you be all right?'

'Yes, thanks.'

'How will you get home?'

'I will catch a cab,' she said.

'Where do you live?'

'Croydon.'

She probably didn't have enough for a cab fare to Croydon on her. I'd slip the hospital twenty bucks, they could tell her it was part of the service.

'I will be all right,' she assured me as I was leaving. I had a feeling she was going to be. If she could hold her own against me she could hold her own against her husband when the time came.

I left at the same time as the ambulance guys. Before the young guy got in the van he stopped and came over to me. 'Look,' he grinned, crinkling the corners of those eyes the colour of unpolluted ocean on a sunny day, 'I can't help feeling I've seen you somewhere before.'

I could have spent all day in those sea-blue eyes, surfing the curl of those thick long eyelashes. My urge to tousle the blond hair was almost irresistible. 'Maybe you have,' I gave him my best smile, 'I do this a lot.' -

Round Green Park opposite St Vincents Hospital men looking for rough trade cruise past the boys at the wall willing to give it to them—at a price. Some of the boys still look fresh and healthy, others are further down the track. There are a lot of occupational hazards involved in working the wall—AIDS, mugging and poofter-bashing.

There were occupational hazards to being a cleaner too. I kept thinking about Yasmina. She was just going about her business, doing her job, when she'd got caught up in something else altogether. She was a minor character, a bit player, an afternoon's event in the mystery of Dolores Delgado, and she had no significant lines to deliver. The person who'd injected her had made sure of that. But now this story had intersected with her own.

She worked six till two. Then she'd go home and prepare something for her husband to eat when he got up at four. They'd have that meal together then he'd go to work. It was probably the only time of day they saw each other. But today dinner wasn't going to be ready at four, and he probably wasn't going to like that. Maybe I was misjudging him, I'd never met the guy. All I had to go on was her reaction to him. I'd given her my number at the pub if she needed to call, plus I told her that Vicki at the hotel would look after her.

I'd rung Vicki to let her know how Yasmina was going and to see if there were any further developments. I asked her about the occupant of room 617. She looked it up. A Mr John Brown. One night, cash in advance. He'd come in during Patrick's shift. That was all she could tell me. He'd gone now, the room was vacant.

That didn't get me very far. I had a name but so what. There were probably thousands of people called John Brown. For some of them it might even have been their real name.

I left the hospital and walked across Green Park wondering whether Bernie had rung yet with the rego number.

But I didn't have to wonder, I could find out. Right now. Though I'd started carrying my mobile phone with me I still hadn't got used to the new toy. I hadn't yet left the 018 number on my answering machine and I wasn't automatically giving the number out. I'd gone the whole hog and bought state of the art, with everything that opens and shuts. Only trouble was I still hadn't figured it all out. But I did know how to use the little gadget that would allow me to ring home and see if there were any messages, which was just what I was about to do.

There was another small problem—it looked so posy using a mobile phone in public I could hardly bring myself to do it.

I found myself a nice quiet back alley not far from where the boys worked their beat. There were a few garbage cans and cats but they didn't bother me. I tapped out my home phone number and waited for the messages to be played back.

'Don't struggle, I don't want to hurt you, just tell me where it is.' That wasn't Bernie, it wasn't even my phone.

I could smell the sweet cloying smell of aftershave; feel the breath against my ear. Clammy, as if it was creeping along a dark dank tunnel. I couldn't turn to see who it was because an arm had me in a headlock. I didn't want to move anyway. From the corner of my eye I saw the thin deadly needle hovering near my face.

'Where's what?' I asked, hardly daring to move.

'You know what I'm talking about. Where is it?' Still the same stealthy voice insinuating its way into my ear.

'I'm . . . I'm not Dolores Delgado.' It sounded so stupid. What did I expect, that he was going to say, 'Oh terribly sorry I've made a mistake'?

He chuckled. 'I know. I parked the car and snuck back. I saw the derelict help you up. I was in the crowd, watching. I heard you speak. That's when I knew you weren't that other bitch.' He chuckled again. It made my flesh crawl the way his hot breath went cold on my cheek. 'You asked if anyone saw who was driving. Well now you know.'

If only he'd get that needle away from my face I could make my move. It was as bad as having a gun pointed at me. I didn't want to argue with him while he had that thing pointed at me.

'OK,' I confessed as if the game was up, 'I'll give it to you. It's . . . it's in . . . can you take your arm away? You're choking me.'

'In your bag, is it?' He started to slip the bag off my shoulder.

I moved. Spun around, released myself from his grip and kicked the syringe out of his hand. For a split second everything stood still. He not believing what happened, me waiting for him to attack me again.

He backed back. Then he turned and ran. I couldn't believe it, he wasn't supposed to run he was supposed to be threatening me, attacking. Had he thought because I was a woman it was going to be a piece of cake, that I wouldn't fight back, like Yasmina I would be too frightened to do anything? 'Hey,' I yelled as he turned out of the lane, 'I haven't finished with you yet.' I sprinted off after him.

But I couldn't get out of the alley.

Three of the boys from the wall were blocking the exit. They had chains. What were they doing here? 'Haven't finished with who?' one of them sneered.

'That guy, he tried to attack me,' I said, desperately. 'Let me through.'

'He's the one running away. Looks more like you were attacking him, poofter-basher!' He swung the chain at me. I grabbed hold of it and yanked it, trying to pull him over. He let go. The three of them together looked mean but they were amateurs. It was small comfort. I'd probably lost the guy by now. I tried to make a run for it again but the other two guys grabbed hold of me and knocked me to the ground.

'Do I look like a poofter-basher?' I screamed in frustration. There was no point in trying to barge my way through. Even though they were amateurs, there were three of them. There'd be one to block my every move. 'I'm a private investigator. Look,' I said, scrambling for my bag. 'Look,' I said, pulling out my ID.

They looked at it, they looked at each other. I stood up. They didn't knock me down again. 'Sorry,' apologised the one who had wielded the chain. 'Round here if a guy comes running for his life out of an alley it usually means only one thing. We've got to make a stand, we can't let them get away with it.'

'That's terrific.' In other circumstances I would have meant it sincerely. 'Now, if you don't mind, you just keep fighting your fights and stay away from mine.'

They backed out of the alley still mumbling apologies. I looked up and down the street. It was pointless. The guy had long gone. I went back down the alley and picked up my things—my bag, the mobile phone. Very carefully I picked up the syringe and put it in my bag. This one I'd hand over to Carol. This one would be accompanied by the appropriate forms.

I came back out onto the street again and walked up to the wall where the boys were working their beat. I had a good view up and down the street. I leaned against the wall and tapped Carol's number on the mobile phone. Now I didn't give a shit how posy it looked.

I was hoping she'd been called back from Mudgee on an emergency. Did they have a contact number for her there? No. She wasn't there on police business, she'd accumulated some flexidays and had gone visiting to the vineyards.

Why didn't she tell me where she'd be in case I needed her? Attacked by a maniac, attacked by vigilantes, a syringe in my bag containing goodness-knows-what. I needed someone to talk to.

I could have walked back to the Royale, it was an easy

distance, but I caught a cab. I'd had enough of the streets for one day.

In the cab I had time to go over it. He was about 45, fair hair, tanned—not a leisure tan, the kind you get working outdoors. He was a neat but dull dresser—black and brown jumper, a collar and tie just visible at the top. What with one thing and the other I hadn't particularly noticed any strangeness about the eyes, just the look of total surprise on his face.

I'd probably taken him unawares by fighting back, men usually don't expect women to do that, but I didn't think I'd got rid of him altogether. 'Where it is?' he had wanted to know. He still hadn't found it, whatever *it* was. He'd watched, he'd waited, he'd been in the room. And now he'd shown himself. He was getting desperate, panicky. Next time he mightn't even bother asking questions.

All the way back to the hotel I thought about it. What was it he was after? I didn't have a clue. No, that was wrong, I did have a clue. He'd started to take my bag off my shoulder. It wasn't much but it was better than nothing. At least I knew it was something that would fit into my bag. That ruled out elephants and double basses.

I came in and flung my bag on the bed. I stood in the centre of the room then I started circling. Whatever it was hadn't been found yet. It had to be somewhere. He'd come to the room looking for it, he hadn't found it. That didn't mean it wasn't there. He hadn't looked everywhere, or maybe he had and just not seen it. What was it, what was its shape, what could it be disguised as? Knowing it wasn't an elephant or a double bass didn't help all that much.

If it was that important Dolores would have hidden it well. Where? Where did you put it, Dolores? Give me a clue. I circled the room looking, looking. I wasn't getting any brain waves. If Dolores was sending me any messages from the other side they weren't getting through.

I searched the room from top to bottom.

Literally.

I started with the light fitting, unscrewing the screws and lifting it off. All I found under there was a light bulb. I looked along the top of the wardrobe. All I saw there was the Japanese business book. It was the right size to fit into my bag but surely he would have seen it when he searched the room.

I took it down and examined it, page by page. Nothing was underlined, no page corners had been folded over, nothing down the spine of the book. I got a nail file and started scratching away at the end papers. I lost patience and started tearing the paper off in strips.

I went through the wardrobe, the plastic bag with the muddy boots. Levered off the heels. Tore back the lining of the beauty case, where I'd found the other passport. Nothing. Did the same with the lining of the suitcases. Went through the dresses, cut open the lining of the leather jacket. Nothing, nothing, nothing.

I went through every drawer, every cupboard, the fridge. Tore open hermetically sealed bags of cashews, beer nuts, the little containers of milk, the sachets of sugar.

Tore open the pillows, pulled out all the stuffing. The doona, lifted up the mattress. If the walls had been papered I would have torn that off too.

I went into the bathroom and wrenched the lid off the cistern, opened the cupboard and pulled everything out, ripped open the new packets of soap, squeezed the toothpaste out of the tube. Nothing, nothing, nothing!

Where should I look next, Dolores? Tell me that! Who are you, Dolores, what am I looking for? Did he kill you, Dolores, was that the man? Why did you die, Dolores, why did you die?

I slumped down on the floor. The whole place looked as if a bomb had hit it. Someone else might have been in here but I was the burglar.

I was losing my sense of proportion. I'd started off circling the room and ended up in a feeding frenzy. I had to get out of here, go back to the pub. To my place.

It was a comfort to hear the same noises I could hear every evening—the distant rumble of conversation down below, the occasional burst of laughter and the high soft sound of pool balls clinking together. Strangely enough I rarely heard from up here the satisfying clunk of the ball going down the pocket chute. Must have been the pitch.

Everything was still here, just as I'd left it, all the familiar objects, all in the same place. It felt cold and clammy the way a room gets if it hasn't had any life in it for a while, but at least it was my room. I opened the French doors to allow a little fresh pollution in. The geranium pots on the balcony were like dust bowls and the flowers were gasping for water. The only thing in the room that seemed to show any life was the light furiously blinking on the answering machine telling me there were messages. They could wait.

I watered the pot plants. Then I sat in the warrior pose and did a karate meditation.

Half an hour later I felt clearer, calmer. Ready to resume my life. I got a can of VB out of the fridge and sat down to play back the messages.

No warning pips or gaps, Steve's voice took me by surprise. It sounded as if he was just around the corner—mellow, assuring, slightly gravelly, like water passing over stones. He was in Bangkok, everything was fine, he'd be back in about a week. 'Miss you, Magnum,' was how he signed off. As if he'd called

111

just the other day, as if he hadn't been away for over a month and all I had to show for it was a postcard where the name and address was longer than the message. Maybe all the other letters and postcards he'd written had got lost, gone to Austria instead of Australia. Yeah, that'd be it.

I was aware that the machine had moved on to the next message. It was from one of my insurance companies. There was a bad back in Ashfield needed watching. Urgent. Phone before 11 a.m. today. Today was yesterday. The only work I'd been offered in weeks and I'd missed it.

The next message was from my friend Otto, enquiring if I was still alive. There were a couple more messages like that.

Then there was Bernie. With details of the Barina. It belonged to a hire car company. Coincidentally enough the one I used when I wanted something faster and less conspicuous than the Daimler. That was going to make finding out who it was rented to a lot easier.

Last message was from Cilla at the club, reminding me that we had a date to go shopping tomorrow and that Jimmy had dropped the photographs in.

That got me going again, but not a frenzy this time, my thoughts were calm and considered. As if I was observing, reading them rather than actively thinking them. The hotel wasn't the only place. There may have been something at the club. It was probably the same guy searching her room as the one Cilla had found in the dressing room. She said he was looking for something.

I rang Cilla and told her I'd be coming over tonight. She said bring your dancing shoes. 'I will. Cilla, you know the other day when I picked up Dolores' things, did you give me every-thing? Could something have been overlooked?'

'What sort of thing do you mean?' I told her that someone had been in the hotel room. 'I kept the dresses and the good stuff for you, the rest I threw away. You went through the rubbish, if there was anything to see you would have seen it, no?' Maybe not. I didn't think there was anything particular to look for then.

Going to the club sounded like a damned good idea. I had the photographs to look forward to. Patrick, the night-shift receptionist, wouldn't be at the Park Royale for another hour yet. When he did start work it was pretty busy for the first hour or so then it eased off. I could talk to him about the mysterious Mr Brown of room 617 later on in the evening. Maybe round midnight he'd appreciate a little company apart from the security guard. I could bring him back some decent coffee.

Meanwhile I phoned my friend at the hire car company. It was just on six. She should still be there. 'Sharon? Hi, it's Claudia.' We had some preliminary discussion about each other's health which in both cases was good. I don't know why I told her mine was good. I had a sore neck and a grazed elbow from this afternoon and two grazed knees from the Celica that hadn't healed up properly yet.

Sharon informed me that my usual Vitesse was out on the road at the moment, what would I like instead? 'I don't want to hire one this time,' I said, 'I have a little problem. Someone is following me—in one of your cars.' Oh really, she said, we can't have that, can we? I gave her the details of the black Barina and asked who had the car out. I waited the fifteen seconds while she brought the information up on her computer screen.

'No-one.'

'No-one?'

'It's here. Came back this afternoon.'

'Who had it out before?'

Thripps, she said, Howard Thripps from Coffs Harbour. 'That's interesting,' I heard her say, 'I remember that name. Just give me a minute, I'll see if I can trace it.' I gave her a minute. She traced it. 'Claudia?'

'I'm here,' I assured her.

'This Thripps,' she continued, 'he had another car out before the Barina.'

'Let me guess,' I said, 'grey Celica?' I stunned her into momentary silence.

She came back on line, 'How do you do that?'

'Cars are easy. Names and addresses I need some help with. What have you got on our Mr Thripps?' She gave me his Coffs Harbour address and a contact phone number in Sydney. 'He didn't take another car out?' No, he didn't. 'Thanks, Sharon. Fancy a drink after work?' She said some other time, she was supposed to be playing squash with her boyfriend. If he shows up, that is. He was late. If he doesn't show, I said, come to the Tropicana, you'll get as much exercise and you'll be having such a good time you'll hardly even notice. OK, she said, I'll give him ten more minutes then I'm on my way.

Thripps. The word was vaguely familiar. I looked it up in the dictionary. Thrips—'any of various small slender-bodied insects typically having piercing mouth parts and feeding on plant sap'.

I shivered. Not that I minded insects, it was something Lucy had said. Oleander leaves. Bufotenine. I wondered if that was the kind of plant sap this Thripps fed on.

I rang the contact number. A recorded message told me that the Yagoona Animal Shelter was open between 9–5, Monday to Friday. I checked the number and dialled again. I got the same message. Very bloody funny, Mr Thripps.

He hadn't hired another car from Sharon. He'd changed companies or he'd finished his business.

I didn't think he'd finished his business.

I put on a slinky black lace dress with a silver belt. Slinky, but short enough to allow plenty of leg movement for dancing. I spent half an hour mussing up my hair and putting on make-up. I didn't have to dress up like Dolores anymore, I just liked doing it. I closed the French doors and gathered up what I'd need for the evening. I was ready for action.

When I opened the door to leave Jack was standing there with his hand up as if he was just about to knock. In his other hand was a sheet of paper. 'G'day,' he said, 'saw you sneaking in. I was just going to leave this, it came this afternoon.' He handed me the piece of paper. It was the fax from Brian Collier. 'Well, I'll leave you to it, looks like you're going out. Have a good time.'

'Thanks.' I came back inside. The fax gave the company number of Royal Dolphin Enterprises, where it was incorporated, registration date and principal activity—tourism and property development for holiday resorts. There were current organisation details, registered office and a list of directors. By far the most interesting of these was the list of directors. There were four of them—Gordon Stanley Schaeffer, Warren Harvey Johnston, David Patrick Turnbull and John Quentin Peterson. They all had Sydney addresses; their dates of birth placed them currently in the 40–50 age range.

'In relation to your current investigation you might find Schaeffer's history and connections of particular interest,' Brian had written. *She had a rich sugar daddy . . . big business tycoon . . . Gordon somebody . . .*

Gordon Stanley Schaeffer was a director of several companies whose properties included, amongst others, the Royale Hotel, Kings Cross. Another of his companies, Royal Blue Finance, was named as financial backer for Green Dolphin Resorts, a $2 company with no other assets than its subscribed capital. Green Dolphin had recently won a tender for crown land on the north coast and had submitted a Development Application to Coffs Harbour City Council. 'He's not a director of Green Dolphin but,' wrote Brian, 'one of the directors of that company will be familiar to you—Dolores Delgado.'

I thought nothing would ever surprise me again after finding out Dolores was a transsexual but she could still reach out from the grave and spin me around. I would have thought it was a joke if she'd told me she was a company director. But here it was in black and white. And black and white when it came from Brian Collier I had to believe. It was somehow disorienting, as if I'd been blindfolded, turned around and when the blindfold had been taken off everything looked different.

Is this the clue, Dolores, is this where I should be looking?

A little chat with Mr Schaeffer was in order. But not tonight. Tonight I had business at the club. I wanted to have a good look at those photos Jimmy took on the night Dolores died before I went calling on anyone.

Despite the smoke, the heat and the plastic, walking into Club Tropicana was a breath of fresh air. It was as if, instead of someone at the door taking your coat and hat, they took your cares.

The coloured lights were on, highlighting the palm trees and the birds on the ceiling. They almost seemed to be dancing. Probably just the air currents. The people were dancing though, to the house band. There was Amadio, bald head like an orb of bronze, grooving away on keyboards. There was Ramón, keeping his hand in by waiting on tables. He was wearing a Hawaiian shirt undone to just above the waist, and white trousers. Tight white trousers. Same look in his eyes as he served the tables of girls on their hens' night. All that advertising and nobody buying it.

In amongst the partying sat a couple who rarely spoke and never smiled. They each had a glass of white wine that stayed full most of the evening and later they drank a coffee. They were here every night, they were Cilla's parents. They were having a great time, she said. Every night? I'd asked. 'Sure. Better than staying home watching soaps on SBS.' She had a point.

Ramón sidled up and kissed me on the cheek. 'Chica,' he said, holding me in a dance position and twirling me around, 'when are you going to dance with me?'

'Right now,' I heard Cilla say, 'I think she would prefer a drink. Can you get Claudia a whisky?' She hooked her arm around mine and took me aside. 'Big news,' she said confidentially, 'she came back! This evening. The woman who came to see Dolores, Margaret Shaver.'

Suddenly something clicked into place. Margaret Shaver. Gordon Schaeffer.

'You sure the name wasn't Schaeffer?'

'Are you hearing impaired? That's the name I been telling you all the time. Margaret Shaver.'

Dolores had a Royal Dolphin credit card. Gordon Schaeffer, one of the directors of that company, was financing Green Dolphin Resorts of which Dolores was a director. She was staying in his hotel. Margaret Schaeffer had come to see Dolores. Was I getting the picture right? Were these three the points of a love triangle?

'What did you say?'

'She asked where Dolores was. She said she has an appointment with Dolores today but Dolores didn't come. I told her to come back later, maybe we have some news.'

'Let me know the minute she walks in the door.'

Ramón came back with the drink. It was mostly ice but it looked and tasted great.

'You said the photos were here.'

'Yes, just a minute I'll go and get them.' Cilla disappeared.

I smiled hello at Cilla's parents. A hint of acknowledgement played around their eyes but otherwise it was like saying hello to a couple of Easter Island statues.

Cilla came back with two envelopes, a slim flat one and a bulkier one. 'Come into the dressing room, it's a better light in there.'

We went in.

'When I went to the safe to get the photos I saw this,' she said, putting the bulky envelope down in front of me. 'Dolores used to keep this in the safe, I'd forgotten about it. It's nothing much, just old receipts,' she said, almost apologising.

She put the other envelope down as well and turned on the bright mirror lights.

I tipped the contents of the bulky envelope out. Cilla was right, nothing much, just receipts and dockets. Beats me why Dolores kept stuff like this in a safe. Surely she didn't fill out tax returns. It was an odd collection—bills from restaurants, receipts from dress shops, from jewellery shops, from designers.

But there was something else. A smaller envelope, about letter size. I opened it up. There were keys and a card. Two keys, larger than normal. The card said TNT Security, Application for Vault Access. The deposit box number had been filled in, there was another handwritten number on the back but none of the other details had been filled in. I could almost feel my nose quivering. This is it, Dolores, isn't it? This is where you've hidden your Maltese Falcon. I felt terrific, as if I'd just won a prize. Then I sobered up. Winning the prize was one thing, collecting it was going to be another matter altogether. I put the card and the keys to one side.

'Important?' asked Cilla.

'Maybe,' I said. 'Let's have a look at the photos.'

I took the proof sheet out of the other envelope and examined it under the lights, looking for familiar faces, looking for anything out of the ordinary. I didn't think the killer would have had his photo taken on purpose as a memento of the occasion, as the groups did, but he might be hovering in the background somewhere.

I looked particularly at the area up near the bar; a lone person was likely to be at the bar, not at the tables with the groups. There was a man in those background shots wearing a dinner suit. Odd, too dressed up. What was it Cilla had said about Margaret Shaver—Schaeffer—looks like a person who doesn't go to clubs much? But this wasn't a woman, it was a man. Looking vaguely familiar. Of course I wasn't looking arbitrarily, I was looking for the man with the needle. The guy in the photo wore glasses and had his hair slicked down. He was about the same age. Take away the glasses, fluff up the hair, it could have been him. Was I clutching at straws?

The proof sheet told a story, like stills from a movie. He wasn't in any of the shots taken earlier in the evening but after interval he was there. Up at the bar. There were no photos of the first part of Dolores and Ramón's routine, Dolores and Ramón weren't going to buy photographs, but there were quite a lot of them dancing with people from the audience. And there he was again. Not dancing with Dolores, but standing nearby. With his hand in his pocket. The next one hand out of the pocket, holding something white, like a folded up handkerchief. Then he disappeared from the photos. There was a gap in the evening that Jimmy hadn't photographed, when Dolores had collapsed and Ramón danced her off stage. Then they picked up again when the conga line started. But my man had disappeared from the camera's view.

I went back to the last photo of him. He was up close to her then he disappeared. She complained that someone had pinched her, the audience participation number ended and she resumed dancing with Ramón. About twenty minutes later she went limp and started salivating.

'You seen this man before?' I asked Cilla.

She looked at the photos a while before she could make up her mind. 'Don't think so.'

'Take away the glasses, imagine the hair is fuller. Could he be the man who was here that afternoon?'

She thought about it, looked at the photos from different angles, put them together and compared them. 'Maybe.'

'What about Margaret Schaeffer, is she in any of the shots?'

Cilla looked through them all again. She shook her head, 'I don't see her.'

I asked her if she could keep everything in the safe till the end of the evening. I had a few dances with Ramón, I had a few drinks, I tried unsuccessfully to get into conversation with Cilla's mother and father. I waited in the dressing room. Margaret Schaeffer didn't show.

By midnight I decided it was time to go. I told Cilla if Margaret Schaeffer did turn up, she could ring the Royale, or she could just come over. I'd be up for another couple of hours at least.

The boys and girls of the Cross were out in force on this Thursday night and it wasn't just because Thursday night is late night shopping. Unless you call shopping for flesh shopping. It had grown old and weary since I'd first come up here as a teenager. I guess it had always been old and weary. But now even the kids looked old and weary. Living fast, dying young and leaving a corpse that was no longer good-looking. The kind of look you get from too many late nights, interiors, smoke and self-induced ravages. From seeing too much of the kind of thing you didn't normally see every day.

The Cross was an old whore, whose make-up was applied with a trowel, who wasn't making the slightest effort to grow old gracefully. But at least there was the trick of bright lights, the eternal invitation to consume, the open all hours entertainment, the punters in from the suburbs on a night out. Six a.m. was when it looked really seedy, or maybe that was just a reflection of how I felt if I happened to see 6 a.m. from the dark side. All the lights had gone out then, fading into the daylight. Two hours later the people of the night would collide with suits hurrying onto the train taking them to the CBD.

Bayswater Road was full of restaurants, or rather brasseries, forever trying to titillate the jaded palates of a town that has every cuisine in the world available to it. You didn't have this choice when you dined out in Paris or Rome. There were some benefits to not having a thousand years of entrenched culture behind you. At Crows Nest there was even a restaurant offering Greek yum cha. Only in Sydney.

Patrick was a trim young man in a dark suit and a white shirt. His hair was close-cropped, he looked healthy and he had an easy yet energetic manner about him. He looked like he came from Perth. He certainly didn't come from around here.

He was doing some business with a woman wearing a forties hat and a long coat. The night wasn't cold enough for a coat. I told myself not to be so suspicious but had a close look at her just the same. 'Margaret?' I said softly. The woman didn't turn around.

When she'd gone I asked Patrick if he could spare a minute. Sure, he said.

'You were on duty last night?'

'But of course. The night-time receptionist, c'est moi.'

'So you did the booking for room 617.'

'617, 617,' he repeated, looking it up. 'Yes,' he said, finding it, 'that was Mr Brown. Brown by name, brown by nature.'

'What do you mean "brown"?'

'Oh, you know,' he said, as if it was obvious, 'he was a brown person. Brown. Dull.'

'What did he look like?'

Patrick's eyes looked sideways as he recalled the image.

'Nothing memorable. Brown hair, medium height, fortyish, no luggage . . .'

'No luggage? I thought you didn't let people in unless they had luggage.'

'Only in the movies,' Patrick said, 'only in the *old* movies,' he added pointedly. I don't know why he felt it necessary to add the old, I was only about ten years older than him, from my point of view it was a mere rien de tout.

The guy who attacked me in the alley had fair hair, Cilla had described her visitor as blond. Was this Mr Brown the same person? 'Anything unusual about his eyes?'

Patrick shrugged his lips, 'Like what?'

I thought of what Cilla said. 'Did they look as if there was another person in there looking out?'

Patrick was looking at me as if I was from another planet.

'Just a thought,' I hastened to add. 'How was he dressed?'

'Geez, you're pushing your luck. You know how many people I've seen come through here in the last six months?'

'I only want to know about last night. That should be pretty fresh in your memory.'

'I thought I was doing well so far, I just can't remember what the guy was wearing so I guess it was nothing memorable. It was brown, but I can't remember if it was a suit or a sweater or what it was.'

'Did you think anything about it? I mean, did you think, what a sharp dresser or what a slob?'

'I thought dull, I told you. But there was something,' he was racking his brains, the effort seemed to almost hurt. 'Yeah, I remember thinking how odd that he didn't have any luggage because he looked like he came from the country. But he said he was from Yagoona. That's in Sydney, isn't it?'

'Yes, near Bankstown.'

'It was latish for a booking, about nine, and he hadn't pre-booked, just walked in off the street. Said something about there being a mix up in his arrangements, that it would be sorted out tomorrow but he needed a room for that night. I wasn't entirely convinced but his money was the same colour as everyone else's and I've had less convincing cases in here.'

'What was unconvincing?'

'He didn't have to give me an excuse, I didn't ask him where his luggage was. This is Kings Cross, you don't need an excuse to stay in a hotel for one night with no luggage. That's why I thought he was from the country.'

The timing was right for it to be the guy in the Barina. I'd got back from Mina's about 8.30. He'd seen me drive in. Time for him to park somewhere, check into the hotel. But brown hair? The guy who'd attacked me was definitely fair. Maybe Patrick was thinking brown because of the name.

'Want a coffee?' I asked Patrick.

'Sure,' he said, 'where are you getting it from?'

'Lorenzo's.'

'I'll have a *macchiata* then.'

When I came back from Lorenzo's Dave, the porter, was hanging round the reception area. Towards midnight things got pretty loose round the Cross and here was no exception. All the day people had turned in for the night and the vampires had come to life.

Despite what Patrick had said about old movies, Dave was straight out of one. He wore a dicky little hat and a bellhop's uniform though I wasn't sure whether he had to or whether he just liked dressing up. But he wasn't standing in the eager, ready-for-anything pose of the bellhop, he had his foot up on a chair, leaning on that bent knee, talking to Patrick, his jaunty cap cocked in Patrick's direction. 'Hi,' he said to me cheerily, 'd'ya get ya flowers?'

'The orchid?' I said, depositing the minitray with the coffees on the counter.

'I don't know what kind of flower it was. The one in the box. Said he wanted to surprise you with it, leave it outside your door.' Dave took his foot off the chair, turned around and sat down on it. 'I said, no worries, I'd do it for him. He said no, it was OK he was a guest, he could drop it off on the way up, which room was it again? So I told him.'

I asked Dave much the same questions I'd asked Patrick. He gave much the same kind of answers, except he was able to add that the brownness the guy was wearing was a suit. And a woven wool tie. I asked Dave if he noticed anything special about the eyes, he said no but there was something special about the teeth. They were the same colour as the guy's face. 'Oh, I wouldn't say that,' said Patrick. They then started to have quite a lively discussion about it. None of it was making me feel any better. I took out the photos and showed them the guy with the white handkerchief. Dave said, yes it could be him; Patrick said no, he didn't think so.

They just confirmed the PI's worse nightmare—ask twenty people what someone looks like and you get twenty different descriptions.

Coogee **was like** Randwick only the closer you got to the beach the whiter the buildings got. Despite the occasional visit to neighbouring Randwick to see my mother I hadn't been to Coogee for years. The Aquarium, where we'd gone for school swimming carnivals, had turned into a food hall. The colonnades were still there, tarted up, and a multifaceted dome. More exciting than swimming carnivals was the day the cops turned up at the Aquarium and arrested Miss Blackshaw for forging cheques. She was my favourite maths teacher. I still believed she was innocent even after she went to trial and pleaded guilty. Life has to deal you a couple of dud hands before you become cynical enough to be a private detective.

Which is why I wasn't really surprised to find the Schaeffers had an unlisted number. I was up bright and early, I'd put the hotel room back together as best I could. Cilla and I had already been shopping. We'd hit the winter sales. It had been frantic. All the expert shoppers were there, hunting out the best bargains, gathering them up as fast as they could, practically clubbing to death any interloper. We managed to avoid the blows long enough for Cilla to get her pink cashmere sweater and for me to choose a swimsuit. It was bright pink with straps that crisscrossed down the back. I'd previously stayed well away from pink but now that I had black hair instead of red, new worlds of colour were opening up to me.

It was Margaret Schaeffer I wanted to see before Gordon, but I was prepared to take either. I didn't expect a big business tycoon like him to be home during the day but his wife might be.

I drove up around the south headland, parked the Daimler near the patch of tough salty grass called Grant Reserve, and walked a couple of streets to the Schaeffer address.

It was fortunate that the wind had swept all the pollution out of the sky because the house looked best against a sky-blue background. It wasn't as flash as I expected; a comfortable suburban brick home in the fifties, it had now acquired a top floor of white stucco. And probably a pool, deck and jacuzzi hidden from view round the back. I pressed the buzzer at the front door and waited. It was all pretty quiet in there. I pressed the buzzer again but there was still no sign of life. Maybe Margaret had gone shopping too. I could wait. But not on her doorstep, I didn't want to scare her off.

It was a warm winter's day, I was at the beach, I had a new pink costume and there was no time like the present to try it out. As I walked back to the car to get it I realised I was parked right near Wylie's Baths, a pool that had been carved out of the rocks at this end of Coogee Beach. It would make a nice change from the surf.

I walked down the steps to the baths and had the odd feeling of being on a film set. The sun-bleached timbers hadn't been replaced in living memory. They looked like they might snap at any moment, like a frail old lady's spindly legs. The decks and support poles were built into the rock face and looked like scaffolding. Some areas you weren't allowed to walk on at all for fear of falling through the rotting timbers. There were one or two hardy souls in the pool below; the water looked relatively clean and washed over the retaining wall from the sea.

I went into the change rooms. The remaining bits of pale green paint were dry and flaky. The floor was best left undescribed and I could almost feel the tinea creeping up between my toes. But what a joy, the thing had not been renovated. It looked like it was on its last legs but at least they were its original legs. It was another site around the city that was in limbo, waiting to be rezoned, waiting to have money spent on it. I hoped it wasn't going to rot away completely while the political wrangles went on.

I stepped over some leathery old sunbathers on the rickety deck and walked down a steep set of steps to the pool. The water was about one degree away from turning into ice, and that was only the opinion of my big toe. Against its better judgement I took the plunge, swam a length, turned and swam back. When the numbness went away I was sure this would be invigorating.

Ten laps later I was sitting out of the wind with a towel draped round my shoulders. I could feel the pleasant tightness of salt drying on my legs. I would have a shower when I got home, I didn't expect there'd be hot water up in the change rooms and I'd had enough cold water for one day.

I'd thought about it swimming and I thought about it now. Dolores' safety deposit box at TNT. I could get a court order to examine the contents of the box but that would take weeks. And it would have to go through 'official channels'.

TNT Stronghold had a 24-hour service. Dolores could go straight in there, any time of the day or night. The man with the needle knew I wasn't Dolores but TNT didn't. I had the keys, I had the access card. I'd forged her signature before, I could do it again. A piece of cake. Unless, like Miss Blackshaw, I got caught.

I slipped my clothes back on over my swimming costume. It wasn't as easy as going shopping. Shops didn't have steel vaults, armed guards. OK, so apply for a court order. It'd take weeks but it would be nice and safe. Then it'd go to the cops, I had no official status, it might never get to me. You think I was going to be content with that? My curiosity was of the scale that I was prepared to rip rooms apart. A few armed guards and steel vaults weren't going to deter me.

I climbed up the stairs, left the baths and walked back towards the Schaeffer residence. People get shot in quiet suburban streets like these.

Their place still looked pretty quiet too, no car in the driveway, no doors or windows open. No heavy display of security, though that didn't mean alarms wouldn't go off if I started exploring on my own. But I hadn't come all this way just to go for a swim. The neighbours might be good for a chat. I went in next door.

I thought I was seeing double when the door opened. They were identical, both peering like squirrels out of their cubby holes. 'Yes?' said the two old ladies more or less in unison. Identical in height, body shape and facial features, both wearing little girl dresses with puffed sleeves that cut into their flabby upper arms. There was one major difference. The one on the right had pure white hair while the other one had dyed hers black. She was wearing an Alice band but it didn't hide the white hair roots.

'Hi,' I said brightly, 'I'm enquiring about the room to let.'

'Room to let? Room to let?' repeated the white-haired one like a parrot. 'Do we have a room to let, Lil?' Lil didn't say anything. 'One of the girls given notice?' the white-haired one continued.

'No,' said the black-haired one, firmly, authoritatively, 'there are no vacancies at the moment.'

'I couldn't imagine there'd be, all the girls are so happy here. Although Jennifer's been playing up lately,' she added confidentially, 'I've had to have words with her.'

Lil cast her sister a silencing look. The white-haired one must have got the hint. 'I'm sorry, no,' she said to me smiling, 'we don't have any rooms at the moment.'

'That's strange,' I commented, 'this is number 24, isn't it?'

'No, no, no,' sang the white-haired one, 'this is 26,' she announced proudly. 'Number 24's next door, the Schaeffers.'

'Oh yes,' I said, as if the light was just dawning, 'that was the name, Schaeffer. Look,' I said, lowering my voice, 'I wonder if you could tell me a little bit about them, now that I'm here. It's hard to know what you're letting yourself in for when you arrive in a new place. Are they nice?'

'Why don't you come in and have a cup of tea,' suggested

the white-haired twin in a neighbourly fashion. 'If you're going to rent a room there we'll be neighbours.'

'Evie,' said Lil in a voice like a rod of iron, 'not today, we're doing the spring cleaning. Remember?'

Whatever it was that Evie remembered it worked. 'Sorry, Lil,' she gulped, chastened.

'It's all right,' I said, smoothing the waves between them, 'I'll be off in a minute. I just wondered if they were people I'd feel safe with.' To say nothing of how safe I might feel with you. I had no idea how well my young-girl-from-the-country routine was working with these two. I knew what my hair looked like when it got wet, I hadn't combed it out, and my entire body was encrusted with salt. But here in Coogee that was probably normal. Besides, what was I worrying about? Here were two 80-year-olds trying to look sixteen.

'Ooh, I wouldn't know about safe,' chatted Evie. 'They're not here all the time. They're quite rich, I think they've got another place somewhere. She's quite nice, what's her name, Lil?'

Lil, so quiet when it came to the girls, was quite happy to supply the name of the neighbour, 'Margaret.'

'Yes, that's right. Margaret. But Graeme, he's . . .'

'It's Gordon.'

'Yes, Gordon. Far too showy for my liking. Has a chauffeur pick him up, you never used to see that in my day. Fancy a chauffeur in Coogee. Don't hold with it myself. All men are created equal.' Lil looked at her sister as if she had broken wind in public and Evie quickly back-pedalled. 'Well, some men are,' she said, somewhat miffed.

'Just the two of them,' I took up the slack, 'no children?'

'The boy's in America. He's at tech.'

'Harvard Business School,' Lil corrected her.

'Is that all, just the one boy?'

'Yes. No, there's the other one.'

'What other one?' asked Lil, interested.

'Oh, he's not a boy, he's her brother,' said Evie, quite pleased that she knew something that Lil didn't. 'He's been coming in and out the last few days.'

'You sure there's someone else there?' said Lil, trying to cast doubt on her sister's small moment of victory.

'Oh, yes,' piped up Evie, 'Jennifer told me.' As soon as she'd said it she clapped her hand over her mouth.

'We'd better ask Jennifer about that, hadn't we?' It didn't sound like it was going to be a friendly interrogation. There was something odd going on in the sisters' house and I didn't particularly want to know about it. It was time to draw this session to a close.

'Thanks a lot,' I sparkled. 'I might just go round the side and have a little look in their backyard, do you mind?' They didn't mind what I did. The door closed as if I wasn't even there. I guess Lil had some chastising to do.

I went round the side of their house and pulled myself up to look over the dividing wall. There were leaves in the pool, it looked like it hadn't been used in a while. Didn't people cover their pools over for the winter? There were no kids' toys out on the back deck, no martinis on the white wrought iron garden furniture, no evidence of life style at all.

I got the not unfamiliar feeling that I was being watched. I looked up to the upstairs floor of the sisters' house. There was a doll standing up at the window, an Alice band in her hair, her arms out in front of her. She was wearing the same puffed sleeved dress as the women who'd greeted me at the door. Jennifer?

I came back out the front, climbed over the side fence into the Schaeffers' place. Just as I got to the front door, a telephone started ringing. It rang for a long time. Wouldn't people like this put an answering machine on when they went out? Maybe they forgot. I knocked on the door. I didn't get an answer. There was no reason for me to, but I couldn't help feeling there was someone in there. That there'd been someone home all the time. Maybe they thought I was a Jehovah's Witness and didn't want to come to the door. Sure.

I looked up at the window. The doll hadn't budged. I gave her a wink. You know what's going on, don't you, Jennifer?

I went back to the Daimler and phoned Vicki at the Royale to see if anyone had called. Despite the fact that she wasn't answering the door to me there was an outside chance that Margaret Schaeffer had actually come to see me. Vicki said that this was a hotel, not an answering service. 'Pardon?' I said. She said Yasmina had told her the pillows in Dolores' room were ripped. Yasmina also had a black eye. I told her it had been a rough night. I'd pay for any damage. She said she'd have to speak to the management about it. First time I'd heard her mention the management. Impression she gave, she was the management.

I roughly knew the procedure in banks with safety deposit boxes but I wasn't sure how things worked at TNT. It was after five. The lawyers and business people had come in and were vying for elbow room on the bar with the singlet and shorts labourers who arrived at four o'clock. I didn't think I ever would, but I missed George, our resident dero. He'd been knocked over on the way home from the pub, nothing serious but they were keeping him in for tests. It was a bit of a shock meeting the wife, Jack said, no-one thought he really had one. A plump woman with grey hair, in fairly good nick compared to him. Funny why a man with a good woman like that at home would spend all his time in the pub, commented Jack. Yeah, funny that, I said, I bet there are good women all over Australia asking themselves the very same question.

'No thanks,' I said when Jack offered me a drink. 'You wouldn't happen to have a safety deposit box with TNT, would you?'

'Anything I need to keep in a safe place I use the pub safe,' replied Jack.

'Yes, I thought that'd be your answer. What about the customers? Some of them must use a discreet private service like TNT to stash their goodies in.'

He gave me an enquiring look. 'I thought if we had any customers like that you would have sorted them out by now.

You could try Marty,' he suggested, 'but be gentle with him, will you? He's a good boy at heart.'

'Relax, Jack,' I reassured him, 'he won't feel a thing.'

Marty wore beige suits and pale green ties and had presence. At least, he liked to think he had. He was a big fish in a small pond. A businessman who 'knew people'. He liked to big-note himself and boast a bit. He was just right for what I wanted. He was drinking alone, his lawyer mates mustn't have come in yet. Things couldn't have been better.

'Marty. How are things going?

He looked me up and down. Not too obvious, but doing it just the same. I'd seen him do it to other women in the pub. Just about every other woman in the pub. He liked to think he was suave, enlightened but sometimes he couldn't help himself. Most of the time he couldn't help himself.

'Fine. Can I buy you a drink?' Hail fellow well met.

'Sure. Whatever you're drinking.' I wasn't taking that much of a chance, I'd drink anything except Coca Cola.

Two schooners of Fosters were put down in front of us without any more instruction from Marty than a hand movement. 'Your health,' I said, picking up one of them. A schooner wasn't really my speed but I had said whatever he was drinking. 'Actually Marty, I've got a little something I need to keep in a safe place. A very safe place,' I added, 'like a safety deposit box in a private security facility. You know a lot of folk around town, got any recommendations?' Marty knew what I did for a living but he was too cool to ask me about it. He liked to imply that he knew, though.

'Depends what you want to know.'

'Nothing personal, nothing you'd get rapped over the knuckles for; just want to know the general procedure at private security facilities.' I meant specifically TNT. Brambles had closed down that section of their operation, TNT was really the only player left in the game.

'Not planning a heist, are you?' His tone was jocular.

'I'm interested in getting a safety deposit box, that's all.'

'You know, if you go in, they'll show you the ropes.'

He'd finished his beer. He looked at mine, saw it was still half full and ordered just one.

'If there's a problem, if you don't want to tell me, that's fine. Thanks for the beer.'

'Hang on, I didn't say that.'

He told me. Took me through it step by step, from outside the front door to the inner sanctum where the boxes were. I even knew what colour the carpet was in the reception area.

By the end of the next schooner Marty was starting to lose it. He moved his barrel chest forward, wedging me against the wall. It wasn't terrific but I've been up against worse walls. 'If you've got something on, maybe I can help,' he suggested. 'I know people who can help.' His eyes were nudging me. He was thinking I was going to do a job on the place. He could help me. All I had to do was lie down for a while.

'Nice talking to you, Marty, see you round. By the way, your tie's dangling in your drink.'

I was back in Dolores' room sitting on the bed. I had the access card in front of me, I had the keys. I sat there jiggling those keys for a good half hour before I could spur myself into action. Time to start the ball rolling, I kept telling myself. No time like the present. All it is is one little phone call. What's so difficult about that?

TNT Stronghold was probably full of security guards bristling with guns who would shoot first and ask questions later. You could get swallowed up in a place like that and disappear without a trace.

The Stronghold had 24-hour access but that didn't mean I had to go in there right this minute. Marty said the usual procedure was to phone first and make an appointment. I could at least give them a call and pretend I was Dolores making an appointment. They couldn't shoot me over the phone, could they?

I dialled the number.

'TNT Security, good evening,' said a woman. She sounded as if she was in her thirties, mellow pleasant voice with enough experience to know what to do if you tried to mess with her. In my best Dolores voice I said I would like to make an appointment to visit my box. I couldn't help feeling as if I was trying to make an appointment to visit someone in jail. After an interview in which I assumed she was keying the name into the computer she said, 'Please state your box number, Miss Delgado.' I read the number on the vault access card. I must have got past the first landmine without it blowing up in my face because she next asked me what time I'd like to come in. 'Ten-thirty tomorrow morning,' I said off the top of my head.

'Fine,' she said, 'you know the procedure.'

'Yes,' I said, 'I know the procedure.'

My appointment wasn't till 10.30 but I was up much earlier than that pacing the floor. As I paced I rehearsed the two numbers Dolores had written on the TNT card—the box number and the PIN number. I'd practised Dolores' signature about a hundred times before breakfast even though I was using her credit card as if it was my own and her signature now came easily to me. If I was a smoker I would have smoked about a hundred cigarettes as well. I tapped the credit card as I paced, wondering just how much longer I had before the golden goose went off the lay.

All the pacing was doing was wearing out Dolores' shoe leather, I was more nervous now than when I started. I went out onto the balcony and breathed in the city. Why was I making such a big deal of it?, I cajoled myself, I was just another person going about my business. Lots of people must pass through TNT, there was a good chance no-one knew Dolores by sight and I was looking more like Dolores today than I ever had. I knew the drill, I had the keys and the numbers, the only person who knew I was faking it was myself. I did some karate breathing. Afterwards it felt better and my pulse was almost down to normal. I looked at my watch. Time to go.

As I walked down the corridor I could hear a vacuum cleaner. Passing room 617 I noticed the door was slightly open. I peeped inside. There was Yasmina, hair pulled back in a new clip, going about her business. I knocked on the door but she didn't hear me. Patrick had said that the guy didn't have any luggage but he might have left some tell-tale sign. I looked around the room but I couldn't see anything, apart from the fact that it was now obviously vacant. 'Yasmina?' I called. Still she didn't hear. I reached around and turned off the vacuum cleaner at the power point but she kept on vacuuming merrily away. She was doing under the bed now. I wanted to give her some warning. I didn't want to suddenly tap her on the shoulder, it would be too much like what her attacker must have done. I went and stood on the other side of the bed so she would see me when she stood up. She did, and with a very surprised look on her face. And a black eye. She took the earplugs of her Walkman out.

'You're back,' she beamed. Then she looked confused. 'No, you are the one who took me to the hospital. Are you the sister of Dolores?' I smiled. She thought I was Dolores' sister. TNT wasn't going to be that hard.

Yasmina noticed the vacuum cleaner was silent. 'I turned it off,' I explained, 'I didn't want to give you a fright. You feeling OK?' I asked tentatively.

'Yes, I'm good.' For someone with a black eye she was sounding pretty chirpy. She gave the bedside table a quick wipe.

'The ah . . . your eye OK?' I ventured.

'Oh that,' she said, as if suddenly remembering it was there. 'That day after the hospital, when I got home it was too late to cook so I went to Kentucky Fried Chicken for my husband dinner. When I come in he say, you late, where's my dinner? I say here, I buy you dinner. He say I wanted stuffed peppers and meat. I say, you want dinner, you eat Kentucky Fried Chicken. He get mad. He say, that's not food for a man, Kentucky Fried Chicken is shit. I say, listen mate, I buy food you eat it. He hit me,' she pointed to her eye. 'So I pick up the Kentucky Fried Chicken and plaff! I hit him in the face, and plaff! I hit him again. Me, I have only one back eye, my husband he has two. I tell to him, tonight you have no dinner but you hit me one more time and you have no wife.' The bruising on the cheekbone seemed a small price to pay considering what Yasmina had gained. 'He doesn't want to go to work with the black eyes so he is staying home for a couple of days. Before I came to work this morning he says I make you something nice for dinner, what you want? You know what I tell him I want? Kentucky Fried Chicken.'

I didn't particularly go for take-away chicken but I'd never be able to look at a drumstick again without thinking of Yasmina.

I could see the TNT tower as the train pulled into Redfern station but the Stronghold centre, which advertised itself for those wanting to do business with it as AUSTRALIA'S FORT KNOX, was about a block away from that. It was conveniently close to the station, though I doubted whether many of the clients would come to do business with their boxes by train.

A Daimler is the right class of car to visit a Stronghold centre but I didn't want to be that visible. I didn't know what kind of car the man with the needle would be driving now, maybe a different car every day, but I did know what he looked like. If I took the train he couldn't follow me by car, he'd have to take the train himself. He'd be easier to spot on the train.

Redfern station has eight platforms, a newsagent's, take-away food and lots of flowers for sale. I walked out of the station and past the koori mural that ran the length of the wall. A rasta-looking guy came by with a ghetto blaster, heavy rap blasting out of it. *TNT get the fuck out of Redfern; TNT get the fuck out now* I heard as he passed by.

The building on the corner of Gibbons and Marian Streets was squat, low-rise. There was an intercom and a written instruction to press the buzzer then stand on the square painted on the footpath outside the door. Considering the treasures hidden inside the building, the outside was very unassuming. This was one place where wealth wasn't flaunting itself.

I pressed the buzzer and stepped back onto the yellow square. It was far enough away from the door that you couldn't comfortably muscle your way in. The karate breathing had lasted till I'd pressed the buzzer and now I was as nervous as a bank robber on her first job.

The crackling voice asked me to state my name and my business. I said Dolores Delgado, that I'd phoned the night before. That was fine, they were expecting me; now, if I didn't mind, would I quote my box number. I reeled off one of the numbers. I had them written on a piece of paper in my pocket as well but I didn't want to take it out in case they had a hidden video camera trained on me, watching my reactions.

There was some white noise that lasted about an hour. Actually it was about fifteen seconds but during that time the concrete of the wall suddenly appeared to be pitted with craters as if I was looking at it through a zoom lens, the relatively quiet Gibbons Street seemed to have ten tonne trucks roaring down it, and I could actually feel the hairs on the back of my neck. None of this was helped back to normal mode by the crackling voice telling me that was not the right number.

At least standing this far away from the door and the intercom they couldn't hear my rapid breathing. 'Ah, that must be my PIN number.' I leaned into the intercom, feeling as if I was shouting. 'I always mix them up.' Somehow it seemed in character for Dolores to be scatterbrained about numbers. Numbers that didn't have a dollar sign in front of them, that is. I reeled off the other number. This did the trick.

I don't know where that voice was coming from but it mustn't have been far away because almost immediately the door was opened by a man in trousers and a short-sleeved shirt. I had expected him to be dressed in a brown uniform with a gun just visible below the jacket but he was in smart casual clothes. He had a moustache and a squat nose that looked like it had been rearranged in a fight but not recently.

He greeted me by name without query. I doubt he knew me, or rather Dolores, he just had that salesman's manner that gets personable straight away. I was after all, as far as he was concerned, a client.

He led me into the reception area Marty had described— puce-coloured doors, mushroom pink vinyl on the floor and dark blue cushion covers on the sofa with small white dots woven into the fabric. There was a low table with a stack of APPLICA-

TION FOR VAULT ACCESS cards on it and underneath, various money magazines including the BRW's annual RICH 200 in case you wanted to see what the competition was up to. As I was to find in every nook and cranny of this establishment, the reception area also had a closed circuit television, or CC TV as they call it in the trade.

Filling in the card wasn't that difficult, particularly after the chilling lesson at the door sorting out which number was which. I filled in the deposit box number, customer name, customer signature.

I knew I was here under false pretences. As I filled out the card, I thought about the alternative. Hand it over to the cops and wait till they get a court order for access to Dolores Delgado's box. But it wasn't an alternative anymore, I was here, it was too late to back out.

The guy with the moustache and the nose, who had now introduced himself as Frank, no surname, led me along a corridor. Before being allowed access to the vault area I had to put one of the keys into a keyhole and tap in the PIN number. While I was doing this, Frank was checking out my or rather Dolores' signature.

The adrenalin that I'd indulged in at the outside door, when I still had the luxury of running away if anything fouled up, was now in abeyance. There was no easy way to duck out now, I had passed through too many levels of security to say, sorry guys, I made a mistake. Though Frank didn't have a brown uniform and a gun I knew that there were people in the building who did. Lots of them. In fact the brochure at reception shows one of the brown-uniformed guards standing in front of the safety deposit boxes, his hands behind his back, and though the photo cuts off at the waist, you can bet he has his legs apart in a stance that says you'd need a crowbar to budge me.

I must have passed the signature test because the door to the vault area opened to me.

With all the trouble the man with the needle was going to, with all the fuss I was going to just to get myself in here, I'd worked up a fair amount of curiosity about just what was in

Dolores' box. To know not only what part it played in her murder but the part it played in the life of Dolores Delgado. Dolores had left a trail, a scent, I was sniffing the air, following it, seeking out its source. There's something alluring about entering someone else's life, following their footsteps, putting on their clothes as if it were their skin and becoming someone else. But what happened to your own self when you did that? These were not my clothes, it was not my skin. By wearing hers my own was in danger of suffocating.

She had been in here just as I was now here, rung up for an appointment, stood outside then passed through the doors. How did you feel when you did all that, Dolores? Nervous, thrilled, nonchalant?

I felt enclosed, confined. This wasn't helped by the fact that the vault resembled a maximum security prison, except that there was carpet on the floor. In front of me were rows and rows of boxes, like drawers in a giant filing cabinet, different sizes but standardised different sizes.

We came to the box with Dolores' number on it. There were two keyholes, one for the key I had and one for the key Frank had. Almost simultaneously we inserted our keys. Frank pointed out the cubicles or, as the brochure described them, the private viewing booths. As with banks, private stronghold facilities have no knowledge of the contents of their clients' boxes, what they don't know can't hurt them. That's the general idea—total privacy and confidentiality, safe from theft or damage, safe from prying eyes. TNT unlocks the box but they don't open it, the client does that in the privacy of the cubicle. Frank would wait till I had finished then accompany me out of the maze.

I took the box off the shelf. Whatever Dolores had been killed for was in this box, the answer to the riddle, the secret of the Sphinx, the Maltese Falcon. I hoped I was looking cool. After all, the box would hold no surprises for the actual box holder. It felt weighty and solid enough but that would be the box itself. Inside could be gold, guns, drugs, heirlooms, papers and documents. You couldn't judge by the weight.

As I approached the cubicle area one of them opened and

out stepped a gentleman whose face was familiar to people who read the business section of the paper. Very familiar. In fact recently he'd come forward in the newspaper and had hit the headlines as his empire came crashing down. He looked like someone who'd gone to a private school and eaten in a lot of restaurants that weren't *nouvelle cuisine*. He had a round face, full lips, a suit made by a Hong Kong tailor and a tan. Our eyes met for a split second before he turned away. Long enough for him to realise that I'd recognised him. Under other circumstances he might have smiled his billion dollar smile, that's right baby, I'll have to come clean, yes, it's me, you've recognised me. I'm rich and famous and I'm magnanimous enough to smile at a nobody like you.

It wasn't what he was doing here that interested me but the fact that he was here at all. He was supposed to be away convalescing in a country that had more sun and fewer laws. For a stay that was going to extend way past the date when he was supposed to appear in court on charges of fraud.

I watched him leave before going into the cubicle. It was hard to tell whether he'd taken something out or put something in. Whatever he'd done in his cubicle would remain without a trace. Once his box was back on the rack he put his arm round his minder's shoulder in that matey gesture. Thing is, it doesn't look so good when you have to reach up to do it, just ruins the line of the suit when the shoulder pad hunches up like that.

I entered the cubicle.

My first reaction was disappointment. I don't know what I expected from Dolores—the lost treasurers of the Incas—but I certainly didn't expect to see a scrappy-looking notebook. There was a bundle of cash as well—$10 000 in fifty dollar notes. It seemed a lot of money to me but it was only a couple of dresses for Dolores. It had to be the notebook that was worth dying for. Unless this wasn't what the man with the needle wanted after all.

On the front it said David Morgan, Atherton Milne & Associates. Further down:

ENVIRONMENTAL IMPACT STATEMENT
for
PARADISE PARK RESORT DEVELOPMENT, COFFS HARBOUR

(Client: Green Dolphin Resorts)

The handwriting was neat and artistic, like an architect's, but not that easy to read. Neither were the diagrams and tables.

It all looked fairly botanical. Tables entitled 'Main Vegetation Community Types in the Study Area', species names in Latin through the text. It would take me hours to sort through these notes. And this wasn't a booth in the public library. It might not have been the lost treasures of the Incas but this document had cost Dolores her life. Before I exposed it to the hazards of the world outside this fortress I needed to at least know why.

I began to turn the pages, one by one. From what I could decipher it seemed to be fairly dry textbook stuff. I was more than halfway through when I came across the first underlined section. 'Phyllis told me she'd unearthed it while digging a hole. She showed me the spot. Wouldn't have believed it if she hadn't seen it with her own eyes—a plant flowering underground, not in a cave but in the actual soil. Only two species in Australia known to behave in this way—underground orchids, *Rhizanthella* and *Cryptanthemis* (see Bernhardt, 1989). Based on Bernhardt desc. most likely to be *Cryptanthemis*. Only three previous sightings.'

It went on to give a botanical description that appeared to be almost in code there were so many abbreviations. There was a rough drawing of it. It didn't look like the orchid in the box, it looked somewhat like a daisy, with outer petals and tiny closed flowers in the centre.

Further along he described how he found other examples of the species by carefully brushing aside debris and soil near the site of the first discovery.

His final recommendation, in capital letters, was that IN VIEW OF THE RARITY OF THIS UNDERGROUND ORCHID, AND THE DIFFICULTY

OF DETERMINING THE EXACT DISTRIBUTION OF SUCH A SPECIES, THE DEVELOPMENT SHOULD NOT PROCEED.

I transferred the notebook and the money to my bag then closed the safety deposit box and locked it. I signalled to the guard that I was ready to leave. 'What were you doing in there, sleeping?' he joked. I smiled. I didn't have to tell him a thing, they were the ones who were supposed to be big on discretion.

Despite the place being like a prison, now that I was coming back to the reception area I didn't want to leave the building. It was fraught with all the dangers of a baby leaving the womb. Out there all sorts of things could happen. Somewhere out there was the man who wanted this notebook. It was safe in here, safe and hidden. But now I was taking it out into the world.

I hoped exposure wouldn't kill it. Or me. But I didn't want to leave the notebook in the safety deposit box and have to come back here either.

I got them to call me a cab. I knew after the first time round the block that no-one was following me but I got the driver to do it another couple of times just to make sure. Then I told him Balmain. He said he thought we were going to Pennant Hills. I said I'd changed my mind. He was smart enough to leave it at that.

S ee Bernhardt, 1989. I didn't have to look far in the library to see. I knew by the title I'd found the right publication: *Wily Violets and Underground Orchids*.

The chapter that dealt with underground orchids was called 'Orchids in the Dark'. The sightings of them have been few and far between. And accidental. *Cryptanthemis* (crypt: hidden, *anthemis*: flowering head) was last found in 1974 in the Blue Mountains when a property owner excavated soil near his house to put in a garage. It has not been seen since. Till now, I thought to myself. It was documented by naturalist Rupp. As the book says, he was 'captivated by an orchid that repeatedly deceived him'. His white flowers gradually acquired splotches of red, the plant looked as if it should poke its fruits out through the soil but it didn't, the plant had fooled him by masking its true method of seed dispersal. The underground orchid has two odours—the little flowers have a sweet and pleasant fragrance, but if the rhizome is cut or bruised it produces a strong stink reminiscent of formalin. Bernhardt concludes: 'Is Rupp's *Cryptanthemis* gone forever or is this species waiting for its own rediscovery?'

Something about that flower reminded me of Dolores.

Is this why Dolores had the notebook, because it described her double in the plant world? Was she hiding it or keeping it safe?

She was a director of the company, Green Dolphin Resorts,

who had commissioned the EIS; it was only natural that she should have it.

No. It wasn't. She might have a copy of the EIS but what was she doing with the botanist's notebook?

Atherton Milne and Associates had an office at North Sydney. It was on the fourth floor of one of those buildings otherwise occupied by advertising agencies. Nice view of the Harbour Bridge, easy access to the station.

The people in the office weren't as snappily dressed as advertising execs but they were doing all right. A guy came over to attend to me. Well tailored—dark blue trousers with a subtle fleck, white shirt, paisley tie. Glasses, dark hair falling onto his forehead, handsome when he smiled. 'Can we do anything for you?'

'I'm looking for David Morgan.'

That seemed to amuse him. I asked him why.

'Mostly they just ring up asking, you're the first one to come to the office.'

'First what?'

'Friend of David's.' He said friend in a way that meant girlfriend. I let it ride. For the moment. He'd slotted me into a category, no point in explaining myself any more than necessary.

'What did you say to the others?'

'That we haven't seen him. I hate to be the one to break it to you but I think he's done a flit. He sent in his last report and a letter saying he'd had a better offer and was off to Western Australia. Must be having a good time in WA, he hasn't even bothered giving us an address to forward his pay to.'

'Can I have a look at the report?'

'People normally go to the local council or one of the government bodies that hold copies of the EIS if they want to look at it but since you're here I don't see any problem. You sure you want to see it? It's pretty technical.'

I continued on with the girlfriend role. 'He didn't tell me he was pissing off to Western Australia. I just want to see what his famous last words were.'

He went and fetched it. A quarto-sized volume. Environmental Impact Statement for PARADISE PARK RESORT DEVELOPMENT, COFFS HARBOUR.

'Here,' he said, opening it and pointing to a section titled Flora, 'that's Dave's contribution.'

There were four or five pages, with tables and maps. Some of them I recognised from the notebook. I read it from beginning to end. Read it again. It concluded that no rare or endangered plant species were located in the area and that the proposed development would not significantly alter the flora of the study area.

There was not one mention of the orchids. So what had happened to them—disappeared underground again?

'This was what he sent you?'

'Word for word.'

Somewhere along the line something had got lost in the translation. But where?

The only way to find out what was really going on was to go to Coffs Harbour and have a look at the proposed development site. Maybe this Phyllis would know, the one mentioned in the notebook. If I could find her.

I went into the nearest travel agent and booked a flight. Coffs Harbour, day after tomorrow. I went back to the pub, made a photocopy of David Morgan's notebook then put it and the money in Jack's safe.

Then I went over to the Royale.

I stayed up late, watched a few videos, had a few drinks and waited for callers. No-one came. I thought about Steve, I thought about my kids. Coffs Harbour was on the way to Queensland where they lived with Gary. The holidays were over now, I wondered how the white-water rafting had been. I wondered if there were going to be more holidays when they'd have better things to do than come and see me. They were growing up. Amy would be going to high school next year. My kids were growing up and I was missing out on it. I'd left my husband but I hadn't left the children. It wasn't like Carol said, to take some tango dancer shopping. I could never leave you,

Amy, David. I explained that all to you. You understood, didn't you?

My father had never explained, never said why he wanted a drink more than he wanted to stay with us. Was he lying in a park, a doorway somewhere, a bus shelter, having this same silent conversation with me?

When my eyes were too blurry to see the video I decided I'd done enough drinking for one night. It was almost 3 a.m. If I'd known what lay in store the next day I would have gone to bed early and got a good night's sleep. God knows, I was going to need it.

It was almost nine o'clock when I woke up. For an early riser like myself that's sleeping in. Kings Cross hours must be getting to me. I hadn't had that much to drink, had I? I would have slept even longer had it not been for the persistent ringing of the telephone.

I picked up the receiver. 'Hello?' My voice sounded as if I'd smoked too many cigarettes though I hadn't smoked any at all.

It was Vicki. 'I'd like to see you downstairs. If you can spare the time.' If I could spare the time? What was she talking about and why was she using that tone of voice on me? I hadn't even got out of bed yet.

'Why? What's up?' I asked, still not fully awake.

'When you're dressed and ready,' she said. She hung up. I didn't even have time to ask—dressed and ready for what?

I had a shower and got dressed. Not because Vicki said so; it's what I normally do first thing of a morning.

I was just about to go downstairs when the mobile phone rang. It was my first incoming call on the mobile phone. I got such a surprise I wondered what it was for a moment. It was Jack. Carol, or as Jack put it, my dry martini friend, had been around. She wanted to know where I was, she was surly. She always is, I told Jack, especially in the morning. No, he said, this looked like more than ordinary morning surliness. She'd demanded to know where I was but he hadn't confessed under the torture. But he did suggest I ring her back, it looked pretty serious. I thanked Jack for letting me know and apologised for any inconvenience it might have caused. I'd deal with Carol later, after Vicki had dealt with me.

She was being her usual amiable self while checking out a Korean couple but when she saw me emerge from the lift the House Full sign went up. 'You have till midday to vacate the room,' she announced. 'I'm sorry it's such short notice.'

'I wasn't aware that I was leaving,' I answered.

'The management thinks it's best you do.' She wasn't even trying to raise a smile.

'Seeing it's so sudden perhaps the *management* has an explanation,' I said pointedly.

Her blusher seemed to be getting pinker by the moment. Much as she would have liked me to she knew I wasn't going to go away just like that. 'In view of the fact that Miss Delgado won't be coming back we need to make the room available to other guests.'

She knew. Somehow she'd found out about Dolores.

'The management doesn't wish to discuss the matter any further,' Vicki said.

The management mightn't but I certainly did. It was time to change my tune. 'What's with this management crap, Vicki? You run the show around here.'

'A decision has been made.' A decision had been made but it wasn't hers. She was only delivering the message.

'Who's leaning on you? Is it Mr Schaeffer?'

I'd guessed it in one. She started to say something but changed her mind. 'Till midday,' she said briskly.

'Perhaps Mr Schaeffer would like to tell me himself what's going on.'

'Read the paper,' she said.

CANE TOAD KILLS TANGO QUEEN

There was a full-length picture of Dolores, the publicity shot of her with Ramón but they'd managed to cut Ramón out of the picture. They made a lot of the fact that Dolores was a transsexual dancer but there wasn't much beyond that. They had reason to believe she was travelling under an assumed name. A police check had revealed no passport issued in that name. The mysterious Ms Delgado, they called her. They had a field day with the cane toad, the intruder who'd slipped across the border, infiltrated as far south as Coffs Harbour, and even made reference to a cane toad that was sighted in Homebush Bay in Sydney after a State of Origin match in which the Queensland maroons thrashed the NSW blues. Ironically enough for Dolores Delgado the cane toad originally came from South America. Extract of toad had been injected into the buttock, the coroner reported. Although cane toad poison had previously killed cats and dogs, this was the first human death. The coroner denied the rumour that licking cane toads produced an hallucinogenic effect.

Though the newspaper hadn't given a specific address it stated that Ms Delgado had been staying in a Kings Cross hotel. It wouldn't take long for someone with a nose for a story to find out which hotel.

It brought it all back again—the stark, crass black and white headlines, the photo, the way Dolores had been turned into a juicy newspaper story, the way they'd sensationalised her death. I could imagine the cane toad jokes already. I knew it would make big news but I didn't realise how I'd feel when I actually saw it. I was affronted by everything about it, by the language they used, the gory details, the speculation, the insinuations you were supposed to read between the lines, as if the dead had no right to privacy.

How come if you're dead, Dolores, if you no longer exist, I still care? How come if you're dead you can still reach out and spin me around?

FUN GIRLS
AUSTRALIA'S LARGEST BED
EXCITING HOSTESSES
UPSTAIRS
OPEN NOW

The neon sign in the hotel across the road was lit up even at ten o'clock in the morning. Kings Cross looked decidedly sleazy. The main drag was full of people for whom the night never ends, who were unaware that they were now being seen in the full light of day. There were skinny girls in skinny jeans and skinny tops, long hair falling over their rough-textured skin. Imploring boys who looked the same. A deal being done in the doorway of Woolworths, in a barber shop a dude smoking a cigar while the barber cut his hair. There were T-shirt shops, camera stores, tourists, prostitutes, touts. Everything and everyone open and inviting, trying to attract to themselves what they needed to stay alive.

I went into Lorenzo's. There were dark timber panels inside, and cream-coloured walls. There were cartoons from *Punch* magazine framed in the same dark timber and posters from the Hungarian Tourist Bureau before 1956 enticing people to visit Budapest, the Paris of the east. I thought Prague laid claim to that title, but never mind. I found a particularly dark and dingy corner, which wasn't all that hard in Lorenzo's.

I ordered a short black and opened the newspaper again. I stared at it without really reading.

The coffee arrived. I stirred it for a long time even though I don't take sugar. I watched the liquid eddy round the spoon. I watched it even after I'd lain the spoon on the saucer and the movement had stopped. Cane toad poison. I took a sip. Injected. Had it been the syringe I'd unsuccessfully taken out to the labs? They'd reached a verdict anyhow. It was officially a homicide case now and Carol's buddies would be all over the place. Is that what she was so surly about, that she had a big job to do? Maybe they would pick up something I hadn't. They had a network with a wide sweep. Maybe it was time for that. Meanwhile, I had a ticket to Coffs Harbour.

I paid for my coffee and left, leaving the newspaper on the table for the next punter.

I wished I could be leaving the hotel and Vicki on better terms but now Dolores was officially dead there wasn't much point in me staying there anyway. I stood across the road looking at it, at its red bricks with white mortar, at the fabulous Hollywood staircase. I could see Dolores and Ramón dancing down that staircase, the Busby Berkeley chorus paving the way. Dolores always was a big Hollywood production.

And now I had to pay for it. Though I'd been using her credit card fairly lavishly the last few days I didn't think Vicki would be impressed if I tried to pay the bill with it. God knows how enormous it was going to be. I expected it to be thousands.

'It's been taken care of,' said Vicki curtly. I guess I should have been grateful but I was too mystified for that.

'Vicki,' I began, 'what do you mean taken care of?' I couldn't believe that Dolores would be so organised that she would have paid for her room in advance. 'Did Dolores pay in advance?'

'It's been taken care of, that's all you need to know.' Vicki was wanting to close this unpleasant episode as quickly as possible.

'Listen,' I said, leaning over the counter towards her, 'Dolores, as you are now well aware, was murdered, so if someone else is paying her bills I need to know.'

'Why? You going to impersonate them as well?'

I packed up Dolores' things. No next of kin had yet been traced and the hotel had no special claim to them. I seemed to spend my life packing and unpacking Dolores' things.

I could vaguely hear the vacuum cleaner further up the corridor, Yasmina at work. Vicki was throwing me out of the hotel, the newspaper was full of bad news and I still had Carol to contend with.

Unfortunately she wasn't sitting at her big shiny desk doing her nails, she had to be paged. That meant she was busy. 'Rawlins here,' she answered brusquely. And she didn't even know it was me yet.

'It's Claudia. Have a nice time in Mudgee?'

'Well, well, my old mate Claudia. How nice of you to call.' The sarcasm was coming through the wires like razor blades. I heard her ask someone if she could use their office. She let me dangle there while she changed phones.

'Carol,' I said brightly when she finally came back on, 'Jack said you called into the pub this morning.'

She informed me she'd been trying to get in touch with me for the past 24 hours.

'Why didn't you leave a message on my answering machine?' I asked. A big mistake.

'Claudia,' she hissed, 'I can barely bring myself to talk to you, let alone your machine. Maybe I'd be better off dealing with your machine, at least it stays in one place. Piss off, Gavin,' I heard her say before she brought her attention back to me. 'I've had a "please explain" from upstairs. Some officious little chemist from the labs at Lidcombe's made a complaint about some possible corroborating evidence not being sent to them at the same time as specimens for analysis. As it transpires a private individual approached them independently and tried to pass it off as police work, naming me as the police officer. You've really dropped me in it this time, Claudia. What could you have possibly been thinking? Is there nothing you stop at?'

I felt like a nail being hammered into a particularly hard piece of wood. For someone who could barely bring themselves to talk to me she certainly had a lot to say. It wasn't just the hammer pushing me into the wood, I was trying to crawl into the woodwork myself. 'I tried to explain but you were in Mudgee,' I said lamely.

'Forget Mudgee. Why did you do it in the first place? Do you realise what trouble you've caused me?'

'I had some things to be analysed, it seemed an efficient way of getting things done. Maybe another chemist wouldn't have let this golden opportunity pass by but this Davidson was Public Service. You know the type, correct channels, no imagination . . .'

'Claudia,' she interrupted, 'you are talking to correct channels, I am correct channels, don't expect to get me onside by complaining about them.'

She was trying to dump it on me but I wasn't going to wear all of it. 'Correct channels didn't want to investigate this one, you might recall.'

She recalled. At least that was what I imagined she was doing in the huge silence that followed. 'It has now become an official homicide investigation,' she said dryly, as if making an announcement to the press.

That was as close as she was going to get to an admission that it wasn't all my fault. But it was enough to make me feel conciliatory. 'I'm going away for a couple of days but I've got lots of stuff I can contribute to the official investigation.' I savoured the words as I spoke them. 'Photos, names and addresses. Think that'll make up for things?'

'What's it going to cost me, more embarrassment?' It was a gentler jibe this time.

'I'll be away, I'll be out of your hair altogether. What can go wrong?'

She thought about it some more then said, 'OK. What have you got?'

'Drop by the pub later this afternoon and I'll show you.'

'Fine,' she said, 'see you then.' Carol and I were at peace. For the moment.

I bundled up all the dresses, went down to the parking area and piled them into the back seat of the Daimler. Then I went upstairs again. The shoes were next then the make-up and odds and ends. Only one book in the room and that was it. I left the bag marked 'Yasmina' on the bed where she would see it.

When all of Dolores' belongings were in the Daimler I went upstairs for one last look. The room was bare now, back to being a hotel room again, as if nothing had ever gone on in there. I took in one last view from the minute balcony. There was a dero pissing now outside AUSTRALIA'S LARGEST BED, two Double Bay matrons waiting at the bus stop. They pretended not to notice but moved aside nevertheless to avoid the trickle when it came their way.

I went downstairs.

'The key,' I said, dropping the card on the counter in front of Vicki.

'Good bye,' she said, 'I hope you enjoyed your stay,' with a plastic smile as if I was just another guest.

'Yeah,' I said, 'I've enjoyed myself immensely.'

When I went down into the car park I was surprised to see a chauffeur standing beside my car, his legs firmly planted, one gloved hand on top of the other at crutch level. Was the hotel supplying a driver to make sure I actually left? Under his arm was a newspaper folded in half. He stepped forward. 'Excuse me, Miss,' he said with no hint of threat, 'could you spare a few moments?' He was a London boy by the sound of it, with enough years in Australia to stretch the vowels out a little.

'For what?' I asked, starting to get suspicious. Boys in uniform didn't speak to me all that much. He was a bit more than a boy when you looked more closely. Thin boyish figure but vertical age lines were working their way down his face.

'Someone would like to have a word with you, would you mind stepping into the car?' A couple of cars away was another Daimler, a '65. You don't get those from hire car places.

'Normally I don't get into cars with strange men,' I said. Strangely, I don't get into cars with normal men either.

'Someone wants to have a little chat with you.' I looked over to the car but the windows had been tinted and I couldn't see inside. At least we had the same taste in cars. Anyone who drives a Daimler can't be all that bad. I wondered if I'd have thought the same if I owned a Celica or a Barina. Probably not.

'Someone wants to talk, I can talk just as well in the open as I can in a car.' I was on the alert but I wasn't all that worried. I wasn't up a back alley with a syringe at my neck. If they were going to do any damage, they would have done it by now.

The window of the Daimler rolled down. 'That's not very hospitable of you, particularly as I've been so hospitable to you. I just want to have a chat about a mutual friend. I'm sure I don't need to mention any names.' I couldn't see him that well, and he was wearing dark glasses, but it looked like the guy who'd brought the roses. Dolores' sugar daddy, Gordon. Gordon Schaeffer. Well, I had said I wanted to talk to the management. I didn't think they were going to do me any harm, they weren't trying to force me into the car.

'How long do you think this little chat is going to take?'

'Just a few minutes of your time, that's all.'

The chauffeur politely ushered me to the car and opened the door for me, the front passenger's side, not the back. I felt better that way. Riding up front I was within arm and leg's length of the controls. The chauffeur couldn't really hold a gun on me with one hand and drive with the other. From what I'd seen of

Schaeffer I didn't think he was the type to do his own dirty work. If there was dirty work to be done.

'Where are we going?'

'Not far,' he said.

It wasn't. He drove down Bayswater Road into New Beach Road and came to a halt alongside Rushcutters Bay Park, near the Cruising Yacht Club. Expensive eastern suburbs real estate on the other side of the road, green water and a fabulous view of the city and the Harbour Bridge without the noise. The engine stopped with barely a sound. There were a few quiet lunchers in the park, a few people sitting in parked cars. Sharon had told me that in this street she'd once seen a briefcase being passed from an unmarked car to one with Commonwealth plates.

'Take a walk, Nigel.' The voice came from the back. A mellow voice but used to being obeyed. The chauffeur opened his door and got out. The sound of his door closing was barely perceptible. I watched the chauffeur stroll across the park to the water. He got to the sea wall and looked over. A smoker would have taken this opportunity to light up but the chauffeur didn't. I got the impression he was very strict with himself. People in uniform often are.

While I was watching Nigel I waited for the person in the back to make the next move. He was taking his time. I don't know what he was waiting for, he was the one who wanted to have the chat. I shifted position so that I could see into the back. I know how capacious Daimler seats are. He almost seemed to be disappearing into the upholstery. It was all right for a look but I wouldn't want to spend hours with my head in this position.

'Mr Schaeffer, I presume?'

'You've been doing your homework, Claudia. You don't mind me calling you Claudia do you?'

'It's your car.'

'Perhaps you can enlighten me. I was under the impression that Dolores was convalescing somewhere. Then I thought she'd run out on me and now I discover she's dead. The papers didn't say anything about her being on a health farm down the south coast, she died at the club. You knew she was dead all the time, didn't you?'

It was uncomfortable sitting like this. Why couldn't we just get out and sit in the park, go for a stroll? I wanted to look at him while he talked. To see what the body language was telling me, the hesitation in the eyes, the expression on his face.

'Look,' I said, 'is there any reason why you're in the back and I'm in the front? You got anything contagious?'

'I thought it might be easier this way. Easier for me.'

Nigel the chauffeur was now skipping pebbles over the surface of the water. I don't know where he was getting the pebbles from, the park didn't seem to have any, only grass and well-swept paths. If the guy in the back wanted to do it without looking, fine. I turned to face the front and put my hand up to adjust the rear vision mirror so I could see him.

'Leave it,' he ordered. 'If you don't mind.' Back to his urbane self. 'I'm not one of those New Age men good at expressing their feelings.'

At least he'd heard of them.

'What feelings have you got to express?'

He paused. 'Let's see what I can find. Anger, curiosity, suspicion. And another that I can't find a word for—the feeling that I'm being played for a sucker.'

Did he mean me or Dolores? I could hear the anger already creeping into the conversation, like a ball of snow that might rumble into a avalanche. It got worse.

'You know a damned sight more about what happened than you're letting on.' He meant me. 'Dolores disappears and suddenly you turn up. You've got her keys, her credit cards. My credit card, I might add. You live in her room, you wear her clothes, you spend her money, my money, you even dye your hair to look like her. You tell me she's off somewhere convalescing. But where is she? Oh, you're very vague about that. A health farm in the country. She collapsed of nervous exhaustion, like all the big stars. Then surprise, surprise—Dolores turns up dead. Now what does all that look like to you?'

I'd already been through this kind of avalanche once today

with Carol. I had practice. I wasn't going to get snowed under without throwing some of it back.

'I'm sitting in your car but I don't have to answer your questions. You're right, I do know a thing or two about Dolores but I think you might know a thing or three.'

'Like what, for example?'

He owned the hotel where she'd been staying, he'd given her a credit card, financial backing for her company . . . And what else? I had nothing to connect him to her death, nothing to connect him to the man with the needle, with Howard Thripps. He was a big business tycoon. He could probably go to jail for that but not murder. He wasn't the type to do it himself.

That didn't mean he couldn't organise it.

'The one or two things I knew about Dolores were shopping and dancing. You knew about her business deals.'

'Her business deals?'

'Green Dolphin Resorts. I believe one of your companies provided financial backing.'

He sniggered, a hint of nervousness. 'You have been doing your homework. But it's not up to date. I did originally agree to provide financial backing but I have since withdrawn it.'

'Why?'

'I didn't think it would be a viable business proposition.'

'Why didn't you advise Dolores against it then?' I turned around. He was getting fidgety. Not giving too much away, the odd hand movement, contraction of a jaw muscle.

'It wasn't really her company, she wasn't going to lose anything, she was just there to make up the numbers. Just a name.'

'Whose company was it?'

The jaw muscle contracted again. 'I don't really know. She told me the names but I don't remember.'

Bullshit.

'Did she . . .' he cleared his throat. 'Did Dolores ever talk about me?' There was an urgency in his voice now. Beneath the powerful businessman with the chauffeur-driven car was a little boy wanting to be liked. And wanting to change the subject. He could change it. I had another pipeline to that information.

Did Dolores ever talk about me? She talked to Mina, told Mina he'd given her that awful necklace, but Dolores herself never mentioned him to me. 'Mostly we went shopping, she didn't talk much about her private life.'

'Then you wouldn't have known she was transsexual?' He said it as if he was trying to trump me.

'I knew. Before I read it in the papers. How about you?'

'We were lovers, how could I not know? I've had lots of women. But she was different. In every way,' he suggested, inviting me to ask more. But I didn't want to know this from him, share this intimacy, dissect her body with talk as the autopsy had done with instruments.

I could see Nigel making his way back to the car.

'Do you know who might have wanted to kill her?'

Nigel's face loomed large at the car window. 'The other side of the park is nice this time of year,' I said to him. He looked surprised but he wasn't going to move till he got an official instruction. It came.

'Go on, Nigel,' said the boss in the back seat.

Nigel left.

'You didn't answer my question.'

'No, I do not know who might have killed Dolores.' He said it as if he was in the witness stand.

'Know anything about orchids?'

'What?' He thought it was a joke. 'You mean flowers, those things that grow in the ground?'

'Yes, those things that grow in the ground.' In this case under the ground.

'I know bunches of roses from the florist's and that's about it.'

Nigel had gone to the other extremity of the park now, had trodden in some eastern suburbs dog poo and was scraping if off.

'How did you meet her?'

'At Surfers Paradise. I'm involved with some people who have a resort complex there. She'd just come back from a club engagement in Tokyo, she looked terrific, she could dance, we gave her a job.'

'Then she came to Sydney?'

'Yes. No, she had an engagement in Coffs Harbour as well.'

'Engagement?'

'In a club there.'

'She wasn't there on Green Dolphin business?'

'I told you, she wasn't actively involved, just there to make up the numbers. A name on paper.'

'What did your wife think about you and Dolores?'

'She didn't know.'

'But she knew about Dolores.'

'No, I don't think so. She suspected there were other women but she never really knew.'

'I wasn't asking, I was telling you. Your wife came to see Dolores. Think she could have killed her?'

'Margaret knew Dolores? No, she couldn't have.'

'Why not?'

'I never gave her any reason to suspect, I was discreet.'

'You blokes always are. Except what's the point of having a good-looking girlfriend if you can't show her off in front of your mates? Wives aren't stupid. They get to do a lot of thinking while they're sitting around waiting for their husbands to come home.'

He was quiet. Time passed, Nigel headed back to the car. He didn't look like he was in the mood to be told to go away a second time. 'Margaret couldn't have killed Dolores, she's not the type.'

'Everyone's the type if they're pushed hard enough. She mightn't have actually pulled the trigger, or in this case, jabbed in the needle but she could have paid for the service. What I don't understand is why Dolores rather than you? Husband plays up, why kill the girlfriend? That's only a temporary measure. You want to get rid of the problem altogether, shoot the husband.'

Nigel was back. He got in the car, started the engine humming and did a U-turn outside the Cruising Yacht Club. It was only a five minute drive back to the hotel but the silence went on forever.

They let me out. I tapped on the back window. I had one more question to ask and I wanted to ask this one up close. The window went down.

'Ever heard of Howard Thripps?'

'Never.' He didn't even have to think about it. The window went up again and the car drove off.

He'd heard of him all right.

I got into my own car and drove back to Balmain. It felt good, like an old familiar friend. It was a slow afternoon in the pub and Jack had time for a game of pool. I told him I was going to Coffs Harbour for a couple of days. He said lately my life seemed to be one big holiday.

I was amused. 'Is that what it looks like?'

Carol walked in and joined us. She had her customary dry martini while Jack and I finished the game. I took her upstairs and gave her the photos taken on the night of Dolores' murder and pointed out the man I thought might be Howard Thripps. She'd never heard of him but she'd see what the computer brought up. I gave her the other passports I'd found with Dolores' belongings. She said she'd try those on the computer as well. I told her there was probably no point in bothering the people at the club but she might try interviewing Margaret and Gordon Schaeffer. Schaeffer she knew. Not the highest flier around but not doing too badly. 'Better get to him quick,' I said, 'I spoke to him today. If he's left any tracks he may start covering them.'

'Thanks for all this, Claudia,' she said as she got up to go, 'you're a real mate. And it's nice to see you making a deposit instead of a withdrawal. Have a nice trip.'

'Want anything? A Big Banana perhaps?'

Carol raised her eyes to the ceiling as if to say, that's all I need. 'This'll do just fine.' She was pleased with the 'deposit'. I hadn't put all my savings into Carol's bank, though. I still had the botanist's notebook.

When Carol had gone I put all Dolores' things in my wardrobe. I'd have to do something with them. Maybe I could auction
them and give the money to a fund for the preservation of rare
orchids. It seemed a waste to dump them in a clothing bin. I
rang the club to let them know I'd be away for a couple of days
but the number was engaged. I rang the hire car company and
asked Sharon whether Mr Thripps had rented anything else.
She said no, the Barina was the last they heard of him. I gave
her my mobile number. 'Call me if you hear anything, OK
Sharon?'

'OK.'

I tried the club again. 'Claudia, you must be psychic,'
exclaimed Cilla. 'I've been trying to ring you. She's here. Margaret Shaver. She wants to see you.'

'Tell her . . . just keep her there, I'm on my way.'

No-one answers the door when I go calling on the Schaeffers
and now both of them, within a few hours of each other, want
to talk to me.

Cilla was sitting at a table with a woman drinking coffee and
sambuca. I went over to them. The woman was dark-haired,
early forties but looked younger. Her style wasn't flashy; expensive clothes but no labels screaming out for attention, good skin,
face lightly made-up, a bit of tension round the eyes but nothing
long term. 'This is Claudia, Dolores' friend,' Cilla introduced
me, 'Margaret Shaver.'

We shook hands. Cilla got up. 'You need me for anything
I'm at the bar,' she said. Margaret Schaeffer was a nice sort of
woman, didn't look like she was going to be any trouble but
who knows.

Unlike her husband, she wasn't slow in coming straight to
the point. 'I want you to know I didn't kill Dolores Delgado. I
read about it in the papers today and thought it best to speak
to someone about it. Someone who wasn't the police,' she added
in a quieter voice.

'Why not the police?'

'Because they might think I was involved. I wanted her out

of the way but I didn't kill her. I thought she had disappeared but when she didn't turn up . . . I'm sorry,' she smiled, 'I'm a little distracted, I'm getting ahead of myself.' She took a minute sip of sambuca and continued. 'She was having an affair with my husband. Now that in itself was not the problem—he's had affairs before, he'll probably do it again. But this time it was different. Gordon was planning to run away with Dolores.' She smiled. 'My husband and I have long ceased to . . . well, you know, but I enjoy my lifestyle and want to keep it that way. I offered Dolores $20 000 to disappear. $10 000 when she bought a ticket out of the country and the other ten at the airport.'

'You gave her the first $10 000?'

She nodded.

'What denomination?'

'It was in fifties.'

The money in the safety deposit box.

Margaret Schaeffer continued, 'She bought a ticket to Bangkok but she didn't show up at the airport. I waited till the plane took off but Dolores wasn't on it. I came here that afternoon but they couldn't tell me where she was. They told me to try the Royale.' She smiled and shook her head. 'My husband owns the Hotel Royale. He'd know if I went there asking after the woman.'

Her story sounded all right but then so did a lot of stories. 'Why are you telling me, Mrs Schaeffer, what do you think I can do for you?'

'I don't know exactly. I explained my involvement to the lady here, Cilla, is it?' I nodded. 'She said that I should tell my story to you. You see, no doubt when the police start to investigate her death they will discover that she was my husband's lover. I recently made a withdrawal of $20 000 from our funds. Now I can imagine what the police will make of that—that I paid someone to kill her.'

'And you didn't.'

'And I didn't. I thought if I told my story to you, you may be able to convince the police I'm telling the truth. I doubt

that a policeman would go further than the most obvious expla-
·nation—jealous wife kills husband's lover.'

'Do you have any proof to back up your story?'

'Well, the people at the club know that I came here to speak
to her. And at the airport, hundreds of people must have seen
me, I waited at the check-in for at least an hour.'

'Did you talk to anyone?'

'Yes. Yes, I did. When I arrived I looked around for Dolores
but I couldn't see her. So I asked the woman at the counter
whether she had checked in yet. She said no.'

I'd get Carol to find out from Thai Airways who was on duty
that day. If Margaret Schaeffer had hung around there as long
as she said she did, if she'd actually spoken to someone, there
was a good chance they'd be able to identify her. And the
money checked out. You wouldn't give someone $10 000 if you
were planning to kill them. Would you?

Her story seemed OK but I didn't like to trust my judgement.
Every time I thought I'd got to the truth with Dolores she'd lift
off the mask and reveal another one underneath. Even after she
was dead. I was enmeshed in deception and fabrication. Some
of it I wanted to believe. Some of it seemed credible. How did
I know Margaret Schaeffer wasn't playing the same kind of games
as Dolores Delgado?

'Here,' I said, giving her Carol's phone number, 'get in touch
with Detective Rawlins, tell her you spoke to me. She was
coming to see you anyway, it would be better if you made the
first move.'

My bag was packed, I'd booked a wake-up call for 5 a.m. An
early night and I would be ready to take Coffs Harbour by storm.
But there was one more thing. The names of the other directors.
What had Schaeffer said? Dolores was only there to make up
the numbers. So who were the movers and shakers in the
company?

I called Brian. 'Remember that fax?' I asked. 'Sure,' he said,
'it's at work. Under lock and key so that all those bright young
pups from communications courses don't start learning the old

dog's tricks.' It wasn't encouraging to know that the information I wanted was at work. 'What about it?' he asked.

'Green Dolphin Resorts. You don't happen to remember the names of the other directors, do you?'

'Direct-or,' he corrected. 'There was only one other apart from Delgado. Howard Thripps.'

Howard Thripps. Company director, killer and full-time maniac.

Where was he? Why hadn't I seen him for days? Had he gone to ground?

This wasn't the first time I'd been to Coffs Harbour but it was the first time in a while. It was like one big suburb, only with banana plantations on the hills behind and a coastline in front. Its contribution to Australian culture was the Big Banana. There were plenty of shopping malls, skin cancer candidates, people in short-sleeved shirts, blond hair, Sikhs in turbans, the odd batik sarong when a hippie came to town. There were cafes where drug deals were done and all the eyes were lazy. It had sun and surf and golf. It had apricot-coloured tourist resorts, some of them left incomplete when the developers scurried into bankruptcy owing local builders millions of dollars. It was the capital of the holiday coast. Something about it reminded me of passengers on the sundeck of the Titanic politely coughing into their handkerchiefs to hide the blood.

Sharon had arranged a car to be waiting for me at the airport, a 4WD. There were a few other vehicles there as well, including a ute that looked like it spent a lot of time in the bush. Maybe the 4WD would look like that by the time I finished with it but at the moment it was gleaming—not a trace of dust or mud to be seen.

I'd asked Sharon about places to stay, somewhere between backpackers and the pricey resorts endorsed by the airlines, now that I'd lost the benefit of Dolores' credit card. Somewhere inconspicuous, modest, where no-one would be asking me too many questions. She told me she knew just the place. Twin Peaks.

I said, c'mon, Sharon, seriously. She said, Twin Peaks. God's honour.

Twin Peaks was on the south side of town; an old-style motel, old for Coffs Harbour, built in the early sixties. The twin peaks were two banana-clad hills behind it, almost identical. The units were red brick with a few straggly flowers in front of each and a white gravel parking area for the car.

I pulled up and went into reception. Behind the desk was a woman in her fifties with bouffant hair dyed blonde and pencilled-on brown eyebrows. She was wearing a light blue uniform with a badge that said MAISIE, above a bust that stuck out like an awning over a verandah. Her smile revealed a set of teeth whiter and more perfect than anything you'd find in nature. I felt immediately at home with Maisie—my mother used to have friends like Maisie when I was a kid.

'Hello, dear.' she said, all bright and cheery.

'Hi,' I said, catching some of her mood, 'I made a phone booking. Claudia Valentine.'

'Ah, yes,' she said, consulting the Domesday Book behind the counter. 'We've put you in number eight. Just the one night is it?'

I had no idea how long my business in this town would take. 'Probably two, I'll pay for one night then see how it goes. That all right with you?'

'That's fine, dear. It's not one of our peak times, I'm sure we can accommodate you on a day-to-day basis.'

I handed over some cash. The place was still old-fashioned enough for her not to think there was anything strange about cash.

'Well, that seems to be that,' she said, closing the Domesday Book. 'Hang on a sec, I'll get the key.' She got the key from a panel behind her and eased her voluminous bust out of the reception area.

It was as if she'd started dressing from the top and lost interest halfway down. The bouffant hair was immaculate, as was the face, the uniform was clean and neatly pressed but by the time we got down past the hemline things had started to deteriorate. She was wearing knee-high stockings and Chinese slippers. Scuffs, Mina would call them. She must have worn them a lot and got used to them because she crossed the white gravel without kicking any of it up in the flip flop movement.

She opened the door of unit eight. I could have predicted exactly how it looked. I've stayed in a thousand motels like this. There were twin beds with orange chenille bedspreads, the smallest bedside table in the world sporting a light that was supposed to look like a lily. A built-in wardrobe, empty except for a couple of wire coathangers and a blanket on a top shelf. The day you'd need an extra blanket in Coffs Harbour would be the day Hell froze over. 'And this is the bathroom,' beamed Maisie, like the proud mother of a child who'd just won a scholarship to Cambridge. Bathroom was a bit of a misnomer because there wasn't a bath in sight. There was a shower recess, a minute hand basin, and a toilet. No complimentary toothbrush but there was a dwarf-sized lozenge of soap.

It was so anonymous and ordinary you'd be at pains to recognise your own face in the mirror. It was great.

Maisie didn't offer to help me with the luggage. Good heavens, this was Australia, she wasn't a servant. I didn't need any help anyway. I hadn't brought much with me. A camera, a few tools of trade, some clothes for flogging around in the bush. I'd left all my black clothes at home because I didn't want to look like a city slicker. No-one wore black in Coffs Harbour, not even the undertaker. On the other hand I hadn't gone as far as baggy shorts. Beats me why people wore them. They looked like you'd got your skirt caught between your buttocks. If people started staring at me too much I could always buy a pair. The shops in Coffs Harbour were full of them.

'If you need anything, just give us a call.' Maisie turned to leave. 'Oh,' she said, 'will you give us your breakfast order before eight o'clock this evening? We bring it round between seven and nine unless you'd like to make a special arrangement.' She smiled and treated me to another showing of those dazzling white teeth.

The breakfast menu was on the bedside table. It had a range of items that you had to tick. It also said that breakfast was served between seven and nine but I guess it made Maisie feel better to remind the guests personally. At least that way you were sure that they knew.

'I'd rather have it closer to seven than nine. That be all right?'

'Yes, that's fine. You need anything just give us a call.'

'I will. Thanks.'

I hardly knew her yet I liked Maisie a lot. I was here off-season, I was a woman travelling on my own, I didn't own a pair of shorts. Yet she hadn't asked me any questions, not even of the seemingly innocuous kind. This was the right place for me to be, even if it was called Twin Peaks.

I had a car, a tankful of petrol and a big day ahead of me. The first item on the agenda was to look at the Green Dolphin Development Application. At 9 a.m. the Coffs Harbour Council Chambers would be open for business.

As I drove into town I couldn't help thinking about David and Amy. I was only half as far away from them now as I was in Sydney. I could keep heading north, I'd be there in eight hours. I could pick them up, take them to the beach for a few days, it'd be great. The part-time parent always has great times with the kids. No fights about eating breakfast, doing homework, tidying the room. What the kids had with me was holidays. Fun and adventure. What they had with Gary and Rachel was acres of farm to play in, homegrown vegetables, security, safety, no pollution. They had cane toads in Queensland but they didn't have people following them, they didn't have people attacking them in alleyways.

Coffs Harbour had the odd cane toad and it had Howard Thripps. Where was he? He hadn't shown himself for days it seemed like. He was around somewhere though. I looked in the rear vision mirror, in the side mirrors of the 4WD. There was no-one following me, there was no-one round for miles. Yet I could feel his presence, smell him almost. I told myself to relax.

I only felt like that because this was his town and I was a stranger in it.

The traffic lights were turning red. I stopped. Huge semi-trailers pulled up alongside me, wheezing and hissing their brakes; the sound of the country grinding to a halt. When the lights turned green, I made a right turn. Peak hour—this was as heavy as the traffic ever got. It was a breeze.

The Council Chambers weren't where I remembered them to be. But it wasn't my memory—the Council Chambers had changed location.

I passed the red brick Town Hall and the Harry Bailey Memorial Library. It was a squat, spread-out building whose dark brick was well hidden by some lush-looking tropical trees.

The new Council Chambers were blond brick. Bigger and more lavish than the Town Hall and Library combined. Business must be booming, living up to the council motto—Progress and Prosper. There was a banner with a sailing ship, two trees and a bull either side. Did this represent the cattle industry or what went on at council meetings? A band of garden bordered the two-storey building—palms and birds nest ferns overshadowing a carpet of native violets. There was a driveway for cars to drop off anyone important and a set of stairs for the rest of us. I walked up the stairs and waited for the automatic doors to open. They didn't. They weren't automatic. I pushed on the glass door and went in.

The pink and grey galah colours so favoured by Sydney decorators had migrated as far north as here. There were potted palms in the reception area, a huge dead tree stump with a polished circular seat fashioned out of it, splendid contemporary works of art on the walls.

It all looked nice and squeaky clean. But what was happening in the back rooms? I went to the counter. Development applications went on public display, I didn't anticipate any problem with asking to see the Green Dolphin DA.

'Hi,' said the young guy behind the counter. Sixteen years old and a face full of pimples. Hair spiky on top, longer at the back. Friendly and keen.

I told him what I wanted.

'Jeez, I dunno,' he mentally scratched his head, 'I'm only here on work experience, I'll have to ask someone else.' He went over and spoke to the woman behind a section of the counter that said CASHIER. He said something to her, she listened, looked over in my direction. I stood there, innocent expression on my face, couldn't hurt a fly.

He came back. 'Which one was it again?'

'Green Dolphin Resorts. G for Green.'

'Yeah, right,' he said and disappeared.

He seemed to take ages. There were some pamphlets and booklets on a display stand. A Public Works brochure—'The solution to our sewerage problem is clear.' The solution was an ocean outfall near Woolgoolga, just north of Coffs. Not everyone agreed it was the solution however. The protests had received national coverage in the media. I passed over a booklet on Building and Renovating and picked up the Coffs Harbour City Council Annual Report.

There was the mayoral message and a photo of the mayor, then mug shots of the councillors on the next page—three women, five men. All smiling happy faces. There were several pages devoted to Major Works and Achievements, and Planning for the Future. The last page listed council staff, starting with the Town Clerk.

It ended with the Noxious Weeds Inspector. It was in exactly the same typeface as all the other names but this one leapt off the page and hit me in the eye.

The Noxious Weeds Inspector was Howard Thripps.

'Sorry I took so long, the aldermen are having a meeting and they wanted me to get some coffee.'

'What?' Howard Thripps.

A manilla folder was placed on top of the lists of names. 'The file you wanted. Green Dolphin.'

'Oh thanks.'

'I'll stay here while you look at it. That all right?' He was like a kid asking his mother if he could stay up late. I smiled at the thought. But not that much.

There were yellow papers with the DA number on it. Green Dolphin Resorts, Paradise Park Proposal. Rezoning and development of a section of crown land, Paradise Park in the Coffs Harbour Shire. The 6.25 hectares would include a hotel with 350 suites, luxury holiday cabins, swimming pool, tennis court and golf course.

There was a Preliminary Assessment Checklist, and other papers relevant to the development. Memos to the Manager, Strategic Planning; the Manager, Social Planning. The notice of Proposed Development for advertising in the newspaper. There was a survey map of the area and an architect's plan laid over it.

I came to the EIS. Atherton, Milne and Associates, the North Sydney address that I'd visited. Don't they have Environmental Consultants in Coffs Harbour? Or did Thripps prefer someone who wasn't too familiar with the area?

I turned to the flora section. Exactly the same as before. No orchids. They seemed to have disappeared even from their home ground.

Apart from this, and the fact that there were no letters of protest about the development, not even from cranks, there didn't seem to be anything out of the ordinary. The final outcome—a two-year lease had been granted to Green Dolphin Resorts.

Which was a $2 company with no other assets than its subscribed capital. That's what Brian's fax had said. I wouldn't have even known what it meant a few months ago but with so many empires crashing and the media revealing who owns what, who's selling what to whom then going on holidays to sunnier climes, you couldn't help but take some of this in osmotically. We were living in economic times.

How was a company that had only $2 to its name going to finance this multi-million-dollar development? There was a letter from Thripps to council saying the project would be financed by Royal Dolphin but there was nothing in writing from Royal Dolphin. How were they going to finance it? Maybe they weren't.

A pair of hairy hands with clean clipped fingernails closed the manilla folder on me. 'This one's not for public inspection. Sorry.'

I looked up. It was one of the councillors, I recognised the face from the annual report. It wasn't smiling now. Rugged and square, a low hairline with steel grey hair combed straight back from it. I suppose he had to comb it back otherwise the hair would get confused with the eyebrows. They looked like a couple of straggly bushes growing out from an overhang. Compared to that stunning feature the rest of him was fairly ordinary. A brown cardigan, beige shirt and grey trousers.

'Not for public inspection? I thought all DAs were open for inspection. What's special about this one that it's not?'

'Nothing, nothing,' he glossed over it. 'The plans for development are advertised and on display but not the correspondence etc. That's council business. Now, if you don't mind I'll just pop it back in the filing cabinet.'

'I'll do it, Mr Pottinger,' offered the kid.

'It's all right, son,' said Mr Pottinger firmly, 'I'll look after it. In future ask one of the aldermen to see that it's OK.' I got the feeling that if I hadn't been there he would have given the kid a good hiding.

'Geez, I'm in for it now, I left the filing cabinet open too,' said the kid once Pottinger had withdrawn. 'Don't know what's bugging him but. Marie said it was OK.'

I didn't know what was bugging him either. The file had nothing incriminating in it. The incriminating stuff had been left out. 'He's probably got PMT.'

'PMT?' The kid couldn't believe I'd said it. 'You mean . . .' His mouth dropped open. Then he grinned. 'It's not once a month with him but, Pottinger's had it all his life.'

It was a pity I couldn't photocopy the contents of the file, particularly the survey map, but I remembered it well enough. Next thing to do was go out and have a look at the real thing. Maybe this afternoon, make a picnic out of it. Pull up at the side of the road and eat my sandwiches in the car like every other Australian.

'Hope you enjoy your work experience.'

'Don't think I want to do this as a job, end up like Pottinger.'

'What do you want to do?' I could feel that motherly tone creeping back into my voice. Get back.

'Work for the railways.'

'Good. See you on a train someday.'

I walked along the mall eating a prawn and avocado roll. Prawn and avocado rolls seemed to be the go in Coffs Harbour. The shops were all open for business, the business being clothes, souvenirs and icecreams. Despite all the clothes I didn't think Dolores would enjoy spending her money as much up here as she had in Sydney. Though she'd been up here. If she was just a name on Green Dolphin paper as Schaeffer had suggested, what had she been doing? Dancing? Coffs Harbour wasn't exactly the Gold Coast but it did have a night life of sorts.

I went into the newsagent and picked up a tourist guide to the area. There was live entertainment at the Hoey Moey and various other hotels—local rock bands and a few big names on tour. There were nightclubs too—Joe Bananas, Midnight Dream. It seemed to me Midnight Dream was more Dolores' pace than Joe Bananas. At the Post Office I called Midnight Dream. I asked if they'd had any tango dancers in the last couple of months, live dancers of any persuasion. The woman couldn't recall anyone like that but if I wanted to make sure I could ring the manager about 5 p.m.

The Post Office, where the public phones were, was at a busy intersection, busy enough to have traffic lights. A lot of the traffic was heavy duty—trucks lumbering up to Queensland, tourist coaches and utes. I didn't really fancy standing here all day trying to make myself heard, and trying to hear, above the noise. I'd be much better off doing these calls from the motel.

The gravel in front of the motel unit made a satisfying crunching sound as the 4WD came to rest. I didn't know a soul in Coffs Harbour. I'd spoken to only three people—a kid who knew nothing, a councillor who pretended he knew nothing, and

Maisie. She looked as if she'd lived here all her life. Or at least her hairdo had. In the stream of fashion some items seemed to get stuck in a backwater. I hadn't seen big hair, as they call it in America where it is rife, for twenty years. But maybe I don't get out enough. Seems whenever you're within cooee of country and western music you get big hair. Who knows what secrets were locked away in Maisie's hive of hair? But before I approached Maisie, I had a few phone calls to make.

None of the clubs, hotels or nite spots that I rang knew anyone called Dolores or a tango dancer by any name. It was the same story again and again—we don't have that kind of entertainment, we have bands. I tried the resorts. No luck there either. One of them suggested I try the escort agencies. It wasn't a bad idea. With the escort agencies I said I was looking for a friend who had been working here up to about a month ago. Her name was Dolores though that may not have been the name she was using with the agency. Fortunately this wasn't the big city, and while there were a fair few escort agencies in the area the list was considerably shorter than it would have been in Sydney.

On the third call I got a result. The voice on the other end sounded fairly businesslike, a well-modulated voice that had benefited from elocution lessons. The only thing the lessons hadn't got rid of was the upward inflexion at the end of each sentence which made all her answers sound like questions.

'Dolores?' she repeated. 'Yes, the name rings a bell. Are you a friend of hers?'

'I am,' I replied.

'Come and see me,' she said. '7 p.m. tonight, the Plantation Hotel.'

That had been easy, I thought, I hadn't even had to ask her.

'Your name is?' she asked before we hung up. I told her. 'Mrs Roche,' she told me.

While I had the phone book with me I looked up Thripps. There was only one in the Coffs Harbour Shire phone book. The initial was H. It was North Street. I found it on the map. North Street was off High Street, on the way down to the jetty.

At the end of North Street was the cemetery. If I could have, I would have looked up Phyllis, but phone books don't list first names.

I went out to find Maisie. She was just turning the sprinkler off. I commented on the flowers and we got into conversation. 'Do you know anyone called Phyllis?'

'Only one Phyllis I know, that's Phyllis Harmon. They call her Mad Phyllis round here. Poor old thing, she went a bit loopy after Blue—the husband—passed away. Don't know where she'd be now, she avoids Coffs like the plague. Reckons the son and daughter-in-law are trying to put her in a home. Probably are,' laughed Maisie, shaking the water off her hands. 'I did see her in town about a year, eighteen months ago. Coming out of the army disposal store. She was humming "Waltzing Matilda", quietly, to herself. Until she got to "you'll never catch me alive, said he", she sang that bit out loud and clear.'

So much for finding Phyllis in a couple of days. I brought the subject round to noxious weeds. Did Maisie know Howard Thripps?

She took off one of her scuffs and knocked some dirt out of it. 'I've known them for donkey's years,' she began, now that her feet were comfortable again. 'I went to school with the sister. Lovely girl, she is. Married money. Don't see much of her nowadays but she'll pop in if she's up this way.'

'And Howard?'

'Now Howard . . . well, I suppose he's all right, but he's not a patch on her. I never liked him that much.' She took a breath. 'He used to, well lots of the boys did, kill possums. But Howard didn't just take pot shots at them like the other boys, he'd set up baits and watch them. Said he was doing scientific research. Can you imagine, a little boy saying that. Still, I suppose it was good training,' she said wryly, 'he ended up being the noxious weeds inspector.'

'No-one makes comments about someone with his name being a noxious weeds inspector?'

'His name?' she frowned. 'Sorry, I don't get it, what's his name got to do with his job?'

I felt ashamed, apparently I was the only one who found it amusing. The only thing about Thripps I found amusing. It would be uncharitable of me to make anything of it to Maisie. I backpedalled. 'A bit unusual,' I explained. 'The only one in the phone book.'

'There was only Howard and Margaret after Mr and Mrs died, and of course she moved out of the area. You wouldn't find her under Thripps anyway. She's been Margaret Schaeffer for a good twenty years.'

I t was still early afternoon. If I kept things moving I could have a quick look around Mr Thripps' residence, a long look around the development site and still be back in time for my 7 p.m. rendezvous with Mrs Roche from the escort agency.

It didn't take long for High Street to turn from shops into houses. Most front gardens sported hibiscus bushes and umbrella trees. In all of them there was a lot of rampant tropical vegetation.

The Thripps residence was no exception. None of the vegetation here though was rampant. The sort of neatness and clipped efficiency I'd expect from a noxious weed inspector, the neatness and efficiency of the person who'd searched Dolores' room. It had its fair share of hibiscus, umbrella trees and that other palmy thing I don't know the name of.

I locked the car, probably unnecessary but years of Sydney don't wear off in one day, and walked over to the front gate. The neighbourhood was quiet. There was nobody about but I knew from experience that news travels surprisingly fast in country towns, about the only thing that does.

The house was small compared to the size of the block it was on. It wasn't Howard who'd married money. It was an old house and an old-fashioned house. Probably the home of the older Thripps before they passed on. The house had a patio built over the garage, a grey concrete block with a simple white painted iron railing around it. The house itself was weatherboard on top and brick below. The windows had fly screens on them and the curtains were drawn, a sensible thing to do on a hot afternoon. Or if you were going away for a few days.

There was nothing in the letter box although Thripps was probably the kind of person who'd arrange with the Post Office to hold his mail while he was away. If he got any mail that is.

I stepped over the low gate and walked up the concrete path to the front door. I hadn't expected anyone to come to the door and no-one did. But now I was on the premises and had done the normal thing first I could look about a bit. I had answers for anyone who enquired what I was doing there but no-one enquired.

Near the house, but separate from it, was an old fibro shed. The door was padlocked. There was a small louvre window with mottled glass making it impossible to see inside. There appeared to be a black cloth up against the window as well. A dark room, Mr Thripps; interested in photography?

The ubiquitous Hills hoist was standing smack in the middle of the yard, the pivotal pole from which all else radiated. Not that there was much to radiate, except down the back where a luxuriant stand of bamboo grew. Strange that he'd let the bamboo grow rampant when everything else was so neat.

As I approached the bamboo jungle something moved. I remained still, alert. It wasn't the familiar sound of a lizard scurrying away, or of a bird fluttering in the leaves. There was a plop then the thing practically landed at my feet. Though I'd never admit it to anyone, if there'd been a chair nearby I'd have jumped up on it. I don't mind smooth little green frogs but this warty brown thing squatting in front of me was the biggest, ugliest, widest-mouthed piece of fauna I'd ever seen in my life. I'd only ever seen them on TV before but this had to be the world's biggest cane toad. It stared me straight in the eye then must have decided I wasn't worth the bother because it then hopped back into the bamboo. I didn't venture any further with that piece of investigation; there was probably a whole colony of them living in the bamboo.

I went back to the shed and walked around three sides of it, testing the fibro. I looked at the window again. What was in the shed that he didn't want people peering in? I could take the louvres out. Middle of the afternoon the neighbours are at work, at the beach, watching TV, taking drugs. But there was always one who kept watch, one like the all-seeing doll called Jennifer. I didn't want someone like her to see me breaking into the shed in broad daylight. I'd come back tonight. Late. The watchers must go off duty sometime.

Some of the lushest country in the world can be found in the hinterland behind Coffs Harbour. Inland and south lies the Bellinger Valley where the grass is greener, the rivers wider. The trees are taller and so are the stories. Rivers have names like the Never Never, settlements are called Diehappy and the Promised Land. But I wasn't going to the Promised Land, only as far as Paradise Park.

Lush wasn't exactly the word I'd choose for what I was seeing through the car windscreen once I got off the Pacific Highway. I'd expected the Tropicana, only with real trees instead of plastic. Rainforests, vines, macaws and monkeys, Tarzan and Jane. Mostly what I saw out the window were thin-leaved eucalypts, grey–green vegetation rather than emerald green.

I continued on now along a road that looked like a recent addition, judging by the raw red wound it left across the landscape. The further I went down the road the greener the grass got, and wetter. White birds circled overhead. Then suddenly the road stopped. I had arrived at Paradise Park.

There were clumps of trees, long grasses and waterbirds. It was OK but not my idea of paradise. I would have preferred Tarzan and Jane. Apart from the road the area was virgin. No fences, no signs of construction, nothing.

I left the car where the road stopped and got out. I could hear the sound of wind in the grass, bird calls, another all-pervading background noise. Air molecules bumping together? The sound of silence? There's nothing quiet about quietness. My city ears kept straining but not one of the sounds I heard could be associated with a human being.

I put on my boots, took the camera and started wading into the long grass. It was squishy underfoot. I didn't imagine orchids that bloomed underground were going to be all that easy to find and 6.25 hectares wasn't exactly a leisurely stroll. But there must be some signs. The notebook had said that Phyllis had found the orchid while digging a hole, that David Morgan had scraped away debris to find them. There must be some clues left behind, something to read.

As I walked I imposed the proposed development plan on the landscape, imagined where everything would go, the hotel, the units, the swimming pool, the golf course. It wasn't a park yet and it wasn't paradise. If they built their artificial paradise everything I was looking at now would change. Would the orchids still remain, unseen, flowering in the darkness of the soil or would they disappear? I thought of people who disappear, those in Argentina where Dolores came from. Those customarily removed from their homes, removed from sight, silenced. Whose skeletons were dug up years later. Would the orchids survive the excavating, the damage to their habitat? Their defence mechanism, the illusion and pretence that had fooled botanists like Rupp, would it protect them against the builders of Paradise Park?

The ground started to squelch, I was glad I'd stopped off at the army disposal store to buy the rubber boots. As well as orchids I was also keeping an eye out for snakes and all the other nasties that keep the Australian bush from being completely user-friendly. The land rose up as I approached a stand of trees and it got drier underfoot. They were long, tall, flooded gums. They weren't going to be standing much longer; this was going to be levelled for the tennis courts. My approach started the birds off—I recognised the throaty chuckle of kookaburras but there were other less familiar calls including a long mournful sound of a lone bird. The grass beneath the trees was sparser, my footsteps crunchy with dry leaves and twigs. I bent down here and had a closer look. Was this the kind of debris that the orchids grew under? I scraped some of it away. A few scurrying ants, a spider hole. I didn't think it was a good idea to keep on doing this with my bare hands. I didn't particularly want to find a funnel-web spider coming home after a hard day's work.

It wasn't long before I was through the trees and looking at a vast grassy field. It would have been quite breathtaking except that the grass wasn't lush green as it was on the other side of the trees, it was brown and dying. Why?

The answer came as a short loud explosive noise. I dived to the ground, stupid really, I should have gone back into the trees but I didn't have time to think about it much less do it. That wasn't a bird call or a car backfiring. The echo of the shot seemed to reverberate forever. Thripps. I had sensed his presence this morning. No cars had followed me out along the dirt road. Did he know a secret way of getting to this place?

Once the bird warnings had screeched away there was silence all around. Bush silence. Loud humming silence, as if every sound in the world had finally come to rest here.

Maybe it was just a duck shooter. I lay there for a long time listening. Long enough to get the cold clammy feel of muddy water seeping through my jeans and the crawling, slithering creatures that frequent places like this trekking up my body like tourists climbing Ayers Rock. The grass may have been brown and dying but the fauna were alive and well. Don't panic, I kept saying to myself, everything will bite you if they smell fear.

And what will happen if I stand up?

I was going to have to find that out, I couldn't stay here forever. Unfortunately I couldn't raise the white flag because the only white thing I had, a tissue, had compacted into a small wet lump in my jeans pocket. If he'd wanted me dead right away he would have kept firing. He wanted me dead but he also wanted the notebook. If I moved slowly and didn't make him jumpy, I had a good chance of being able to stand up without getting shot. I gingerly raised one hand in the air. Silence. So far so good. Then the other. Then I stood up, keeping my hands in the air, though what I desperately wanted to do was to brush off the crawly things. I could feel them in my boots, inside my jeans. I looked down. I was covered in leeches. Hundreds of them were making their way up my boots, onto my legs, looking for a free spot to start sucking. And country people think life in the city is tough.

I still couldn't see anyone. 'Thripps?' I called.

There was some movement in the clump of trees on the other side of the brown grass. I caught sight of some colour that wasn't green. Then the figure approached and stopped, a good twenty paces away from me.

It wasn't Thripps at all. It was a woman with arms as long and skinny as the rifle she was holding. Her skin was sun-wrinkled and leathery. She was wearing a dress that would have looked good in the fifties but was now faded and worn. Below the dress were rubber boots. Well at least I had the right footwear for the occasion. Whatever the occasion was.

'Friend of Thripps, are ya?' The voice was not friendly. She looked mean, the rifle looked mean. I had the feeling that if she didn't like my answer I could be lying on the ground again, this time dragged down by bullets.

In the nicest calmest voice I could muster I said, 'Sorry, I didn't realise it was your land, I thought this was Paradise Park.'

Her mouth curled down in contempt. 'Over my dead body are any mongrels gunna build anythink here. And I'll be taking a few of yous with me. You might be the first. What do ya think about that, eh?' she said, brandishing the gun. She meant business.

I had to convince her I was not one of those mongrels and I had to do it quickly. 'I'm not with them. I thought you were Thripps shooting at me, that's what he'd do if he knew I was here.'

She eyed me suspiciously. She was listening but she hadn't heard enough yet. The trick now was to try and keep the gun out of the conversation, to put things on a more friendly footing. 'Do you mind if I put my arms down? They're really getting sore.'

She thought about it for a minute. 'Go on,' she relented, 'put 'em down, but keep 'em where I can see 'em.'

Slowly I lowered my arms. My legs were so itchy it was driving me crazy. I rolled up my jeans to find my legs were black with plump leeches drinking themselves to a stupor on my blood.

'Any chance of getting the leeches off my legs?' I asked hopefully.

'You can have a go. There's not much point, they'll only jump back on.'

'You wouldn't happen to have a match, or some salt, would you?'

'Forget about that rubbish,' she snorted. 'If you're quick you can pull them off and flick them away. But you've got to be quick, before they latch onto ya fingers.'

As I pulled the little suckers off the blood ran down in rivers. But I wasn't quick enough in flicking them away. They latched onto my hands. I rubbed my hands hard down my legs, they latched on there again. I could move them around but I couldn't get rid of them.

'OK, that's enough of that. Stand up and leave ya hands where I can see them. Now what are you here for?' she hissed.

'I came to see the orchids.'

She jerked the rifle up at me. 'What do you know about the orchids?'

'That if the building goes ahead they'll be destroyed.'

'That's what the botanist or whatever he calls himself said. He told me they'd be protected, that the law wouldn't let the mongrels build on top of them. So much for that!' she scoffed. 'Next thing I know they're building a bloody road down to the place.'

'It's not too late, they can still be saved.'

'Ha! What do you think happened to that grass you're standing in, that it just died of its own accord? That was Thrippsy, bloody bastard. Reckons he was spraying to kill off the midges. He was spraying poison into the ground. You know what he says to me? Points the spray at me and says, "You better get out of here otherwise I'll think you're a midge as well." '

Jesus Christ, Howard Thripps had poisoned the orchids. Did he know where they were or was it just random selection? Was he going to come back and do the whole 6.25 hectares?

'Did you tell anyone, about what Thripps did?'

'Told Blue. He said stay put.'

Blue. Mad Phyllis' dead husband. Stay put, don't go into town, they might put you away.

'Who else do I tell anyway? The council? Those mongrels are Thrippsy's mates. They were all down here the first time, Thrippsy, Pottinger, a few other council blokes. Old Mr Thripps was all right, can't say the same for the son.'

'So you wouldn't be upset if he went to jail?' I suggested.

'Jail? If I'd had the gun with me then I would have shot the bastard meself.'

'Then you'd go to jail,' I pointed out, 'you wouldn't be able to stay out here.'

'That's just where you're wrong. I'm staying put. This is my place. Anyone wants to try anything I've got the gun with me now. You can't trust anyone anymore. That botanist and his girlfriend, they said they'd do something but they never. They never stopped Thrippsy coming back with the spray.'

'His girlfriend?'

'Yeah, she was a bit like you come to think of it but a foreigner. She's got all the right gear on but it's, you know, like the stuff you see in magazines, wouldn't last a day in the bush. All nice and friendly too but she never done anythink about stopping Thrippsy.'

'She couldn't. Thripps murdered her. He can't go ahead with the building if he's in jail, he can't come back out here and kill the rest of the orchids.'

'How do I know you're not all talk too?'

'You can't know for certain till it happens. That's the chance you'll have to take. You live out here, you take chances all the time, Mrs Harmon.'

'What did you say?' Suspiciously, as if she hadn't heard properly.

'You can't know for cert . . .'

'No, not that,' she interrupted, 'what did you call me?'

'Mrs Harmon. You are Phyllis Harmon, aren't you?'

She looked confused, as if she was unsure whether that was her name. 'No-one's called me Mrs Harmon for years,' she said quietly. 'The rest of them, they call me Mad Phyllis.' She was silent for a moment. 'What's your name?' as if noticing me for the first time.

'Claudia Valentine. Do you need anything from town?'

'Like what?'

'I don't know,' I shrugged, 'tins of bully beef? Toblerone?'

Her face started to light up, then she broke into a cackle of laughter and thigh-slapping. 'Toblerone? D'ya hear that, Bluey? She wants to bring me some Toblerone. I got a bloody crateful of the stuff. When I come out here I bought a bulk supply. Bloody stuff got weevils in it. I had to dig a hole and bury it, that's how I came across the orchids in the first place. Talk about chocolate and flowers, that's a good one, isn't it, Blue?'

I could hear the laughter all the way to the car.

Thripps had killed Dolores and he'd poisoned the orchids.

Could he really do it that way? Does spraying the top of the ground kill what's under it? Probably, if you knew what kind of poison to use. And Thripps would know. If that didn't finish them off the building would.

Somehow, out of all of it, that seemed the worst thing, that he'd killed the orchids. They were in the wrong place, they couldn't run, move out of his way. The camouflage hadn't worked when the predator was Thripps. Noxious weeds inspector. Eradicate, eradicate.

I didn't even know such orchids existed up to a couple of days ago. I'd never seen them, I didn't care if they were beautiful or ordinary. I felt no desire to enfold them in my loving arms or to 'collect' them, take them home and label them. But did they have to die just because they were there? Were they just more noxious weeds that had to be eradicated to make way for Paradise Park?

There was Phyllis, in the bush with her gun and her memories, ready to shoot anyone who was going to destroy all that. And here I was on the road that was bringing the people who were going to do it.

Something about the bush unhinges your mind, any minute now I'd be thinking about all creatures great and small, about the meaning of life and the cosmos. It was time for me to get back to town.

I looked in the rear vision mirror for a last sight of Phyllis and her gun. All I could see was dust.

I got back to the motel three-quarters of an hour before I was due to meet Mrs Roche. I spent half of that time cleaning up the leech bites and putting on the Stingoes I'd bought at the chemist on the way back. I wasn't sure what one should wear for a meeting with the manager of an escort agency but it probably wasn't rubber boots. Or at least not the practical kind.

Though I'd left my black clothes at home I had packed a navy dress with white spots on it and some dark stockings. My legs already had whitish spots on them from the Stingoes but at least the dark stockings would cover them. I put on Dolores' leather jacket and a pair of high heels. The high heels were a bit of an indulgence but I'd become rather fond of wearing them lately and this would probably be the only occasion I'd have here to wear them.

The Plantation Hotel had a feel of Raffles about it. There were light-coloured timber supports, ceiling fans, tall stools with short backs. It was very tasteful. The woman I took to be Mrs Roche was sitting on one of the high stools. She was wearing an apricot suit, pale stockings and beige shoes. She had a wide face, heavily made-up but you didn't notice that till you got close up, and champagne-coloured hair that had had a lot of treatment to give it a casual wind-blown look. She smelled vaguely of powder, perfume and cigarettes.

'Mrs Roche?' I didn't really have to enquire. We each knew who the other was. We were the only people in the bar not wearing shorts. 'Claudia Valentine,' I introduced myself.

'Would you like to sit at a table?' she invited.

'Here is just fine,' I replied.

'A drink?'

What a perfectly charming woman. 'Sure. What's good round here?'

'I've having a Virgin Mary.'

'That'll be fine.'

The drinks came, we got the preliminary chitchat out of the way then came to the matter in hand—Dolores. Apparently Dolores wasn't one of her girls at all. 'Oh?' I was confused. 'But on the phone you said . . .'

'I said the name rang a bell. Actually I have a bone to pick with your Dolores, or whatever her name is. I had a gentleman, a Japanese gentleman call up the agency asking for Dolores. I said we had no-one here by that name. He described her, in much the same way you described her. I said we still had no-one like that. Apparently she had turned up at his hotel as a, what was the word he used? A gesture of goodwill. That had been sent by Pink Panthers. You must understand, I take a fairly dim view of girls operating on their own and passing themselves off as Pink Panthers. It's bad enough they work here for a while then take clients with them when they leave.' She paused to give weight to the seriousness of this.

'Look, I don't know what Dolores was doing up here, but she won't be doing it again. She's been murdered.' Her eyes widened slightly but she didn't lose her apricot cool. She took another sip of Virgin Mary.

'I see. I guess it's pointless then trying to sue her.'

Under the circumstances I didn't find the comment all that humorous. 'If you can tell me anything about the Japanese man, or anything at all you remember.'

'As I said, I remember the woman's name because she was trying to pass herself off as a Pink Panther. As for the man, what can I say? He was awfully sorry to disturb me, could I put him in touch with Dolores? Actually, he gave the impression that he was ringing on behalf of someone else. That's not unusual. I said I had a range of attractive intelligent girls as escorts, if he described his requirements perhaps I could find someone suitable.' Never let an opportunity slip by. 'But no, it wasn't for the service, he needed to speak with her about another matter. Well, quite frankly as long as it didn't concern the agency or my girls I had no interest in this other matter whatsoever. I did ask, though, if he happened to come across her could he let me know where she could be contacted.'

Dolores seemed to have cut quite a swathe around Coffs Harbour. The botanist's girlfriend, escort girl for the Japanese. What else, Dolores, what else? Haven't I heard everything yet?

After I left Mrs Roche I came back to the motel and changed clothes. I wasn't going snooping around Thripps' in the same clothes I wore to talk to Mrs Roche. I wondered who the Japanese man was who'd enquired after Dolores. The book in her room. Was he the Japanese she was doing business with?

I checked my camera. Despite the rough treatment it had suffered this afternoon at Paradise Park it seemed OK. It was small, nifty and could take pictures in the dark. I put the camera, torch and a few other things in a bag. I started up the 4WD and crunched out over the gravel.

It was after midnight, the roads were quiet. It made the 4WD sound like a tank.

I didn't drive straight to Thripps', I went round the back way and parked behind the cemetery. I thought of the cemetery in Randwick where I'd parked to go and see Mina. You were watching me that night, Mr Thripps, are you watching me now? Watch carefully, because I am coming after you.

I put on my gloves and made my way through the cemetery. If you can get over the fact that there are a lot of dead people lying under the ground, and personally that didn't worry me, cemeteries can be very welcoming places. There are tombstones and shadows, lots of places to run and hide. And with what I was about to do, the thought of somewhere to run and hide was quite comforting.

I came into Thripps' the back way, over the fence and around the bamboo jungle. I watched carefully where I was putting my feet. I didn't want to tread on anything that croaked. The back of the house looked quiet. So did the shed. Near the Hills hoist was a dog bone, quite a big one. I hadn't noticed it there this afternoon.

Between the house and the shed I could see up to North Street. There was a vehicle up there that hadn't been there this afternoon as well. A ute. Dusty from what I could make out. I remembered seeing a ute like that parked at the airport. There were probably lots of them around Coffs Harbour.

I watched the house. Not a movement. I picked up a small stone and threw it at the window. Not hard enough to do any damage, just to make a noise, to make anyone inside who heard it come and have a look. I waited. No-one came to investigate.

I crept over to the shed. I already knew how I was going to get in but I walked round the shed and checked it. Just to make sure. Everything was still and quiet, there were no lights on in any of the other houses in the street, everyone was asleep.

Taking the louvres out took time but not a lot of effort. Once I'd loosened the brackets they slid out relatively easily. It took time because I had to do it without making any noise. As each louvre slid out I placed it neatly against the side of the shed. I'd put them all back once the job was done. Nice and neat, Mr Thripps, you couldn't do a better job yourself.

The trick now was to get through the space.

The curtain I'd seen behind the louvres was a blessing in disguise because it would probably hide any torchlight coming from inside the shed. I chinned up with the torch and shone it in. Directly below the window was a sink, dry and a bit dusty, as if it hadn't been used for days. I dropped back down to the ground and got the bag with the rest of the things. I chinned up to the window again and lowered the bag in. I heard the soft sound as it came to rest in the sink. Now all I had to do was get myself in.

The space where the louvres had been was adequate but only just. Think like a snake. I wriggled through it head first.

I could hear a fridge humming. Howard Thripps obviously wasn't one to bother about turning off the electricity when he went on holiday. Which was odd, seeing how neat he was about everything else.

I shone the torch around. Neat as a pin. At one end were the tools you'd find in any country shed—hand saws, lathes, hammers—neatly arranged, no wood shavings, no nails lying about. Then there was chemical apparatus. It was like the labs at Lidcombe in miniature. Bunsen burners, test tubes, pipettes; I took photos of the lot. Looked to me as if a bit of distilling was going on in here. I shone the torch next onto rows of jars and containers. They had labels—Dacthal, Dalapon, Glyphosate, Passtox. Thripps' tools of trade.

On one shelf there was some printed material. Sales brochures from chemical companies, detailing the latest line in weedicides. About as interesting as the magazines at the labs had been. Then there was an exercise book. ENDANGERED AND EXTINCT SPECIES on the front. In capital letters, except for the 'i's which were dotted as if they were lower case. A neat person like Mr Thripps, you'd think he'd know not to mix lower and upper case like that.

The handwriting in the book was small but in the same capitals. It was set out like a botanical work—genus, species etc.

Cryptanthemis morgani. Cryptanthemis I recognised, but not *morgani*. I read the description. It was similar to the one in David Morgan's notebook. Morgan, *morgani*. 'Cryptanthemis *morgani* named after its discoverer, David Morgan. Now extinct.'

Which one was now extinct?

I turned the page. Genus—*homo*, species—*sapiens*, specimen *Davidus Morgani*. I read a description of a man aged 24, brown eyes, blond hair. The width of his forehead in centimetres, length of his nose, size of his ears, circumference of the skull. My eyes were riveted. I didn't want to read this but I couldn't help staring at it. It was macabre, the description of David Morgan, of a person, cut up into centimetres like this. I thought of Nazi doctors in concentration camps, the experiments. They measured their 'subjects' like this. Where was the body, did

Thripps dig a pit and bury him after measuring him, bury him under the ground with the orchids then spray the lot?

I shut the book. In the torchlight I could see the swirl of my breath. My ears were ringing.

I flicked the torch around the shed. Just a shed, Claudia, it's just a shed.

I put the book in my bag. What I could have done with now was a stiff drink. I shone the torch on the fridge. A fridge in a shed usually is full of beer. I doubted though I could bring myself to drink anything that belonged to Thripps.

I opened it. There were bottles of liquid, brownish coloured through to clear. I slipped a couple of those in my bag as well.

Beside the fridge was a freezer. I lifted the lid. It looked like about a year's supply of dog meat in there. He'd probably bought a whole carcass, had it cut up and put into freezer bags. I started to dig around to see if there was anything underneath. I could feel the cold through the gloves. I moved one bag that had something spherical in it. The plastic was frosted over, it crinkled as I picked it up and lifted it out. The roundest part felt as if it was covered with fur. I didn't think they left the fur on when they butchered an animal. The other side wasn't so round, it was bumpy. I peeled off the plastic and shone the torch on it.

Christ! It was a head, it was David Morgan's head! Looking blankly through frozen eyes. I flung it away and heard the dull thud as it hit the floor. I banged into the freezer reeling backwards. The lid crashed down, knocking the torch into the freezer. I was surrounded by blackness, I felt sick, I retched, I could taste vomit in my mouth. My eyes were stinging, my lungs were burning. There was a peculiar smell. The darkness was so dense I could hardly breathe. I had to get out. Where was the window?

I felt the edge of the freezer and pulled up the lid, feeling the cold air as it escaped. I had a strong resistance to putting my hand back in there but I needed the torch. I was disoriented, I couldn't tell where the window was anymore. I was getting stomach cramps, my eyes and lungs were burning. Why was it getting worse and worse?

I closed my eyes but the burning didn't stop. I groped around for the torch but all I felt were lumps of frozen meat. I had no light and no idea where the window was. I would have to work my way around the shed in the dark. My hand found the corner of the freezer then moved onto the fridge. The fridge. There was a light in the fridge. I pulled open the door and let out a square of light.

There were swirls of smoke everywhere or was it my eyes? I could vaguely see the shelf of weedicides. The window was opposite that.

But that was where the smoke was coming from, jets of it, coming in through the window. 'Thripps,' I called out, 'Thripps!' I was shouting now, making as much noise as possible, I wanted someone, anyone, to come, I couldn't get out through the window, that was where the poisonous cloud was coming from. I heard a dog bark, then a car start up. 'Thripps!' Running away, like he did in the alley. 'Thripps!'

I found the door. Padlocked from the outside. I was going to die in here. I started banging on the walls. Walls. Fibro. Hand-saw, tools. Outside, fresh air, green grass. The hammer. Get the hammer. Pick up the hammer and swing. Pick up the hammer and swing. Over and over in my mind, slow and heavy like the batteries wearing out.

Pick up the hammer and . . .

I did it. Heard the sound it made, the fibro cracking clean away. And again. Felt the fresher air come in. Saw the grass.

I woke up in Coffs Harbour Hospital. Whatever they'd done to me made me feel a whole lot better than I'd felt last night. It was early morning, the room was full of sunlight. 'How long have I been in here?'

'Two nights,' said the nurse. 'Can you handle some breakfast?'

'I could eat a horse.' I wish I hadn't said that, it made me think of the freezer in Thripps' shed. I changed my mind. 'I'll just have a cup of tea, thanks.'

After the cup of tea I was visited by a couple of police officers. They told me the neighbours had telephoned about the noise coming from the shed. Several neighbours. I told them Thripps had trapped me in there, turned on the spray then pissed off. They already knew I was a private investigator because they'd looked at my ID to find out who I was. I told them I was up here working on a case. They asked if it was to do with the body in the freezer. I said no, another one.

'Quite a busy boy,' remarked one of the cops. 'Pity we can't find him. He's missing and so is his ute.'

I love the smell of pollution in the morning. You don't really notice it till you have a break from it. There was a lot of dirt around Coffs Harbour but it didn't have a brown cloud hovering over it like Sydney does. Even so, Sydney pollution was a million times fresher than the atmosphere in Thripps' shed. It had been only two days, I'd been held at gunpoint, nearly poisoned to death, spent time in hospital. But I felt good. The leech bites were itchy now, the only physical reminder I had of my 'holiday' at Coffs. There was something else irritating me—where was Thripps? He was hiding somewhere, he wasn't going to come after me when he was in danger himself. I wanted to know where he was hiding because we had some unfinished business.

'G'day, Jack, what's happening?' I breezed into the pub.

'Have a good holiday?'

'Not the sort you'd get on an eight-day package tour but it was pretty interesting.'

'Your man's back.'

My heart did a double flip. 'Steve?'

'Came round yesterday. Left you this.' Jack reached behind the bar and brought out a large square gift-wrapped package.

You sneaky bastard, Steve, no letters, hardly any phone calls and you think you can fix it all up with one magnificent present. Well, you're damned right. I was smiling all over.

'Got a pair of scissors, Jack?'

'Got a sharp knife. That do?'

Jack looked on as I cut the ribbon and the bits of sticky tape. Inside was something hidden in masses of pink tissue paper. 'What is it?' said Jack, as curious as I was.

'Don't know yet,' I said, lifting out something made of brown leather, 'it looks like . . .' I stopped. It was a pair of lederhosen.

Jack could hardly keep a straight face. 'You joining the Boy Scouts?'

I, on the other hand, had no trouble whatsoever keeping a straight face, in fact you could have ruled lines with it. 'Boy Scouts don't wear shorts like these.'

His mouth was twitching, any minute now he was going to break out. 'One word, Jack, just one word.'

I put the garment back in its box and took it upstairs. Down below I could hear Jack whistling 'I love to go a-wandering'. In spite of myself, I couldn't help smiling. May as well try them on, I thought, maybe they looked better on than they did in the box.

I don't know who Steve got to model them but they fitted like a glove. Or at least they were holding onto my buttocks like a pair of hands. Very sexy. Quite short and revealing every contour. I take back everything I ever said about shorts. Still, unless I had an armed guard with me, they wouldn't be leaving this room.

I rang Steve's number. 'Hi,' said his answering machine, 'I'll be in Canberra till tomorrow but if you've got long legs, red hair and a pair of lederhosen come by any time tomorrow. I'm all yours.'

I hoped his boss was going to ring up to see how the trip had gone. Or one of those blokes he plays squash with. A man could get into trouble leaving messages like that. Trouble with a capital T, just like the straps of the lederhosen. I didn't leave a message, I'd call back later.

I rang Carol. She had some news but not much. She'd heard about what happened at Coffs Harbour. No luck locating Howard Thripps though. I told her that Howard Thripps and Margaret Schaeffer were brother and sister. Margaret Schaeffer hadn't mentioned it when she called to tell her story. I guess if I had a brother like that I wouldn't mention him either. Carol seemed to think Mrs Schaeffer had been telling the truth. The person from Thai Airways had verified that a woman answering Margaret Schaeffer's description had waited at the check-in counter and had enquired after a passenger, Dolores Delgado. She remembered the name because the passenger had not checked in or taken the flight.

Gordon Schaeffer they hadn't spoken to yet. He was away on business but his wife assured them he would be in touch with them as soon as possible. She was staying for the meantime at the Palm Beach apartment and could be contacted there.

She hadn't told me anything that I didn't know already. 'I haven't finished yet,' said Carol, 'I'm sure you want the news on your friend.'

Outside of Australia Dolores Delgado didn't exist. Buenos Aires had never heard of her. No official passport had been issued in this name. Interpol didn't know the name either. It was a clean alias, no track record. So was Valerie Estevez. On the other hand, Lola Montana had form. She was involved in shonky property deals in the hotel and entertainment industries. Last job was in Florida. Stated occupation was artiste. Bullshit artiste.

The thing I kept thinking about wasn't the morality of being a liar and a crook, a swindler, but how she could live this double, or rather triple life without the people close to her knowing. Maybe there were more than three aliases. Maybe whenever she got caught she just fabricated a new identity and dropped the old one, like a snake shedding its skin. I guess if you make the big change from male to female the rest is easy. For the short time I was working for her she treated me as a confidante, telling me little secrets, as if I was her best buddy. But the secrets were all bullshit.

Who did she tell her true self to?

I pulled the top off a can of VB and listened to it hiss, took the beer out onto the balcony and sat out in the crisp winter night. The soil in the geranium pots was moist. It must have rained while I was away. The truth about Dolores was that she was an invention, everything about her was made up, she wasn't real. Yet I had spent days and nights with Dolores, she made me feel things—intrigued, deceived, betrayed. How could she do that if she wasn't real?

The beer can was empty. But I hadn't had enough. Any more drinks on my own and I'd get dangerous. I came inside, put on a pair of shoes and went downstairs.

It was almost closing time but the pub was crowded. Jack saw me come down. 'VB' I mouthed to him. By the time I got to the bar the can was there with a glass.

And an envelope with my name on it.

'It came in earlier,' said Jack, 'by courier. I thought you'd be down before this.'

I poured half the can into the glass, and took a mouthful. My name on the envelope was typed. Inside was another name and an address.

Howard Thripps' name and the Schaeffers' address.

He'd had plenty of time to have come down to Sydney, even if he'd offloaded the ute somewhere on the way he'd have had plenty of time. Was this an invitation or a warning? Surely he wouldn't send it himself. I knew too much about him now, it wasn't the kind of lure the invitation to lunch at the Ramada had been. Even Thripps wouldn't be this obvious, would he? But he was desperate. Maybe he thought he had nothing to lose.

I didn't care who'd sent it or why, I was pleased just to know where to find him. Because I had unfinished business with Howard Thripps.

I left the beer and went upstairs, got my car keys and put on clothes that allowed me plenty of freedom for action.

Twenty minutes later and a clear run through I was in Coogee. I rang Carol on the mobile phone and let her know what was going on. 'Give me an hour, Carol. If I haven't rung back by then send in your heavies.'

I parked in the street parallel to the Schaeffers' then walked the short distance to the house.

It was in darkness, as was the sisters' house next door. Only Jennifer kept her eternal vigil at the window. It was Jennifer who'd 'told' the sisters that Margaret's brother was staying there. I bet she knew everything that went on in this house.

I went into the Schaeffers' front garden. A dog started to bark. From inside the house. I stopped in my tracks. The barking stopped too. The dog bone on the lawn at Thripps', which part of David Morgan was that? I didn't even want to think about it.

I took another step forward but there was no more barking. A dog doesn't suddenly stop barking like that unless it has been given an order.

I looked up at the window next door but Jennifer was no longer there, she'd been replaced. By a bigger shadow. One of the sisters, I presumed. I gave a little wave but the shadow didn't wave back, it moved away. The creature in my stomach stretched out. I could feel its sharp little claws. My heart was beating fast, my skin seemed to be crawling. The night was closing in, I felt like I was suffocating. I was out in the open air but it felt like the shed. I wasn't ready for this. Maybe I should go back and wait in the car for an hour till Carol and her troops turned up.

My mind got made up for me. By a hand grabbing my hair from behind and a knife blade at my throat. 'You're so smart, bitch, aren't you? You know just where to find me. Who was it, those geriatrics next door?'

My answer came so fast he didn't even have time to savour his moment of victory. I kicked hard, up and back. I heard him groan and felt his grasp loosen. I turned and sliced at his neck with the side of my hand. He was on the ground in two seconds flat. Then I saw what the blade was—a machete. It was big enough and sharp enough to cut someone's head off. David Morgan's. Mine. I picked up the machete and flung it way over the fence.

Thripps had done some damage to his jaw on the way down, probably chipped it on the corner of the step. There was the glisten of blood near his ear. He put his hand up to it then looked at the blood, aghast. People always do that. What did he expect, strawberry jam?

Without a weapon he was nothing. He just sat there kind of stunned, like a rabbit mesmerised by headlights. He couldn't run away this time, there was nowhere left to go. I saw now what Cilla had meant by someone else looking out from his eyes. It could have been the effect of the night shadows but it was as if his eyes were struggling to look out over the dark puffiness beneath them, like a child pulling itself up to look over a high wall.

'Bitch, you made me bleed.' Soft slow voice but full of venom now. Poisonous. I felt rage shoot up inside me like a spasm of pain. I made him bleed? What about what he'd done to me, what about my eyes, my lungs burning, my stomach retching, what about the car accident? What about David Morgan and the orchids? 'What about Dolores?' I shouted at him.

If I laid a hand on him I would kill him. I couldn't wait the hour till Carol was supposed to come. I was almost shaking with the effort of holding the rage in. 'Get up, arsehole,' I ordered, 'we're going inside to call the cops.' He smiled weakly, 'But you don't understand, she was a bitch, she deserved it.'

Deserved it?! She deserved it?! It screamed in my head like a chattering monkey. My mind went blank, all I could see was red and all I could hear was the chattering.

When it passed I realised I'd been kicking him. He was holding himself rolled up in a ball, protecting himself. I was disgusted. With myself, with him. Disgusted with him for being someone I could do so much damage to if I fought him, disgusted with him for being someone who could do so much damage if I didn't fight.

'You mind your manners, boy. I hear you say bitch one more time and your head and your body are going to part company. Now get up, scumbag!'

'But you don't understand, she was untidy,' he whimpered, 'she was . . .'

'One more word and I'll kill you. Now get up!' I wrenched

him up and twisted his arm behind his back. I started to push him towards the front of the house.

'No,' he said, 'front door's locked.'

I dragged him round the back of the house. I could feel eyes watching from Jennifer's window. 'After you,' he said in his soft slow cunning voice.

'Not into a strange house,' I said, 'you go first.'

He went in.

'Prince!' A split second before I heard the growl I remembered the dog. The image of the dog springing into action, heading for my throat. I slammed the door on him. There was a whimper but it didn't take the Doberman long to recover. I leant my back against the door and felt the thud every time the dog on the other side leapt up at it. Then it stopped. From somewhere else inside the house I heard him call to the dog. 'Prince!' Jesus, he was letting the dog out the front door.

Howard Thripps by himself I could handle. The dog was another matter altogether. The image of him springing into action. The sleek black body, the pink underbelly, the sharp white fangs. It was time to run.

I couldn't go round the front, the only way out was over the fence into the sisters' place. But on this side of the fence grew some kind of thorny hedge, presumably a natural deterrent to intruders. I could scale the fence but I couldn't run up over the hedge. I needed to climb up on something first.

I was just about to use one of the wrought iron garden chairs when the dog came hurtling round the corner like the dog that guards the gates of hell. The minute his front paws left the ground I grabbed the chair and held it between me and the dog. His jaw closed round the iron leg of it. I was hoping it would break his teeth but it seemed to have very little impact. As soon as the dog realised the leg wasn't mine he let go and came at me from another direction. I fended him off again.

I wanted to laugh. It must have been the adrenalin. It was as if I was looking down and seeing myself as a lion tamer, but instead of a lion I had a dog and he wasn't getting any tamer.

The dog was going to be able to keep this up longer than I

could. The chair wasn't exactly the lightest item in the world, particularly when I had to keep moving it around. I couldn't stand here forever fending off the dog.

I waited for the dog to pounce again and threw the chair right at it. It got the dog, but the weight of the chair threw me off balance. I teetered, stepped back and got tangled up with the pool cleaner. Next thing I knew I was falling backwards. Into the pool. Christ, I thought, this is the end. There was nothing in the pool I could use as a weapon.

The dog came limping towards me but when he got to the edge he stopped, he didn't enter the pool at all. Just stalked around the edge, frustrated, growling, ranging around.

The dog was afraid of water!

The pool wasn't deep, I made my way to the middle, as far away from the edge as I could and stood there panting, turning as the dog circled, watching his every movement.

But Howard Thripps wasn't afraid of the water. He must have been there all the time, lurking in the shadows, while I was so occupied with the dog. As soon as he took stock of the situation he jumped in. Whether he had a second wind now, could see I was flagging, or whether he was just plain desperate I don't know. He lunged at me and tried to jab me with a syringe.

I reached out and grabbed him by the wrist and pressed on the pulse.

'Drop it,' I snarled. I could feel his grasp weakening but he didn't let go. 'Drop it!' I repeated. This time I helped things along a bit. I swung his arm up, causing him to fling the syringe into the water. Then I punched him in the solar plexus. He didn't bend over, he teetered back. I grabbed hold of his shirt front and kept him upright.

'Is that all you've got left, one little syringe? Did you leave in such a hurry you forgot to pack the sprayer and the weedicide?' I spat at him.

I could hear the dog still yelping, it was a wonder no-one had come to see what all the noise was about.

'Why did you kill Dolores?' He was still winded from the

punch in the gut but I wasn't going to wait till he'd gathered strength. 'Answer me!' I shouted, shaking him.

'She was having an affair with my sister's husband,' he whispered.

'Why didn't you kill the husband then if you were so worried about your sister's honour? Margaret didn't even care!'

'I couldn't kill Gordon,' he said, horrified at the idea. 'She was just a bitch.'

I grabbed him by the throat and pushed him under water. What would you know? my mind screamed, what would you know? I could feel him struggling under my hands, trying to pull them away, squirming like a worm. I could stay like this, holding him under, it would be easy. Only a few more minutes, he would drown.

I heaved him up. He gasped for air, opening his mouth like a fish. He didn't want to go under again. 'She . . . she found out about the orchids,' he spluttered. 'The bitch was sleeping with the botanist. She tried to blackmail me, said she'd tell the Japanese. She knew about the orchids.'

'You killed the botanist and poisoned the orchids,' I snarled.

'I had to, I had to put it right again. If there was any problem the Japs wouldn't buy the development. I had to get rid of the problems.'

'Then you came looking for her.' Dolores knew she was in danger, that's why she left and came to Sydney.

That's why she hired me.

It wasn't just to go shopping, she was buying protection.

Why didn't you tell me that's what it was, Dolores? I could have saved you.

I kept hitting at him, lashing him across the face, again and again. For Dolores, for David Morgan, for the orchids. For me. He was almost unconscious before I stopped.

I became aware of people clapping. I looked over towards the fence. There were the two sisters with a ringside seat.

I pulled his head up out of the water. The dog was growling, but it was a low pointless growl, almost as if he'd forgotten he was still doing it. He was looking at me in a different way, too. As if I was his master now.

But I didn't know how things would be on dry land. I still had to get out of the water and though I had Thripps in tow I wasn't sure the dog wouldn't go for me again. As long as there was water between me and the dog I'd be all right. The sisters were still looking over the fence. 'You got a garden hose?' I asked them. They went through their routine of repeating the question to each other, but eventually they produced one. 'Train it on the dog, will you?'

It worked a treat. I got out of the pool dragging Thripps with me.

I hardly noticed the dolls sitting, standing and lying around inside the sisters' house. 'Ooh, it's a long time since we've had a man in the house, isn't it girls?' cooed the white-haired sister, Evie.

Carol arrived, and a couple of her heavies. I looked at my watch. It had been an hour, almost to the minute. The longest hour of my life.

The sisters were fussing around like a couple of chooks with their chickens. They'd cleaned Thripps up as best they could, combed his hair and propped him up in a chair.

'What happened to him?' Carol asked me quietly.

'We had words,' I said. I told her what had happened and what I'd got out of him.

The sisters offered everyone a cup of tea and they brought out their best biscuits. 'I'm afraid not,' said Carol, 'we'll have to take him back to the station for questioning. Thank you for all your help.' The sisters looked disappointed but it didn't matter, they always had the girls. 'Something very weird going on in here,' said Carol out the side of her mouth, when the sisters went to put the biscuits back.

'Weird? You don't get out enough, Carol, that's your trouble. By the way, you might find some useful bits of evidence lying around next door. Beware of the dog.'

'How did you know he'd be here?'

'I got a message.'

'Who from?'

'When I find out I'll tell you.'

'Want to come to the station while we question him, prompt him in case he forgets his lines?'

'No,' I said, 'I don't want to be in the same building as him, I don't even want to be on the same planet as him.'

'Will you be at home if I need you?'

'Later. Right now I'm going dancing.'

Carol was looking at me strangely. 'Are you all right, Claudia? Do you want one of the boys to see you home?'

'Does he know how to dance?'

I declined the offer of a cup of tea as well, and thanked the sisters for the use of their hose and their house. 'Bye bye,' I said to them. 'Bye girls,' I said to the dolls. The white-haired one giggled and nudged the other one. I felt as if I had become a member of a somewhat dubious club. I couldn't really blame the old ladies and their dolls. Reality is so slow and boring.

By the time I got back to the car the adrenalin had worn off and I was pooped. It had been a hard night. I didn't have all the details and I was too tired to care. Thripps was now in the long strong arms of the Law, Carol could beat the full story out of him. The sun was rising brilliantly over Coogee Beach as I drove past. I was too tired to even stop and look.

Fortunately, back at the pub it was too early for the deliveries so I was able to creep upstairs unseen. I took my clothes off and crawled into bed. Bits of me felt sore but not as sore as bits of Howard Thripps must have been feeling. I'd check it all out later. Right now I had one overwhelming priority—sleep.

I got about four hours of it. I don't know if it was the sound of the phone that eventually did it but I woke up to the tail end of Carol leaving a message on the answering machine. She had Thripps' confession.

I sprang out of bed, still a bit punchy, and called Carol back immediately.

Thripps had started off trying to drag Schaeffer into it but eventually it transpired that Schaeffer didn't have very much to do with it at all. Thripps told his mates in the council he had Schaeffer's backing. It sounded good—Schaeffer was his brother-in-law, he was a big name. On the strength of that, and some monetary persuasion, Green Dolphin won the tender. But apart from the costs of preparing the development application and bribing the council, Thripps didn't need financing because he was going to on-sell to the Japanese. Schaeffer introduced Dolores to Thripps. Dolores had a Japanese contact looking for a potential development package. What Dolores wanted for bringing the buyer into the deal was a hefty spotter's fee. And she wanted to see what other loopholes she could exploit, what else she could get out of them. 'Wheedle' was the word he used, Carol told me.

Everything would have been all right had it not been for the orchids. The botanist knew about them, Dolores knew about them. Thripps had to weed them out. ' "The bitch got what was coming to her" ', Carol repeated his words, ' "she was a whore." '

'Sleeping with everyone else except him, was that it?' I asked.

'Something along those lines,' replied Carol. 'Plus she tried to blackmail him. She got friendly with the botanist, supposedly just to see how things were going. Thripps had the council in his pocket, he didn't envisage any problems. But to a botanist underground orchids are big news. He wasn't going to keep quiet about them and neither was Dolores, once she found out.'

'So she threatened to tell the Japanese buyer if Thripps didn't increase her already substantial fee.'

'And the National Parks and Wildlife Service. You know,' Carol continued, 'the funny thing is, he kept going on about some notebook. Kept saying it was the only thing he'd left undone. The man's obsessed. He's up for murder, twice, he's eradicated an entire floral species, he's looking at a life sentence and his only regret is a notebook. You wouldn't know anything about that, would you?' It sounded nice and friendly but I knew Carol.

'Now that you come to mention it, yes. You can have it any time you like.'

'I like as soon as possible. I'll send a courier.'

'Fine. You said Margaret Schaeffer gave you a contact number at Palm Beach. You got it handy?'

'What do you want to see her for?'

'Just a bit of a chat.'

'It was her, wasn't it. It was Margaret Schaeffer who told you where to find Thripps.'

'That's what I'm going to find out.'

'Mrs Schaeffer? It's Claudia Valentine. I'd like to come and see you.' 'I thought you might.' Almost as if she'd been waiting for me to call. I asked her if now would be convenient. Perfectly convenient, she said.

When I was ready I asked Jack for the envelope from the safe. I took the $10 000 out and wrote Carol's name on the envelope with the notebook in it. 'A courier will be coming to pick this up, can I leave it with you?'

'Sure.' He took it and propped it near the till.

I must have been mad taking the $10 000 back to Margaret Schaeffer. Dolores would never have done it. Shop, she would say if she were here, buy dresses, spend it, that's what money is for. But I had enough dresses. I'd glutted myself on spending.

Another fine sunny day in Sydney town. Glints of light dancing off the harbour as I crossed the Bridge, the sea and the sky overloaded with blue. Midday weekday. A good time to be driving up to the northern beaches.

Margaret Schaeffer's apartment was off Ocean Road, on the surf side of Palm Beach.

She opened the door. 'Come in.' I came in. White walls, slate floor. An entire wall of glass on the side looking over the sea. 'Would you like some coffee?'

I said yes.

We sat outside on the patio, only marginally less glary than the white walls inside. The coffee pot and cups were already on the table. She poured, her smooth brown hand set off by the sleeve of her white cotton jumper and elegant gold jewellery. It was a lot more elegant than the necklace Gordon had given Dolores. She had the looks, she had the money, she had the class. She had everything that Howard had missed out on.

'The police have arrested your brother, Mrs Schaeffer.'

'Yes,' she said almost to herself. 'Is he all right?'

I'd beaten him to a pulp, he'd had four hours of relentless

questioning from Carol, he was going to spend the rest of his life in jail. 'As well as can be expected. So am I, Mrs Schaeffer, your brother almost killed me.'

'I'm sorry about that.' She selected a cigarette out of a pack and lit it. 'First packet of cigarettes in ten years,' she exhaled the smoke, 'ten years. You never know, do you? I'd rather you called me Margaret, if you have no objections.'

'I have no objections to that. I can't say the same about being set up.'

'Set up?' she said. She ashed absentmindedly. It didn't matter, the wind whisked it away immediately.

'I get a note with an address for Howard Thripps. I go there and find him waiting for me with a machete and a dog. What's the story?' I wasn't menacing, I just wanted an explanation.

She went through the motion of ashing again but there was nothing to ash. 'It was Howard who was being set up.' She looked out at the sea, at the surfers skipping the waves. 'I'm sorry about the dog, I thought he'd left it in the kennels. And the machete,' she added.

'You set up your own brother? You must have known I'd tell the police. Is that what you wanted?'

She got up and went to the railing, leaned on it, her back to me.

She turned around. 'Let me tell you a story,' she began. 'When Howard and I . . . when Howard was young we had a dog. It was Howard's dog. Dad gave it to him on his seventh birthday. We'd had other dogs but this was Howard's own special dog. It was his to look after, to feed, wash, make sure it didn't get into any mischief. Well, it got into mischief. It started to go off hunting, killing people's chickens. It got the taste for blood. Dad told Howard if he couldn't control the dog he'd have to get rid of it. Howard cried, he said he'd do better, he'd tie the dog up at night, he'd control it. But he couldn't. It was partly Dad's fault, he expected too much of Howard. One day the dog mauled a baby in a pram. They came around and said they'd have to take the dog away. Dad said he'd take care of it. He took the dog out into the bush and shot it. While Howard was at school. Howard came home and the dog was gone.'

She flicked the smouldering cigarette butt over the balcony. There were tears in her eyes. She came back to the table and sat down. 'I did offer Dolores Delgado that money to go away but it was not for the reason I said. I didn't do it to preserve my lifestyle with my husband, I barely see Gordon anyway. I wanted to make sure Howard couldn't get to her.'

'Two more days and she would have been safely in Bangkok. I admire your altruism, Margaret, there are lots of wives who'd be quite happy to see their husband's mistresses dead.'

She shook her head, a wry expression on her face. 'It's not a question of altruism, I'm afraid. I didn't care about Dolores, it was my brother I wanted saved. I didn't want him ending up a murderer. That was before I knew about . . . the other things,' she said darkly.

She took out another cigarette, then offered me one. 'I'm sorry I didn't offer you one before, I'd forgotten the etiquette, the whole . . .' She stopped. The small talk, etiquette, it all seemed futile.

She lit the cigarette. 'Howard became like that dog. After he found you in his shed he fled, came down here begging me to help him. He was mad, he told me everything, what had happened in the shed, Dolores, the botanist fellow, everything. I was horrified. I knew then that something had to be done. I told him to stay at Coogee and wait there till Gordon came back.'

She poured more coffee into our cups, adding milk to her own. 'He wanted to be like Gordon, a big important man,' she said ironically. 'This Paradise Park business was his chance. So when things started going wrong he just . . .' she couldn't finish the sentence. 'You saw the results.'

Yes, I saw the results, I was almost a result myself.

'You decided it was time to have him put down.'

'Yes,' she said simply.

'Wasn't there a risk that he'd murder me too?' I tried to say it as if it was another person, as if it wasn't me. 'Didn't you consider that you might be adding one more murder to the list?'

'I didn't want hordes of police coming for him like a hunted animal, cars all over the place, loudspeakers. He needed to be handed over to them, I thought you might do it more quietly.'

'Like your father taking the dog out into the bush.'

She didn't answer. Well, she'd got it both ways, me and the police.

'What will happen to Howard now?' There was anxiousness in her voice, guilt, dilemma. It mustn't have been an easy decision to make, to know that your own brother had gone so far there was nothing left to do.

'I wouldn't bother waiting up for him.'

He was a mad dog but he wasn't the only one. I wished now she hadn't sent me that message at all. Because then I would never have known how close I could come to killing a man. Now I knew. And no matter what kind of scumbag Thripps was I had to live with that.

I was almost all the way back to Balmain before I realised I hadn't given Margaret Schaeffer the $10 000.

I called the club and told them that Howard Thripps had been charged with Dolores' murder. 'That same man who came here?' said Cilla. 'I knew he had a bad look.' I gave her an abbreviated version of the story.

'So,' she said when I'd finished, 'when are you going to come and dance with Ramón?' I'd grown quite fond of the club, of Cilla and all the other people there.

'I'll be in from time to time.'

'No, serious,' she said, 'you come, we pay you. It's a job. You dance good. Maybe not the main attraction but a guest spot, like your mother did.'

A month ago I would have thought the idea was crazy. But now? The more I thought about it the better it got. I was good with my legs, I'd seen the routine so many times I knew it off by heart, I had the dresses, the shoes, why not?

'When do you want me to start?' I grinned.

'You see Ramón, you practise a bit. When you're ready, you dance, OK?'

'OK.' I didn't even ask about the pay but who cares.

I'd just finished leaving a message on Steve's answering machine when I heard a knock at the door. Boing! My heart stretched out on elastic—it was him, that's why he wasn't at home when I called, he was on his way over here.

'Just a minute,' I called seductively. I put on the lederhosen, checked them in the mirror and went to the door. I looked like a million bucks.

But it wasn't Steve, it was Jack. I didn't know where to put myself.

'Hope I'm not interrupting anything,' he said, looking me up and down.

'Certainly not. What is it?' I asked, briskly changing the subject.

'There's a lady downstairs wants to see you. Danny's mother.'

I didn't know any Danny. 'Who?'

'She said you'd know.'

I still couldn't think who it might be. 'She have a gun or anything?'

'No,' laughed Jack. 'She looks like the kind of little old lady you'd sit next to in church.'

'What would you know about church?'

Jack ignored the question. 'Will I send her up?'

'Isn't that what you're doing already?'

'Pardon?'

'Just give me two minutes to get dressed.'

'That all it takes?'

'Some days I'm quicker than others.'

I shut the door, took off the lederhosen and put on a sensible pair of dark green trousers. Danny's mother? Maybe it was someone after a missing person. Maybe she was offering me work. Two jobs in one morning, things were looking up.

There was a tentative knock at the door. I opened it to find exactly the kind of little old lady you'd sit next to in church.

Her white hair was softly permed, she wore no make-up. Her skin was wrinkled but it had once been fine. White blouse with a touch of lace on a Peter Pan collar, a dusky pink skirt with matching jacket. Beige handbag and beige shoes.

But I'd never seen her before in my life.

'Miss Valentine?'

'Yes,' I said.

'I'm Dorothy O'Riordan, Danny's mother.'

I was still none the wiser.

She opened the beige handbag and took out a photo. 'This is a photo of Danny when he was a child. I believe you knew him as Dolores.'

I hope she didn't notice how much my jaw dropped open. I couldn't believe it, this little old lady standing in front of me was Dolores' mother? Where was the woman from the high society of Buenos Aires? Where was the woman who'd been swept away by the bandoneón player?

'Danny kept this photo, I thought perhaps you might have seen it, they told me you were looking after his things.'

It was the photo of the little boy I'd found in Dolores' suitcase, and I remembered now what it had said on the back—'Danny's first haircut.' She had others as well, at the beach, playing with Christmas presents, a class photo from Earlwood Public School.

She spoke in a quiet unassuming voice. 'I hope I'm not disturbing you. All these years I've wondered if Rex and I had done something wrong. After Danny . . . after he had the operation Rex wouldn't have him in the house. It's not like it is nowadays with all the young ones. Rex had lost a son, as far as he was concerned he was dead. It was very difficult for me, very . . .' Her lip started to quiver. She regained her composure with quiet dignity.

'Now that I know my son is really dead I want to give him a proper funeral.'

I really didn't know what to say. This woman's child seemed so remote from the Dolores I knew. Yet here she was standing in front of me, with her lifetime of sadness.

'Would you like a cup of tea, Mrs O'Riordan?'

'Thank you,' she said politely.

'Come into the kitchen while I make it,' I invited.

On the way to the kitchen she caught sight of the kids' toybox—water pistols, Lego, the sheets of drawing paper. It was a bit out of date now. They were growing up, they would want other things to play with.

'You have children, Miss Valentine?' She sounded surprised.

'Yes,' I said, putting on the kettle, 'I don't have them with me all the time, they live in Queensland with their father.'

She looked at my sympathetically, assuming I'd feel the same way about absent children as she did. She didn't understand. It was different for me. But I didn't want to have to go into all of that right now. 'English Breakfast be all right?'

'Whatever you have, thank you.'

I served the tea and even managed to find some Arnott's Scotch Finger biscuits that weren't too stale. 'Will you talk to me about Danny, please? Tell me what he did, the life he had.'

What could I tell her, what do you tell someone who asks you that? 'She . . . I'm sorry, Mrs O'Riordan, it's difficult for me to think of Dolores as "he".'

'It's all right,' she said simply. As difficult as it was for Mrs O'Riordan to think of her son as 'she'.

'She was the sort of person that made everyone around her feel good. She was generous, she was friendly. She lived her life as if every day was worthwhile. She was the most fascinating person I'd ever met.' She betrayed and deceived. She was a liar, a blackmailer, a con artist. She had three passports and none of them were in the name of Danny O'Riordan.

She sat staring into space, a wistful expression on her face, imagining her child's life. I swallowed a mouthful of tea to get rid of the lump in my throat.

'Can I ask you something, Mrs O'Riordan? I always thought she came from South America, do you have any relatives there?'

She smiled. 'No, no-one. I think it was the films. He always liked that actress, the one who wore those big hats covered in fruit. Carmen Miranda.' She sat quietly sipping her tea. 'There is one more thing,' she hesitated, building up the courage to ask, 'why did they . . . why did he die?'

I took a slow quiet breath and gathered up biscuit crumbs with my fingers. If Dolores had remained Danny O'Riordan would she be dead now? 'The man who killed Dolores was mentally unbalanced.' It seemed such an inadequate way to describe Thripps. 'He'd killed other people, he tried to kill me.'

She sat there slowly shaking her head at the state of the world, at the sheer waste of lives.

'Thank you,' she said, rising to her feet, 'thank you for your time, thank you for telling me. I wonder, is there anything Danny would like to go in the coffin?'

The first thing I thought of was the Barbara Cartland eyelashes but I couldn't bring myself to tell her that's what I thought her son would like to be buried with.

'I've got all her things here, let's have a look through.'

I showed her Dolores' dresses, the shoes, the poster of her and Ramón. She spent a long time sifting through Dolores' things, carefully, gingerly, as if she didn't feel comfortable doing it.

'What about these?' I said, holding up Dolores' gold dancing shoes.

She looked at them, put out her hand and touched the shining gold leather.

'Yes,' she said finally, 'I think Danny would like that.'

I took Mrs O'Riordan out the side door so she wouldn't have to go through the bar. It had been a strange experience. I felt close to her yet we had nothing in common. We hadn't really even been talking about the same person. There were no traces of her son Danny in the woman I knew as Dolores Delgado. Danny had left home a long time ago.

I guess everyone invents themselves to a certain extent but Dolores went the whole way. With her the makeover was total. She devoted herself to it with the same passion she devoted to everything else she did. Her life was her masterpiece, her greatest performance. I knew it was a lie, a fabrication, but it enticed me. I wanted to step into that life, to feel it, to know what it was like to be her.

Would I have felt the same about Danny O'Riordan, would I have been as intrigued by his story? If I hadn't invented myself, if I'd stayed married to Gary, would I have ever met someone like Dolores Delgado?

As I came back into the bar I heard the sound of balls from the pool room. Sounded like a break. 'What's down?' I heard a familiar voice. George. The old codger had conned some poor sucker into playing with him.

'Nothing yet. Take your pick, sport.' This time the elastic on my heart boinged right out. That wasn't some poor sucker, that was Steve! Playing pool with George.

Though my heart was spurring me on like a jockey in sight of the finishing line I didn't want to miss the scenery by galloping too fast. I sauntered over to the doorway and stood and watched.

Steve had let his hair grow long enough to make curls down the nape of the neck. I liked that. Curls on the back of the neck always got me going, even on Greek statues. I hoped he'd stop before it was long enough to put in a ponytail. Though Steve's hair was still black I'd seen too many men with grey ponytails trying to hold onto a decade they were too stoned to remember at the time it was happening.

George circled the table like a toothless shark—not really up to the job but still with the instincts.

'Smalls?' he said after a time, 'I'm on smalls?'

Steve didn't show any exasperation at all. 'Whatever you like. There's nothing down yet.' Steve looked up as he spoke to George.

Such a pleasure to see those blue pools surrounded by black lashes. These lashes didn't come off at night like Barbara Cartland's. They stayed on all night. On and on and on.

Those eyes washed all over my body, onto my face, till they got to my hair.

'G'day,' he said, 'what happened to that wild red-headed woman who used to live around these parts?'

Most people had got used to my hair being black but I'd forgotten this was the first time Steve had seen it. 'She's still around. Only the red's gone, the wild and the woman are still the same.' But not completely the same.

'What have you been up to?'

What had I been up to? I'd had a client called Dolores Delgado, I'd lived her life. I'd learned to dance, I'd learned to shop. I had a wardrobe full of fabulous dresses, I had $10 000 in my pocket. I'd almost been murdered in a shed in Coffs Harbour. I'd almost murdered a man myself.

'Nothing much.'

'I missed you.'

'Me too.' And your letters and postcards. I'd get to them in the fullness of time. But right now it was spring again. The birds were twittering and rosebuds were opening. He looked good, he sounded good. He was going to feel good too.

The game only took ten minutes but it seemed to go on forever. Finally the black went down.

'Go again?' asked George hopefully.

'No,' said Steve, shaking his head, 'we were just leaving.'

'We were?' I commented.

'Come out to the car, I've got something for you.'

We went out to the car. He reached into the back and produced more presents. A bottle of vintage Veuve Clicquot and . . .

I started shaking my head in disbelief.

Steve was dismayed. 'What's the matter? Don't you like orchids?'